THE
AFTERMATH

A hundred years ago, The Sisters came, a string of asteroid strikes that destroyed human civilisation and brought on a decades-long winter.

Now, communities are starting to rebuild, and trying to piece together the knowledge that was lost. The old tools are broken, superstition is rife, and the land is hard and unforgiving.

And some, inevitably, have dreams of conquest.

The Aftermath tells the stories of a future on the edge of survival.

First published 2018 by Solaris
an imprint of Rebellion Publishing Ltd,
Riverside House, Osney Mead,
Oxford, OX2 0ES, UK

www.solarisbooks.com

ISBN: 978 1 78108 566 0

10 9 8 7 6 5 4 3 2 1

A CIP catalogue record for this book is available
from the British Library.

Designed & typeset by Rebellion Publishing

Printed in Denmark

HAVEN

SOLARIS

PART ONE

An English
Settlement

CHAPTER ONE

FORKTONGUE DAVY HAD visions. From time to time his Da would pat him on the left shoulder, in a kindly manner, and say, "Senses working overtime, lad?" Smile at him. "Senses working overtime" was a phrase *his* Dad had used before him, and his Granddad before that, going back into the horizoning haze of recorded time where history had been swallowed by the coming of the Sisters. Who knew what it meant? Different people on the Hill had different theories. *Overtime*, according to Aunt Eley, *overtime* was a special kind of work, a punishment. There had been a time when everybody worked, and then at the end of the workday everybody had gone home, except for the wicked who were compelled to work over the usual time. So the phrase just means: your fits are a punishment. "But why am I being punished?" Davy asked. "Why are any of us?" Eley replied.

Aunt Eley was so old it looked as though her brown face had been erratically ploughed by a tiny ploughshare. She had married Uncle Sunil long before Davy was born, and the two of them worked Oak Tree Farm, a tiny smallholding a mile away.

Their bodies were bent with age, but their farm was too small and poor for them to be able to hire any help.

Da's theory was different. "Lad," he said, "it's like this: your senses, you see—your *senses* are bound in time. Sight, hearing, all that. What happens in your young head is that occasionally your senses drift away from time, fly over it like a red kite." It was true, Davy pondered, that he sometimes saw stuff ordinary people couldn't see. So in a way the phrase made sense to him. Especially the *working* part of the phrase—when the visions came it didn't feel like dreamily floating above things. It felt like struggle, inside him yet beyond his control. He saw strange people, who sometimes spoke to him. He saw a gigantic face floating through the sky. He peered into unsettlingly labyrinthine underground spaces. He saw himself painfully sprouting wings from his shoulders.

Usually the visions would begin in eyeball-aching drizzles of sparking lights and a migraine that pincered his head from the back. More often than not these would lead straight to blackout, and he would come round lying on the floor, bruised or cold; sometimes with people gathered around him.

"Senses working overtime my arse," said his Ma. She was a practical human being. The backbone of the whole farm. Her genius was running things, fixing things, objective and to the point. She was the family's boss. Stray too far from common sense and you invited her ridicule.

It was something of a puzzle to Davy why she had married Da in the first place. Opposites attract, his sister Sue said, but that seemed to Davy merely a contradiction in terms.

"Senses working nothing," said Ma. "You have epilepsy, my boy. That's all. It's just a medical condition, like a sprained ankle or a bladder infection. You can read about it in the big medical book Mama Patel keeps in her house."

He couldn't, because he couldn't read. But he liked the sound of the word. *Epi-lep-sy*, the *p*s fumbled by his forked tongue. It was a word that resonated, somehow. Something happy. Some portion of lucky. Of see. Hap. Luck. See. Not much like the actual experience, of course. But a hopeful way of framing his life, nonetheless. Maybe he would be lucky! Maybe he would be something special.

He wasn't the only person who thought like that. One time Mother Patel told him, "You're blessed, blessed." And when he asked her how that worked, exactly, she said, "I tell you, three times these fits will save your life, young Davy. Three times!"

That didn't seem very likely.

"You'll be transfigured into an angel, boy! An angel!"

That seemed even less likely.

The fits tended to come on him when he was physically worn out, or very hungry. He quite often drifted between regular senses and senses-overtime as he was going off to sleep. But they could come at any time.

Sometimes the fits made him thrash about like a fish, and one time he fitted so hard he put his shoulder—his left one—out of its socket. It went back it when his Ma leaned on it, and the going-in hurt like he was being stabbed; and the joint ached for a week afterwards, and often gave him twinges. And once he had bitten a piece out of his tongue; hence his nickname. His tongue had lolled to the side and his left canine tooth had stamped a neat plug out of the tip. Before that accident he'd been a chatterer, a rapid speaker. Afterwards he'd had to learn to speak anew, and now he enunciated slowly and carefully.

Physical exhaustion brought on the worst of the fits, which was awkward because working a farm inevitably entailed a good deal of physical exhaustion. His Da and his sisters did their best not to overload him with work. But one of the helps, young Sam Parkinson, had absconded—stealing one of their horses and a backpack full of food into the bargain—which was a shock. Everybody had liked the lad, and trusted him too. And then, much worse, young Byron had died. What happened with Byron was that an impacted tooth went bad. It wasn't pretty. In less than a week one whole side of his head had swelled, his features stretching and bulging until they resembled a face drawn on a giant lumpy potato. Soon after that he'd stopped breathing.

Some years it was possible to recruit new farmhands from wanderers or passers-through, but the last few years had been hard and few people ventured onto paths. The worst of it had been a full-scale war that had broken out between two powerful families in an area twenty miles west of Davy's home, a territory called The Parish. This had been a short but very bloody conflict that had drawn in all the local families, big and small, and had escalated rapidly for reasons nobody was quite sure about. Suddenly the area was gripped by major catastrophe—so much so that militia squads from distant parts of the country marched in formation to join the fighting. Who knew why? Shillingford Hill hadn't been directly involved but that didn't mean the families living there weren't affected. A couple of lads from Mother Patel's farm had hiked west to try their luck. They hadn't been heard from again. And when the conflict ended—abruptly—stragglers fleeing the battlefield had caused all sorts of trouble on the Hill as they passed through, stealing chickens, breaking walls, that kind of thing. Then the Monsoon had come and everything had stopped.

Eventually the rains cleared, and it was time for the hardest part of winter. Davy was busy taking the cows out for winter forage at dawn and bringing them in again by dusk. The land was frosty, but the beasts could get to the winter grass and there was a field of turnip stubble sloping down the hill, protected from the easterlies by a hedge, that helped them fatten. It was cold work, though, for Davy. He dressed in as many layers as didn't actually restrict his motion: two layers of gloves, hat and scarf, two sweaters with his hand-me-down big coat over the lot. But tending the cows was still a freezing job, no matter how much he stamped and stalked up and down, or tucked his hands under his armpits. When it snowed the cattle refused to root around to find the grass beneath, so they had to be in-wintered inside the farm, which made life considerably less uncomfortable for Davy. But there was next-to-no forage and the cows grew hungry and restless and unhappy. As soon as the snow thinned he was sent back out on the hillside with them, although it was as bitterly cold as before.

After the war, all the families on the Hill arranged a temporary moot, and called it a parliament, and decided some kind of collective action was needful. In practical terms that meant a tax, something the smaller families grumbled about more than the larger families, since they could afford it less. Davy's family, the Higginses, was not the poorest farm on the hill, but neither by any stretch was it rich. Still, it was agreed: pool wealth, send a party up to Abingdon to buy extra weapons—since the land between the hill and the town was almost entirely flooded, that meant a boat—and take a person from each farm to make a work-group to go round strengthening defences, shoring up or elevating walls, making gates stronger. This last point was debated fiercely, since it amounted to a poll tax on family labour, and (the argument went) the larger families could obviously spare more people than the smaller. But it was eventually decided. Ma, who always negotiated for her family, tried to get the parliament to accept a pig as their contribution to the tax, and held out for a long time on a pig and a goose. But she rode home in a foul mood having had to concede a whole cow.

Slaughtering a cow was a whole day's work; but killing a second could be folded into that same day at the cost of only a few added hours. So Ma decided—arguing with herself vocally, as if she were two different people—to reduce the herd from five to three.

"It's a good call," Da said. "The weather's so cold now the meat will keep, and the beasts aren't going to get any fatter whilst this weather holds."

"Isn't it nearly Christmas, anyway?" Sue suggested, to try and cheer Ma up. "You can give a flank to the church."

Nobody knew exactly when Christmas was. The local priest, Annie Hacault, claimed to keep a careful itinerary of days and weeks from one solstice celebration to the next, but nobody had ever seen her calculations, and the general suspicion was she picked a date at random at some point in midwinter.

The Hillingdon church, a flint-wall structure over a thousand years old, was in impressively sturdy nick, compared with all the wrecks of much later-built properties that still littered the landscape. Christmas was the year's big festival. Intimations of its coming would start when Pastor Annie visited the various farms on her donkey. She boasted about churches up Oxford way where the priest received a tithe from the community—or at least a twenthe—but the Hill was not wealthy enough to subsidise her like that. She kept geese and chickens on a smallholding on the hill's east shoulder and nobody begrudged her food when she came visiting. She brought God with her, and a little God was always welcome. Farmers, forced into an existential passivity not comfortable for a human spirit, are necessarily a superstitious people.

"Give a whole flank to the church?" grumbled Da. "A leg would be enough, surely?" But Sue's was a canny idea: it would be a large statement of Higgins generosity, and since the whole Hill would eat, the family would gain greatly in status. And so it was agreed. Which is to say: Ma said so, and everybody fell into line.

Another thing that happened, as soon as the Monsoon stopped falling, was that Denny White threw his wife out. Half a year pregnant, she was, but he chucked her out the door regardless. At least he waited until the rains stopped, people said. You have at least to give him that. But he was a sour, jealous man, was Denny, and prone to irrational rages and conspiracizing. In this case he got it into his head that the child Gal White was carrying was not his, and so he threw her out. She went first of all to the Singleton's compound, but Bella Singleton, despite her considerable matriarchal authority, decided that taking young Galadriel in would be too much like putting temptation in the way of her husband, Tubb. So Bella fed the lass and listened to her weepy story and then, firmly, sent her on her way. After that Gal made her way to Annie's house, but the priest was practical-minded about the limits of Godly charity, and the paucity of her own means of subsistence. And so Gal ended up at the gate of the Higgins's farm, looking pale and ill. Ma took pity on her. Given the young woman's reputation, some on the Hill considered this foolishness, but people who thought Ma was making trouble for herself didn't know Ma. She was a woman with command over her husband close enough to trust him with a young girl in the house. Of course, there was also old Jeff to consider, but if he tried anything then old Mary, his wife, would surely cut his cock off with a pair of scissors. The only other man in the house was Forktongue Davy the epilept, thirteen years or thereabouts, and presumably beneath even Gal's notice. So Gal joined the farm, and did housework in return for food and shelter. Davy got into the habit of watching her, sly and secret, as she moved from room to room, or settled with a look of exhaustion into a chair, or went onto all fours, her baby-bump swaying in a counterweight motion, to scrub the floor. If she noticed him watching her she made no sign of it. And Davy had no illusions about his own allure. Still, the old proverb about hope springing eternal is more appropriate to the sexual daydreaming of teenage boys than to any other aspect of human life whatsoever.

Ma decided they would butcher the two cows as soon as Annie did her rounds with the announcement that Christmas was coming. That meant that for several weeks life went on as normal. Da grumbled that Christmas in January was one thing, but that it would be a spring Christmas if Annie didn't get her act together soon and make the announcement, but Davy didn't mind the delay. Anticipation, it occurred to him, was a sweeter pleasure than consummation. Christmas would come eventually. He took the cows out, and thwacked them with a stick, and tried to keep warm; he watched as Gal got rounder-bellied, and dreamed hopeless dreams of her amplitude and beauty. His sisters, and Julia in particular, smirked at him. He didn't like that.

The Thames immediately after the Monsoon was wide and fast, but as the season settled into its full chill ice formed in the bends of its course, chunks of it breaking from the edge and sailing downstream.

One night Davy woke in the dark, scared awake by a strange dream—not bad, exactly, but disorienting. There was a tall man in his room, and he opened his arms, only they weren't arms they were wings, great black wings, wings so long they scraped both walls with their scratchy feather-ends. *I'm still dreaming*, Davy thought. But, as if impelled by a force outside conscious control, he slipped from the bed and walked across to the man. He couldn't make out the entity's face. An angel, or an apparition from some other realm. Davy walked, or sleptwalked, past this being and out onto the upstairs landing. The moon was shining right through the big window. Davy's breath was spectral in the moonlight. Sue was sobbing in her room and, without thinking what he was doing, Davy's steps took him to her door. He eased it open and looked inside. Julia was already there, comforting Sue. The sisters were hugging one another. But Julia didn't look like Julia. Her waist was too round. And Sue wasn't sobbing, she was making a different sort of gasping noise and, without fully registering what was happening Davy retraced his steps to his room. It was empty now, and he got back into bed and fell asleep again.

In the morning he sat quietly at the breakfast table whilst the others chattered on. He thought back to his night-time visitation.

It had been a strange sort of vision.

It was two days after this that the temperature really plunged. There was an antique thermometer hung in the downstairs hallway, but it only went down to minus ten and this cold snap sunk the temperature well below that. Davy got up in the morning to windows thick crusted on the inside with ice, and doors sticky in their frames, glued by the frost. Da got a fire going and everybody jostled in front of it as they chewed bare bread and drank water so cold it scalded the mouth. Gal stayed in bed and cuddled her own pregnant belly, but everybody else got up because there was work to do. Da and Ma, Julia and Sue, Biddy Dexter, who was a distant cousin, Old Jeff and older Mary. They went about their various tasks, and Davy wrapped himself up as much as he could and went out to the cows.

The five beasts were standing close together in the yard, leaning body against body, motionless as stone. Great cauliflower bursts of breath, white as the ice coating the ground, emerged intermittently from their nostrils. The nearest cow watched Davy warily, the creature's brown globular eye rotating in the surrounding string of white-pink lining. None of them wanted to move, and for a while Davy thrashed at their behinds with a stick to no effect.

He saw that the water trough was iced over, and only when he tried to break the surface crust did he realise that it was iced through entirely—a block of ice, big as a coffin. That might explain the beasts' reluctance. It meant coming back in the house and getting Da to warm a pan in which water had been left overnight—not to boiling point, but enough to melt the rustling chunks of ice out of it, like butter on a hot griddle. He heaved this out to the cows and one by one by they each took a turn drinking. Davy had to go back in twice to refill the pan.

That loosened them up, and they responded now to Davy's thwacking. He took the beasts out of the compound and led them up the path, through the trees and up to the open land at the summit of the hill. Puddles were saucers and half-moons of pure silver locked hard into the ground. Each breath was a giant feather of surrender that sprouted in front of his face and dissolved into the air. The frost on the twigs was so thick it looked as though the trees were coated in rabbit fur. Every now and then one of the cows would harrumph, and a great gout of steam would boil into the clean air from its snout. But they were hungry, and now that they had drunk it didn't take much from Davy's switch to get them moving.

A large spider's-web stretched from bough to trunk , frozen solid: the centre a hexagonal badge of whitework from which radiated a spread of kinked and angled needles of white linked with sharp lined crossbars, like an arachnid diagram crocheted in white.

Sometimes, before he had one of his fits, Davy could sense something tingling or gathering in the recesses of his brain. A sort of dissipated tingling of intensities, as though some mighty insight were gathering on the edge of comprehension—the key to the cosmos, perhaps, waiting to reveal itself. As he came out of the woodland and onto the clear brow of the hill, Davy felt something like that. The sun, low in the east, shone right in his face. Below him a great hump of shadow, cast by the heaped Chiltern highlands opposite, bulged over the flat lands and the flooded plains of the west. Towards the edge of this huge darkness was Didcot, a town long since under water. Its tops of blocky towers and old church steeples stood proud of the flood and shone bright in the sun.

He scanned the whole scene. To the west the sky was butterfly-wing-blue, incongruously summery in the freezing air. Shielding his eyes to look east, the horizon over the brow of the opposite hills underpinned pale lemon and beige suffused in pink, and the sun a blob of red-wine shining. The whole curve of the Thames was white as a blanched rib bone—completely frozen over. Davy had never seen anything like it in his life. He stared, amazed at the beauty of it all. His heart hammered with it. Could *beauty alone* bring on an epilepsy in him?

Maybe it could.

Maybe he could hold it back, though. Sometimes he was able to.

The cows were grunting unhappily, and they were not feeding. One lowered its huge head, lifted it again. "Come on girls," Davy called. "Fill your boots. Your hooves, I should say." He kicked at various clumps of taller grass, ice scattering like sparks, but the cows just stood. Vacuous animals. They must be hungry, why wouldn't they eat? "What do you want me to do, light a fire?"

"I for one would applaud a fire, this cold morning," said the stranger.

Davy turned and saw him—a tall man, old, dressed all in leather with a scarf tied under his chin and over his head and a hat on top. He was standing a few yards away, and yet Davy could see no footprints in the frosted grass leading to his position.

"Good morning good sir," Davy said, or rather squeaked, and his head buzzed and his balance tipped up and for a moment he thought he could even see the great blackfeather wings unfurl from the stranger's shoulder blades. He almost fell down, had to put a foot out to prevent slipping over. Dizzy. But then the buzzing receded and the rainbow sparks shrunk in intensity and he looked again. It was just an old man, out early. A stranger.

"Something strange about your speech, boy," said the man.

"I could say the same of you, sir," Davy replied, emboldened by who knows what—his near-miss fit maybe. "I can't say I can place your accent."

"You speak careful," noted the stranger, "and there's a hiss at the edge of your words. Not a trouble with your teeth, I think?"

"My tongue, sir, has a notch in its end," said Davy. Because the stranger was standing with the rising sun behind him it was hard to make out details. He was carrying a pack, though, and a tube poked from this. In itself, this meant little, for it was a rash stranger who walked the countryside unarmed. But Davy glanced at his cows nonetheless. If the stranger decided to take one, what could he do?

"A notch, did you say? Was it cut out for thieving, maybe?"

"No sir!"

"I'm messing with you, youngster," said the stranger, and he laughed a little laugh, phlegm audibly vibrating in his throat. "I heard all about your forked tongue. You're Davy, ain't you?"

"I don't see as how you can know me, sir, since I don't know you," Davy returned, a little more boldly.

"I've been here a few days, chatting with your neighbours. You're right, my lad: my accent betrays me. I'm from the North."

"Oxford?"

Again the gurgly laugh. "Further north than that. Now, Davy." The stranger stretched out his arm and pointed east. "What can you tell me about that place?"

Davy, uncertain about what he was being asked, said, "Chilterns, you mean?"

"I mean a particular part of it. I mean Benson."

Davy looked where the old fellow was pointing. "You mean Rafbenson?"

"I mean Rafbenson, very particularly."

"But why ask me, sir? I've never been."

The Thames skirted the Hill, turning in a broad arc as its course changed from running east to running south. At this point the flow was wide and fast, and crossing it was difficult even in a boat. There was a chain ferry at Goring to the south; but that cost money, and to travel seven miles down there and then seven miles back north only to stand on the far bank and look west at your own Hill would be a strange way to waste your time and your cash. The alternative was to take a boat north-west into the flooded land, and work your way across less rapid waters round north and east. But there was rarely a call to go east. As far as Davy was concerned the Chilterns might have been France. Or the moon.

He'd heard of Rafbenson, of course. It was supposed to be one of the old sites, where the mechanised armies of the world pre-Sisters had stored their machines. It was set in a declivity in the western flanks of the Chiltern hills, and by a quirk it was a location that got colder than anywhere else in the whole country—a microclimate of high land, said Ma. An ancient curse left over from the warriors of the vanished age according to Old Jeff . Jeff said he'd been there once, as a young man, and that the whole compound was deserted, yet pristine—protected by malign charms from the decay and overgrowth that had claimed the rest of the pre-Sisters world. Ma rebuked him for his crazy superstition, but Jeff had shaken his head, firm, and repeated that he knew what he knew. When Davy pressed him, Jeff had said, "They have caverns beneath, and in the caverns are… in those caverns can be found…" That was Jeff all over. No matter how many times Davy cried, "Are what, Jeff? What are in the caverns? What's down there?" Jeff only looked shrewdly at him, and touched the side of his nose with one thumb-knuckle.

"I've only heard stories," said Davy to the stranger.

"Stories of war machines. Yes?"

Davy looked past the stranger, across the river valley: the forested uplands of the Chiltern Hills crusty with white frost. Where the sun was yet to penetrate, the mist patched out swathes of the landscape. It was too cold for birds to fly.

"Caverns beneath an ageless building," said Davy. He did not mean to say this. He did not want to talk to the strange man at all. But something drew the words from him.

Something was awry with the whole encounter. Davy lifted his switch, and looked again at the cows. If they weren't feeding, there was little point in keeping them up on the hill; and if this stranger—who hadn't even given Davy his name—wasn't planning on stealing one of the cows he was very likely planning something else nefarious. A shiver of fear went through Davy. Fear, or cold, or both together.

"I'll be taking my cows home now, sir."

"Go home," agreed the stranger. "You'll find your priest there—Annie, she's called, I think? She's doing her rounds, and announcing that Christmas has come at last."

Despite his increasing sense of unease, this made Davy's heart leap a little. Christmas! Naturally it was exciting. And, suddenly he wanted to be back at home: warmth, family. Home.

But now the stranger was pulling off his gloves, and tucking them one after the other into his greatcoat pockets. Underneath the gloves were more gloves: fingerless wool ones.

"Davy," he said. "I want to tell you something before you go. Before you go home."

"Home," Davy repeated, staring at the stranger like a mouse incapable of fleeing a cat.

"Yes. It's about Benson, you see. It's about what's hidden at Benson. What's there is very important, my lad. It's very *very* important—do you see?"

"I see," said Davy, although he didn't. The tingling was starting again, low down at the back of his skull. The green-tinted white of the surrounding fields, and the pale sky above, began to spume outwards with rainbow hues. He angled up his cattle switch in one hand, and grasped the end of it with the other. He held tight. Like the handlebars of a bike. The world hummed.

"Very important for the future of this land. Of this world. You see things, don't you? Visions." With his bare fingers, the stranger was unbuttoning his outer coat. Top button. Next one down. Third button. Fourth.

"Visions," murmured Davy.

"You've seen the great head flying through the air, high as the clouds. Yes? You've seen visions of the sealed room under Benson. You've seen a lot. Well, my young friend, I want it—I want what's in that room."

"I can't help you."

"Harp and carp, Davy my boy, and you just come, come with me."

The stranger flung open his coat and the tails flapped and snapped and, without any kind of jolt or sense of transition, they blossomed into mighty black feathered wings, two filled arches of darkness flanking his form, and the sky streamed with colour, and voices babbled up like floodwater all around him. The last thing Davy saw before consciousness jumped out of his head and fled away was the stranger taking the first step towards him.

CHAPTER TWO

THEY CALLED HIM Hat because he always wore a hat. Sometimes they called him Hat the Boat, because he had a boat. They didn't call him anything else, because, frankly, they didn't often have occasion to talk to him, or about him. He kept himself to himself, and rarely walked the land, and he was happy with that, and doubtless they were happy about that too, or would have been happy if it ever crossed their minds.

Hat's was a flat bottom barge. Hat carried whatever people paid him to carry, down the Thames as far as Marlow, and up the Thames to Goring and sometimes a little beyond, to where the river widened into the great lake and marshland stretched below Oxford. He didn't venture any further north or east than those two termini for a good reason: his mode of passage was not a motor, but a hand-winch. The way it worked was as follows: Hat tied a hundred-metre metal cable to a tree or other bankside firmness, and then manually cranked the boat up along it. It was a painstaking but reliable mode of proceeding, slow enough when moving against the current, but steady. He had little competition. Few boats wanted to waste what fuel they had going upstream, fighting the strong downflow push of the Thames, especially after the Monsoon. Sails were no good, oars were hopeless—although some strong lads made a bit of money delivering letters and such upstream by canoe, the sheer physical effort in it wore out the strongest, nearly killed the weaker ones. Even beasts of burden could make no headway, hauling boats. But Hat could: he tied the boat by steel to a strong tree and then, taking as long as it took, winched the whole thing upriver, one hundred metres at a time. "You could walk it quicker," people said, which was true (and which was why he rarely acted as postman). But as he would have told them, if he was a telling-people-things kind of person, you can't carry twelve hundredweight of potatoes, or coal, or spare parts, by foot.

He was known, and he was reliable.

He had a code-lock on the winch, and without the winch the barge was useless. Once, years ago, a group of leery lads had tried to steal his boat—*had* in fact stolen it, technically. They'd waited until he hopped onto the bank and then come at him with guns out. "We're having your boat," they said. It was autumn, and the boat was full of cobbed corn from Wooburn. Hat had just stood there, on the bank, and the lads had jumped onto the boat laughing at how easy it was. But then they realised they couldn't operate the winch without the code, and without the winch the boat was a dead weight. So they hopped onto the bank again and said, "What's the code, hatty-man?" He said, "I won't tell you." They threatened him with their guns, and one of them slapped him a few times, but he just shrugged. In the end they'd filled bags with cobs, making barely a dent in the cargo. "You know who's trading this corn?" he asked them. "You know whose corn it is you're stealing?" "Does it belong to the Master of fuck-should-I-care, old man?" one of the lads replied, and Hat had waited until their laughter died down to explain, "This is Wycombe's corn, you know. They own the farms that grow it, round about Wooburn way. They won't be happy you're stealing from them." "Bunch of fucking women?" another of the lads yelled. But the news had discombobulated them, Hat could see. Nobody crossed Wycombe. Not if they could avoid it. People who crossed Wycombe rarely prospered, and were often punished out of all proportion to their transgression. But then again, Hat could see the lads thinking (because they were young), *Fuck it. It's only a few cobs.* So they filled their bags and ran off. As a malicious parting shot one of the boys disconnected the cable from the tree to which it was hitched, and held a gun on Hat as his boat began to drift downstream. But then this guy ran off as well, so Hat was able to jog down the bank, jump in the river at a point beyond the boat and swim out to it. He dropped anchor, and splashed through to the land to reconnect the cable. And then he simply resumed his painstaking passage upstream.

Coming downstream was in a sense harder, especially the in period after the Monsoon when the flow was most rapid. The problem here was slowing down; and using the anchor as a break tended to wear it out and risk snapping the chain, neither of which would be cheap eventualities to repair. So what Hat tended to do was winch downstream in reverse, tying the tether to a tree and then unwinding it as slowly as he could. Sometimes Hat passed down in double-cable-length portions— he'd fix the boat at the stern, tie the forward cable to some downstream marker, get on board and let loose: then that scary-exhilarating acceleration as the stream whisked him away, and the cable swinging taut about as he passed its fix, swinging the whole boat around, and then the final hundred metres before the jolting stop. Then do the whole thing again. He liked this less, because it was less controlled and it kept jarring the boat and tethers in ways that clearly weren't good for their long-term health. But it was at least faster.

If he had a base it was probably Henley, although he slept on the boat and went ashore as rarely as he could get away with.

But Henley was a good place to moor if he didn't have a specific cargo to deliver. People would sometimes pay him just to take them across the water—if, say, they had some reason not to want to get themselves, or what they were carrying, wet. It was easy enough: paddle over the far bank in his coracle, taking the cable with him, paddle back and winch the whole boat over. Though it wasn't complicated it was laborious and exhausting, and he charged quite a lot for it, which meant he didn't do it often. Otherwise he just waited for contact, or news of possible jobs. When somebody came to him with a cargo, and an offer of pay, then off he went.

Being alone didn't bother him.

Quite a few of his jobs came from Wycombe. They valued reliability and rewarded competence, did Wycombe. The only problem was that they weren't very patient. When they wanted something done they wanted it done straight away. Hat wasn't exactly a hop-to-it sort of fellow. Slow and steady, his motto.

One brisk autumn morning a woman woke him by kicking the side of his boat. Hat put his head abovedecks. He was naked, with a blanket wrapped around him, but of course he was wearing his hat, so he looked decent putting his head above. "Hello Hat," she said. Hat recognised her. He'd had dealings with her before. She was called Eva, and she didn't take any shit.

"Hello," he said.

"I've got a docket from Henry," she said.

Henry was the bigwig who ran Wycombe. Hat had never met him; and nor, so far as he knew, had anybody else. Kept himself to himself, did Henry, which was (Hat had to concede) quite a clever play for a dictator. Lurk in the shadows. Become more than a mere man. Still, it struck Hat as puzzling that a community otherwise entirely made up of women was happy with a man ruling them. Wycombe was women-only. Hat wasn't stupid: he had considered the possibility that Henry was a mere fiction, a fake dictator that this women's commune projected out onto the world. Maybe the reasoning was that other groups would be more likely to leave them alone if they thought them governed by the all-powerful and pitiless boss-feller. That didn't seem very likely, though. Hat had plenty of dealings with women from Wycombe and the one thing you had to concede to them is that they were no retiring blossoms. On one memorable occasion Hat had watched as one of the warriors from Wycombe had intervened in a Henley riverside brawl—two drunk men swinging at one another with meaty fists, and a lot of shouting. He reckoned it had been the shouting that annoyed her—Denise was her name. Anyhow, she walked right up to the two of them, flashed a truncheon from her backpack, played the coconuts like a sideshow at a fair—*clock, clock*—and the two brawling men were lying the ground moaning. That wasn't even the most of it. Then she'd crouched down, hauled the two bodies towards one another such that their heads bonked together, and then pushed a cord through their ears: an actual *needle*, punched through the cartilaginous flap of one ear and then straight through the same portion of the other guys ear. How they'd howled! Denise had tied the cord into a quick knot and walked away. It had been quite something to watch those two angry drunk hulks get to their feet with a great deal of ow-ow-owing, and fumbling at the cord together to get it untied. At least they weren't fighting any more: shuffling away together to find someone with scissors who would cut them free, and wincing and complaining that the other wasn't in step and that it was tugging on their ear most tenderly.

On the morning in question it was a different Wycombe Warrior who roused Hat with a boot-kick alarm call. "Take the docket, Hat," she said.

"What is it?" he asked.

"Take it and you'll see."

The fact that Hat could read and write was another reason

people liked to hire him. Sometimes people even paid him to take dictation, such that he wrote out letters for them, and afterwards delivered the epistles to family up or downriver. Combination scribe and postman. That was rare, though.

Eva wasn't about to jump onto Hat's boat. So Hat had to pull himself up on deck, wrap his blanket like a toga around his naked body, and come over to the riverbank.

The docket, neatly hand-written, spoke of picking up three hundredweight of what it called 'miscellaneous electrical parts and components' from a trader in Pangbourne. "Fair do's," said Hat. "Then again, I have no immediate cause to go so far upriver."

"This docket gives you cause," said Eva. "What we're paying you gives you cause."

"A cargo would give me cause," said Hat. "No point in hauling this boat empty-belly all the way to Pangbourne."

"How long until you get a cargo?" Eva pressed. "Henry says this is kind of urgent."

Hat nodded. Everybody knew that it was Amy, Henry's second-in-command—or perhaps the de factor ruler of Wycombe, if Henry was just a fiction—was a tinkerer and builder of electrical things. Presumably she was the one impatient to get her hands on whatever the trader had pulled out of the factories and storerooms of Swindon, or Southampton, or wherever this stuff had been sourced.

"Couple of weeks, maybe," said Hat, scratching his beard. "I heard rumours Old McCormack is waiting on some coal, pulled from an old store, out of the water somewhere in Surrey and dried out. If that comes overland maybe he'll pay me to take it upriver."

"Get dressed," said Eva. "Come ashore and I'll buy you breakfast and we'll see if we can work something out."

Hat knew when somebody was trying to butter him up, but he was not about to pass up a free breakfast. So he went downbelow and dressed, and pulled on boots, and followed Eva into Henley—a town that boasted no fewer than three taverns. He had pulled-pork and beer for breakfast, and also an egg, and Eva talked him into going up to Pangbourne straight away for one-half over the usual fee. He tried, weakly, to argue for double money, but Eva pointed out, not unreasonably, that so sumptuous a breakfast was probably worth a half fee anyway.

So, full-bellied, he went back to his craft, the docket tucked inside his shirt, and readied the boat.

It didn't have a name (unless 'Hat's boat' counted as a name) but he knew the barge like he knew his own body. In point of fact, since his own innards were something of a mystery to him, he knew it rather better than he knew his own body. At any rate, he knew something was wrong as soon as he pulled away.

He didn't do anything straight off, though. He moved the boat upriver, a hundred metres at a time, in the same methodical way he always moved it. Round the bend of the river, to where the Thames bulged into a huge almond-shaped loch at Shiplake. Here the best way through was to stick to the right bank, past the meadows where the Chaudreys pastured their cows on the green slopes. There was a particular old oak that overgrew the water, a tree of which Hat was especially fond. He tied up his steel cord, walked back to the boat, winched himself up alongside, and then sat on the deck and smoked a cigarette out of the small store he'd been husbanding. It was corn-silks, not tobacco, bulked up with bagasse, but it was better than nothing. Chaudrey's herdsboy was sitting on a stone halfway up the hill, watching him. They knew one another, and the boy knew Hat wasn't about to try anything, but neither party had any desire to open a conversation with the other.

Eventually he finished the cigarette, and called aloud. "Might as well come out now. We've left Henley."

He wondered if he was going to have to winkle the stowaway out by main force, but after a little while she came up from below. A young girl, couldn't have been much more than fourteen or fifteen: a skinny, big-eyed, brown-skinned thing. "Hello," she said.

"Don't recall inviting you on board," said Hat.

"I stowed away," said the girl. "I'm sorry, but I have to get away. On the run. I have to get up the river. Will you take me? I don't have anything to pay you with, but I will have one day, so I can give you a promise-note, yeah? I'm Amber by the way. What's your name?"

Hat looked at her for a while. "People call me Hat," he said.

"Can I hitch a ride, Mr Hat? Please? I'll be no bother and I could help out with the cooking and washing and..." She seemed at a loss. "Stuff."

"Don't need help," said Hat. "Who you running from?"

"Running?"

"You said you were on the run."

Amber sat herself on the deck. "Don't freak," she advised him. "When I tell you, I mean."

"All right," said Hat.

"I'm from Wycombe. I don't mean the camp followers part, the shanty part. I'm from actual Wycombe. Inside the cordon— inside the town itself."

"I see," said Hat, slowly.

"I'm on the run from them. I know people are scared of us, of them I mean, and that we go after anyone that crosses us and so on. I know people think we have wonder machines and so on. But you'll be fine if you just take me upriver. I promise. And, later, I can pay you, when I have money. I promise I will. I mean," she leapt to her feet again, "I could just set off on foot. But it's a long way, and everyone knows it's not safe for a young girl, out in the wilderness. Who knows what bad things might happen to me, or what bad people I might run into?"

"You might have run into one already," Hat pointed out, "in me."

"You're saying you might be a murderous rapist or rapeous murderer?"

Hat nodded his head, slowly, to convey the magnitude of the risk Amber was taking.

"I don't think so, though," Amber said. "I think I trust you. You *are* trustworthy, aren't you?"

"I'm," Hat replied, gravely, "afraid so."

"I knew it. And you'll help me?"

"I run this boat upriver and downriver, you understand," said Hat. "That's my living. Downriver of Henley it's all Wycombe territory, more or less. Give or take. If I piss them off, I'll be in trouble."

"Oh they won't know," said Amber. "Won't ever know. I'll hide. And anyway, we're going *up*river. That's where I need to go. Or what else will you do? Kick me off the boat, here? Anything could happen to me—I could get murdered. Or raped and murdered. Or raped and *not* murdered—do you want that on your conscience?"

"I didn't invite you on the boat," Hat pointed out, mildly.

"But I'm here now, so you have to deal with it. Don't you? You must have had stowaways before."

"No," said Hat. He rummaged his fingers in his beard and then dropped his hand. "Never."

"So this is a first for you! It's win-win, it really is."

"Not saying I'm agreeing to take you anywhere," Hat said. "But where *would* I be taking you, if I agreed to take you anywhere?"

"I need to get up to Oxford."

"I don't go so far up. And soon it'll be the Monsoon, and I'll be mooring-up for the duration. And after that winter. You'd best get off, go back to Wycombe, hope you've not been missed. You and I can talk again in the spring, maybe."

"Oh I can't go back," said Amber, matter-of-factly. "That's not going to happen. So it's kick me off here or go on with me."

"You got on at Henley," Hat said. "If you get off here it's a short walk along the river back to Henley. You'll be fine."

"No you don't understand. I'm on a mercy mission."

"Mercy?"

"Yes. And Wycombe doesn't take kindly to what I have in mind. I have to get to Father John."

"Father *John*?"

"Yes, I know it sounds crazy, and I know he's like a hundred years old and far far away, over the hills and far away, but I have to reach him. I have important stuff to tell him."

"No girl, no," said Hat, in a low voice. "That's a bad, bad idea. He's a wicked fellow. Don't do that. Don't go to him."

"I must."

"I shan't take you. I'm hardly the only boat on the river. You'll have to find another."

"So what will you do?" Amber stood up to look more defiant. "Will you throw me off?"

"No girl," said Hat, in a yet lower voice. "I won't lay hands on a woman, and surely not a girl."

"Then you'll just have to get used to me." And she went down below again.

In the event, the voyage with the girl did not go the way Hat thought it would. Which is not to say he thought it would go any particular way, of course. Hat made his way upstream, and passed slowly over the remains of drowned Reading, taking the cable out in his coracle and affixing it to the various spire-tops and fixed points that poked over the waterline. There were groups living in the southern islands of this territory, and others who lived in the rising land further south; and they could get testy, and sometimes fought one another. But they generally didn't bother Hat. Finally the river narrowed again, Hat cranked his way round the corner at Mapledurham, and got to Pangbourne. Here he found his contact and presented the docket, and loaded three large sacks and one crate of assorted electrical parts that hustled and maraca-shook like shingle. Then he set off downriver. It was before the Monsoon, and the river was fairly gentle, so he drifted some of the way.

Amber emerged when she realised they had changed direction. "This is the wrong way," she said.

"For you," he told her. "But the right way for me. And it's my boat."

"Go back!"

"No."

"Please?"

"See," said Hat, scratching his beard, as he tended to do when thoughtful, "when folk say that, does it mean *they're* pleased to be asking, or *I'm* to be pleased to obey them? Because if the latter then the word don't apply. Since," he explained, to the girl's puzzled face, "it don't please me, see."

"I can see I'm not dealing with a reasonable man," said Amber. The boat was close enough to the shore for her to jump off, and jump she did, landing in the long grass on the bank where Purley once stood. She made a disrespectful gesture and set off back upstream towards Pangbourne. Hat did wonder if that would be the last he saw of her. He wondered that for a while, and then he settled himself by the tiller, and lit another cigarette, and watched the world drift past his prow, and stopped wondering altogether. Little good ever came of wondering.

CHAPTER THREE

DAVY WOKE WITH a pain in his arm. He was lying awkwardly on it—his left arm, sore from the shoulder down to the wrist. Rolled to free it, and brought it out: it flopped weirdly, and he had to hold it by the wrist to move it. It wasn't broken. It was just numb.

He was lying on a mattress in a bare grey room. The mattress was sheetless, spongy, stained. It smelt strongly of mould and damp. The walls were grey because they were bare concrete. There were a few scabs and patches of old plaster, but most of this had long since fallen away. The surface of the concrete was scuzzy and soft-looking, as if coated in spores. Light came in through a glassless window opposite him, and through gaps in the flat ceiling above him.

Very cold. The light was ice-bright.

Davy sat up, slowly, registering stiffnesses and aches in various joints. The problem with his left arm, he realised, was that the seam of his sweater, or jacket, or maybe both, had dug into his flesh and cut off the circulation. Sensation was pulsing back in, now: acid flushes of pain up and down the limb. He tried rubbing it. He stood upright and fell straight back down on his arse. The soles of his feet hurt. There was a bitter, dusty taste in his mouth and his head throbbed. He got, more carefully, upright again. Looked about him. He needed a drink of water. Indeed, now he came to think of it, he needed a drink of water very badly indeed.

There was a doorframe, and no door, and through it Davy staggered into a corridor. At the end of this was a doorframe with a door in it, but the lock had long since rotted out and the bottom was a ragged selection of wooden stalactites. Davy pushed this open with his foot, squinting against the light and stepped outside.

He was in a courtyard. Two-storey buildings on three sides, and a wire fence directly in front of him. Old leaves were wind-heaped against the flank of the right-hand building, each individual leaf engraved in filigree patterns of wire-work silver by the frost. The sky was white. The courtyard was filled with various pieces of junk: an indecipherable chunk of metal rusted bark-brown and bark-rough all over, a heap of ruined boots, a mess of old cardboard.

There was the stranger. It was the man Davy had met on the hill, still in his long leather coat and hat, sitting with his back to the wall of the building on Davy's left.

He was grinning.

Davy shrieked a small shriek, turned to scurry back inside. But he still felt dizzy, and his arm was still buzzing, and his legs refused to move him in the direction he aimed at. He slammed into the side of the door frame, bounced back hopping on one foot and almost fell over. Then he tried again and bolted back inside. His head was ringing.

He stumbled back into the corridor, slipped and fell. It was blind panic, a stupid thing, and it stymied his coordination, but it meant that he stayed down. The floor was slippy, and as he thrashed his legs trying to get up, he made a low moan that rose, quickly, to a yell. The stranger was going to get him! The man would be on him in a moment!

Nothing happened. Struggling to contain his terror, Davy slipped onto his back and looked through the open door. Nobody was coming after him. He could see the stranger's boots resting in the thin snow. Motionless.

Cautiously, Davy pulled himself upright, and leaned against the doorjamb, looking out into the courtyard. The stranger wasn't moving. His eyes, twinkly in the white daylight, did not blink.

Davy took a step closer. The white patches on his coat were frost, not scuffing. His beard was stiff with ice.

Relief passed through him, and in its wake a sense of foolishness. Then his thirst reasserted itself. He went down on his haunches and tried to scrape up a little snow, but though it was perfectly white on its surface it came up in his hand gravelly and brown.

The stranger would have a water bottle. Perhaps he would have food and Davy was, he realised, very hungry. When had he last eaten? How long had he been in this place?

Where *was* this place?

It took a deliberate concentration of courage to search the stranger's corpse. Davy stood up, and then thought better of it. He crouched down again, settling his thighs on his calves, and then shuffled forward, like a duck. He wasn't sure why, but it felt less alarming to approach the dead body this way. When he was close enough he reached out and unbuttoned the greatcoat. The buttonholes were large but the cloth was so rigid with the cold that it took an effort to force the buttons through. He opened the coat, the cloth creaked and bent like cardboard. Underneath was a second coat, thinner and not quite so frozen, and Davy got this open. Underneath that he found a number of small sacks attached to the fellow's belt, and one of these was a leather water bottle. It was held on the belt by a snap-button loop that Davy eventually released. The contents were slushy with a squashable quantity of half-water half ice. Another pouch held some old bread, a gnarly cube of cheese, some chestnuts and an apple so withered and wrinkled it looked a hundred years old.

There were other things hanging from the belt, but this was enough for Davy to be going on with. He retreated from the terrifying deadness of the stranger, sat himself on the step by the broken door. The water bottle was leather with a metal screw-lid sewn into its mouth, and as he lifted it to his mouth Davy had a sudden horrible thought. What if the stranger had died of some unspeakable plague? What if he were about to contract that same hideous sickness by sharing the man's water? Perhaps gritty snow from the ground was a better bet.

Try the apple, maybe. It might be plump with sweet juices. He gobbled the whole thing quickly down, core, seeds and all, but the flesh was as dry as old bread and the bad-taste thirstiness remained in his mouth.

He was being foolish. There was nothing wrong with the water. He lifted the water bottle again, and palpated the squishy leather sack, feeling the ice-slush crumble beneath the pressure of his fingers.

"If you had the maths," said a voice, "you could calculate how long he has been dead—from the temperature of that water bottle, I mean. It was close to his flesh and would have been body temperature at his death. Now it's slush. Soon it will freeze solid."

Davy fell backwards in startlement. Freezing water splashed from the water bottle onto his chin and neck and the unexpected unpleasantness of the sensation made him yell.

Whoever had spoken was now laughing.

"Who are you?" Davy wailed. "Who? Who?"

A hand grasped his sleeve, and pulling him upright. Standing in front of him was a person in a bulky blue coat and chunky leather trousers. The person's features were completely hidden by the balaclava, but when she spoke again Davy could tell it was a woman.

"You're easily startled. Drink, why don't you. You must be thirsty."

"I don't know," said Davy, his heart running in his chest like a dog chasing a rabbit. "I don't know. Maybe he had the plague?"

"It wasn't the plague that killed him," said the woman. She stepped back, and Davy could see that in her left hand she was holding a pistol.

She saw him looking at the weapon and winked.

"That?" he asked.

"You should thank me," she said. "He meant you no good at all. It's Davy, yes?"

"Everybody seems to know my name," Davy said. And then, because he was so desperately thirsty, and he didn't know where he was, and none of it really mattered, he took a swig from the dead stranger's bottle. The water was so cold it scalded his throat, but it took the bad taste away and it felt good to drink. After he had finished he gasped, and gasped, and then, fearful that the woman would steal it from him, he took a chunk out of the cheese.

"I can imagine you're hungry," she said, transferring the pistol from her left to her right hand. "He's had you here for days."

"Days?" Davy repeated, dismayed. "Why?"

"He was supposed to bring you to us," the woman said. "But I suppose he got—what? Greedy? Yes, let's say greedy. So he brought you straight here instead."

"Here?"

"You're in Benson, my lad."

"Rafbenson?"

"You can certainly call it that."

Davy looked around him. "How did I get here?" he said.

"He carried you, I suppose. Or maybe dragged you."

Davy remembered the iced-over river. Maybe he wasn't as catastrophically exiled from home as he thought. If he hurried due west, maybe the Thames would still be all ice and he could just walk straight back to the Hill. A spark of hope in the kindling of his heart. He took another bite of cheese. His hunger was deep enough that these first few bites only made him more ravenous.

"I'm Steph, by the way," said the newcomer.

"Pleased to meet you miss," Davy mumbled with a mouth full of cheese.

"Well, come along then. There's no point in loitering here. We really need to get going."

Davy looked up at her. "I do have to get home," he said. "It's Christmas soon, and my family will be—have I really been away for days? They will be anxious. Have I really been here for *days*?" The thought of what his Ma would say when he finally stumbled home shivered fear through him. Oh, she would be so *cross*.

"Put that thought out of your head my fellow," said Steph. She aimed the gun at him. "We're going quite the other way. How old are you anyway?"

He stared at the gun pointed at him. He knew what it was, and understood the threat it represented, and yet he couldn't quite grasp what was going on. "I've got to get home," he said again. "My Ma will be furious. I mean she will be so worried. I'm," he added, "thirteen."

"Small for your age."

"I have to get home," said Davy again.

"I say you're twelve. OK? If anybody asks."

"But I'm thirteen," said Davy.

"Twelve," said Steph firmly. "Now: to your feet."

"But why?"

"Because you need to be upright to walk, you plughead. And you and I are going for a little walk."

"Why am I *twelve*?"

"You just are. All right?"

"I don't understand," said Davy. But he got to his feet. The insides of his mouth were gummy with a layer of cheese, so he took another swig from the water bottle.

"We need to go through there," Steph said, pointing at the building to Davy's right. "In through that door."

Davy went over to the door. "I have to get home. My Ma will be really worried."

"Through you go."

On the other side of the doorway was an old classroom: desks pushed against wall, chairs stacked in the corner. A large whiteboard filled one wall, speckled and cracked with age. "Keep going."

He went through into another room, and then into a kind of hallway. Black leaves were strewn all over the floor, dry as burnt paper. There was a double door; one panel still in place, the other broken diagonally at top and bottom, leaving just a ragged triangle attached to its hinges.

The two of them stepped outside. The prospect was of flat land overgrown with shrubs, bindweed carpeting the ground; and in the middle distance the edge of a forest.

Steph was still training the gun on him. "Stop there for a mo," she said. "Stand by the wall. Stand there, facing the wall, and put your hands behind your back."

"I have to get home," Davy said again. But he did as she told him.

"Sure. For Christmas, you said. And maybe you *will* get home for Christmas. Just not this year, OK? And probably not the next either. Look, I'm ready to believe you'll be a good boy, but I don't want to take any chances. So I'll going to cuff you, OK? It'll only be until we get to Wycombe, and these are regular-sized cuffs and your wrists are nice and skinny so it won't hurt."

"I don't understand, why do you want me?" Davy asked, tearfully.

"You're special, my boy," she said. "And there's a *lot* at stake. A lot. Put your hands together, behind your back."

He did so. He was still holding the water bottle—holding it, now, behind him—and she took it from him. He turned his head to look at her.

She chuckled. Then she made a sharp *shh!* noise, and slapped the hand holding the cuffs hard against the wall. It was as if she meant to punch the building really hard, and it made Davy wince to see it. It must have hurt her knuckles to bang the wall so forcefully. The hand that had banged the wall was holding something too: a screwdriver, maybe. Or was it a pen? It looked more like a pen than a screwdriver.

She had dropped the handcuffs. She had thrown down the water bottle.

"Fuck," she said, in a strangulated version of her normal voice.

Davy, without really thinking, bent down and picked up the cuffs. He offered these to her, but her right hand was still against the wall and she was trying to reach round for something with her left. She was reaching round, he saw, to retrieve her pistol from its holster.

She wasn't holding the pen in her left hand. Of course she wasn't. The object stuck straight out from the palm of her hand. And it wasn't a pen. It was a crossbow bolt.

It all came together in Davy's head. He understood what had happened.

"You stay there," Steph said, in a fierce voice. "You just stay right there, Davy boy." She had pulled the gun from its holster with her free hand.

Davy ran.

He sprinted straight for the forested horizon. The ground had long ago been grass, but was now completely overgrown with bindweed which had been rendered slipperier by a thin layer of snow. Davy got six strides away from the buildings before his right foot vanished somewhere behind him, as if yanked back by a rope. He tried to stop his fall with his left foot but the angle was such that it also slipped backwards. He lurched forward, a comedy tumble, ducked his head and, without intending to, rolled a somersault as neatly as a gymnast. The next thing he knew he was back on his feet, skidding to a halt. Panting.

Behind him there was the hammer-blow clamour of a gunshot. It battered his ears and he flinched so hard he almost doubled up. But Steph wasn't shooting at him. She was shooting past him, towards a copse of overgrown bushes near the corner of the main building. Shooting at whoever had pinned her hand with that crossbow bolt.

Davy took a deep breath and set off running again. He had got halfway to the treeline when a second shot banged the air hard and sent rumbling echoes rolling round the flanks of the Chilterns.

CHAPTER FOUR

HAT THE BOAT brought his cargo of electronica down to Henley where a message left at his usual tavern told him to ship it further downstream to Marlow. That was as far east as he usually went, since beyond that point the river spread into treacherous shallows, reefed with underwater obstacles, with ruins and roofs and other hidden prominences, and was besides prey to odd currents. Plus the people down that way were all barbarians. Eventually you got to London, which was a desert, threaded with desperate stalkers hoping and mostly failing to scavenge useful tech. Still, Marlow wasn't a problem. He went that far, and there were six agents of Wycombe waiting for him in the town. They took the parts, and paid him, and then they asked him about his stowaway.

It occurred to Hat that he could, perhaps, lie. But, scratching his chin, he wasn't sure he saw any point in that. "Girl called Amber?" he asked. "I gave her a lift to Pangbourne."

"And why would you do that?" asked one of the women, in a tired-sounding voice.

Hat considered this question for quite a length of time. "She asked me," he said, finally.

"She's very young to be roaming about on her own," said another of the women. "Bad things might very well happen to her."

Hat nodded slowly.

The first woman sighed. "Look, Hat," she said. "If you see her again, do your best to get her to come back. If needs be, lock her on your boat and come find us. You'll be rewarded."

Hat looked placidly at her, which was his way of saying not-on-your-nelly-my-girl without having to open his mouth. But she took it for compliance, of course, and the six of them went off: four armed, on horseback, two driving the cart with all the stuff in it. Hat took his pay downbelow and stowed it.

Then he had a little lunch.

Over the fortnight that followed he made his way slowly back up to Henley, picked up Old McCormack's cargo of coal and took it up to Goring. It was unloaded by a small group of armed men who called themselves Guz. Hat had no idea what that name meant. But gangs came and went, tribes spring up and fell away, and some of them managed to stick around. Best policy was: not to judge.

Hat got a drink in his usual tavern, and chatting with people heard that these 'Guz' soldiers had secured a good swathe of the land west. Not the whole of the Downs west of the river by any stretch, but a fair holding. They wanted the coal to fuel restored steam engines, or something, for some big project. Nobody seemed to know, and Hat didn't really care. The Monsoon was due in a week or so, and he had to figure where to wait it out. Since he now had quite a bit of money he was looking at somewhere he could enjoy some good food, and maybe even a proper cigarette. He could do worse than Goring. The ferry there meant that a lot of traffic east-west came through it, so it had plenty of options in terms of lodgings and food. Henley was probably a better option, because all those travellers brought Goring as much trouble as they did wealth. But he didn't happen to be in Henley. He happened to be in his usual tavern, in Goring. He bought himself his usual beer.

It was warm inside, with the fire, and one pint became two, and the morning became the afternoon. Hat began to feel proper cosy.

"You got a daughter, Hat?" asked Agnieszka, the landlady.

"I do not."

"I didn't think she was old enough to be your daughter. To be honest, I wondered: maybe granddaughter."

Hat thought about this, and rummaged in his beard with his fingers-ends for a while. "Who's this?"

"Girl was asking after you. Said you were called Boat, and that you owned a Hat, but we knew who she meant."

Hat nodded. He sucked his upper lip down into the space behind his lower teeth for a while. Then he took another swig of beer. Then he said, "What did she want, Agnieszka?"

"Wanted to know if we knew you. Wanted to know where you were likely to be. 'On the river,' I said. 'Where on the river?' she insisted. 'Between here and Marlow,' I said. 'That's a lot of river,' she said. 'We could go on all day like this,' I said, 'or you could take my hint.' 'And what hint is that?' she said, getting all bristly and cross, the way the young do when their impatience isn't catered for immediate-like. 'The hint that I don't fucking know my dearie,' I said, and she went off."

Hat nodded and thought about this for a while. Then he asked, "She didn't say why she wanted me?"

"She didn't say why she wanted you," Agnieszka confirmed.

One of the tavern's features, of which Agnieszka was particularly proud, were its windows: two big ones, either side of the main door. The glass in these had been salvaged from various places: eight panes, four on each side, and all made of a kind of toughened glass with a graph-paper matrix embedded into it. This let in a lot of light during the daytime, and was clear enough for Hat, looking out, to see the first transparent beans and specks of rainfall start to cluster on the outside. There was a pittery noise. Then, incongruously, a huge rolling whomp of thunder. This died away and the rain skittered on the window and roof for a while, and slowly died away.

"Odd," said Agnieszka, "that one trump of thunder, and then no others."

"Didn't sound very far away," Hat agreed.

There was a renewed pattering outside, and it got louder. Then the door smacked open and a breathless youngster was yelling, "Is Hat the Boat in here? They said he was in here."

"I'm here," said Hat getting to his feet.

"It's Hat the Boat's *boat*," the lad said, and ran off. Hat went after him, and most of the people in the tavern followed as well. The rain was stronger now. The cobbles gleamed wetly like a thousand frogs' backs, and the unpaved areas were turning to mud slidey as snailslime. Hurrying down to the river, Hat turned the corner and saw his boat with its arse in the air, and its prow underwater.

He stood watching as the water around the rear half of the boat churned and bubbled and made a series of gurgling noises, and then, with a sort of sigh, the back end of the boat slid under the water. A great bubble, like a Kraken's fart, broke the surface, and finally the water settled.

It was gone.

The crowd had swelled to several dozen people. For a long time nobody said anything. Eventually a local called Charlie Charnock came over, slapped Hat on the shoulder and said, "Sorry mate." A murmur went round the crowd.

"What happened?" somebody asked.

"It was an explosion," said somebody else. "A boom-boom explosion! Knocked a hole in the hull we think. That's what Gerry reckoned, anyway. He heard explosions when the Guz soldiers were testing some fusées, out Aldworth way."

"An *explosion*?"

"Were you carrying fucking dynamite, Hat?"

Hat scratched his chin through the hairs of his beard and shook his head slowly. "Coal," he said. "But we unloaded it yesterday."

"Coal dust can blow," said somebody. "I've heard that. Blow up, it can. Anybody else heard that? Coal dust can float in, like, a confined space, and then ignite. Like a bomb. I've definitely heard that."

"Flour dust too," said somebody else.

"In this weather, though?" asked Charnock. "Come on—how damp is this air? That can't be it."

"Then what? What could it be?"

There was nothing else to see, and people began drifting away, earnestly discussing possible causes of the catastrophe. Hat stood staring at the now-placid surface of the water. From time to time he acknowledged the people who came up to offer commiserations before they went back to work, or back to the tavern. It occurred to him that nobody from Guz had come down to see what was going on. Soon enough it started drizzling again, and the river was covered in a tinselly sheet of silver and mauve prickles.

Hat was alone. "Bugger," he said.

CHAPTER FIVE

Davy ran into the woods, and only when he was properly in amongst the trees did he stop to get his breath. The sun was white-yellow, near the southern horizon. He couldn't be sure if it was morning or evening, but he knew which way was north, and that meant he could work out which way was west. Through the trees, then, and a few miles to—he hoped—the river. If it was still frozen he ought to be able to cross it, and then he'd be on home turf.

Merely thinking the word *home* made his heart gabble faster in his chest. A magic charm of a word. He wanted to be home more than anything in the world.

One last look back, out through the trees at the edge of the forest. The roofs of the various structures comprising Rafbenson were just visible, past the scrub, but Davy couldn't see Steph, or her assailant. Beyond, the north-east flanks of the Chilterns, heavily wooded and glinting frost in the sunlight, made an impressive backdrop. There had been no further gunshots after the two that had dinned his ears and terrified him as he ran, which either meant that the assailant had silenced Steph, or that Steph's second shot had hit its mark.

Either way it would do Davy no good to hang around here.

He turned and started through the trees. Bare black trunks, glittery branches and here and there a shaggy-dark fir tree. The ground was a thin layer of old snow over a layer of compressed leaves. His feet moved with barely a swish. It was savagely, sadistically cold. Every breath was a wraith. Shivers and twitches kept going through him. He had lost all sensation in his feet and gloved-fingers.

Inside the woods it was hard to see exactly where the sun was, and so hard to ensure that he was still going west. A life on the heavily forested Shillingford Hill had taught Davy how easy it was to go astray when travelling through woodland. But better to keep moving, and to put distance between himself and the crazy folk behind him—people who wanted him a prisoner or a corpse, of maybe first the one and then the other.

It was eerie in the silent wood, and grew eerier. Light dimmed, seemed to thicken, as he jogged on through the trees. His absent feet were an amputee's phantom appendages. It was only the right-left-right-left sense of impact, the jar as each hit the ground, that told him he had feet at all. Davy's gasping-breathing ground a lopsided rhythm into his inner ear. Everything else was silent with the perfect silence of a winter forest.

Was he being followed? He had a nasty sense he was. He stopped and looked back. There was no-one behind him. No-one he could see at any rate. He leaned forward and rested his hands on his thighs, until his breath slowed and settled.

When he turned to start again he found himself face-to-flank with two blue-brown deer. Roe-deer. They were standing, only yards in front of him. Their eyes were globes of polished coal, and every hair in their coats stood out in Davy's mind as sharp as if they were specifically pricking into his skin. He could *feel* the vivid particularity of that visual texture. The suddenness, and the vividness, made the pitch of Davy's thinking tilt, and colours began to flit and gather out of the bare surroundings.

One of the deer put its head down, slowly, and then, suddenly, the two beasts darted off. Not so much running as bouncing on their sinew-springy legs, away through the trees and gone in a moment.

Davy shut his eyes and tried to calm himself. It was a relief when the prickles of an incipient fit faded and fell away. Senses not working overtime, not right now. He couldn't afford it. Lose consciousness here, and he would die of hypothermia.

He had to get on.

He picked up speed again and threaded his way through the trees. At one point he crossed an old road: now only a corridor where the trees gave way to a few yards of bush. Abandoned cars, each entirely consumed with the black-red smallpox of rust, sat in twos and threes. He passed over and back into the woodland. Trees all around, and a deadweight of absolute silence. Then, without any warning, he came out the other side of the wood. The trees opened to a downslope covered in shrubs and bushes, and there was the Thames.

It was flowing.

The near and far banks were both crusted with solid ice, it was true. It looked, incongruously enough, like the fat that gathered at the top of a stew the day after it is cooked—when you lift the lid on the leftovers gone cold. White with a slight tinge of grey, thick and somehow greasy-looking on the Thames's farside. The thickness was harder to gauge on the nearside where the scrubby growth obscured the details. But there was no mistaking it: the middle of the river was black and open, and occasional floating pads of ice whirled downstream with alarming rapidity.

Davy looked past the river at the rising hills beyond: home, blanketed in purple woods, with stretches of dishcloth-coloured mist threading in and out of the trees.

Ravens flew, north to south, creaking out their warning song in their hard, dry little voices.

He might have burst into tears. But he didn't. He wasn't a little child, after all. Thirteen was a man's age. (Why had the woman Steph insisted he was twelve? What was *that* about?) He had to gather his thoughts; he needed a plan. Somehow he had to cross the river.

He could go south—he wasn't sure how far it was, quite a number of miles certainly, but if he stuck to the east bank of the Thames he would eventually get to Goring where there was a ferry. It was a long walk, and he had no supplies, and there was no way to live off the land at this time of year. Worse, he had nothing with which he could pay for a ferry crossing, and the Goring folk were unlikely to advance him any credit.

There was something else: two rival sets of people were, it seemed, intent on taking him as their captive. He had no idea why, but it was a fact. The stranger in the leather jacket and the woman, Steph, was two. Then again there was whoever it was who'd shot Steph in the hand with a crossbow bolt. Maybe that guy was a third party and *three* tribes were out to get him. Davy pondered the odds of getting down to Goring on his own, pursued by three determined sets of people and decided they were slim. And Goring was the obvious move for a person who wanted to get back to his home on the Hill.

What else could he do, though? To the north the river widened into a long broad lake, edged on both sides by frozen marshland. Pretty much all the land between here and Oxford was a morass. It was possible to pick a way through it, if you knew what you were doing, had some sense of the old causeways and paths, and if it were summer, when the river was less swollen. But alone, with the Thames in full spate, north was a hopeless option.

What did that leave? Going back east was out of the question. And that only left one way. At least, Davy told himself, go down to the river and see what's what. Maybe somebody has left a boat tied up? It was a foolish thing to hope for, of course, but Davy couldn't think what else to do.

Try to swim it? The mere thought of the cold of the river made him shudder. The reality would murder him.

Take a look, anyhow. Take just a look. He picked his way down the slope towards the river. The closer he got the louder it was: a rushing sound overlaid with snaps and thwacks as ice broke away from the edge and floated away, or banged into other ice. The shrubs became smaller and then gave way to sedge: sharp blades of frost stiffened grass that broke under his feet like twigs with a series of crackling detonations. Though the marsh was frozen his feet began to sink into it.

He was hard by the river. There were no boats. Davy thought again about swimming over. There was no guarantee he would survive the cold of it. He put a foot on the ice at the river's edge and it wheezed audibly under the pressure. His other foot, and the ice groaned and wobbled. It was a hundred feet or so to the unevenly crenulated edge of the shelf of ice, and after that was only freezing fast-flowing black water. It was going to be lung-seizingly cold and the flow was such that he would be swept far downstream immediately. He would probably be pushed under the ice-shelf.

He would not survive immersion.

He decided against going any further in that direction.

As he picked his way back onto the bank, and crunched his way carefully up through the frozen sedge, he felt once again as though he was going to cry. Once again he fought the urge back.

There was no point in delaying. He was not going to die of thirst, with a river right next to him, but he was going to get pretty hungry over the next few days, and the sooner he set off the sooner he would reach home, and food, and shelter.

The sooner he *might* reach home.

He resolved: he would walk to Goring and see if he could work off a passage over the river. He had no illusions about his scrawny frame or physical incapacities, but there had to be some kind of work he could do. Or maybe somebody would take pity on him, and let him across without payment. Or maybe he could strike some kind of deal: the Higginses were not a wealthy or powerful family, but the Hill was a solid parish, dependable and reliable, and surely somebody would take his word as an IOU. Then—well, he wasn't sure of the road west from Goring, but if worst came to worst he could walk north along the far bank of the river until he saw some bit of the uplands that looked familiar.

As he crunched up to where the sedge ended and the scrubby bushes started, it began snowing. He looked up. A slow-motion tumbledown of miniature white flakes, so soft they landed right on his face and he barely felt them. Like albino flakes of soot. Ten million of them, all around, muffling even the roar of the river. To his right Davy could see them falling onto the black surface of the Thames where they survived for a second, whirling downstream before dissolving into nothingness.

The fall thickened, until his surroundings became blurry. Davy started walking, picking his way through and sometimes around the bushes that grew on the eastern flank of the Thames. The snowfall increased in intensity. Visibility fell away, and his path began to meander. He knew he was stepping too close to the water when the bushes stopped and he found himself scrunching onto the sedge; but when he adjusted his path further away from the bank it was harder to know that he was drifting. A wind started up and suddenly the snow was boiling all around him, the flakes larger and harder and he began to fear that he would be unable to struggle on, and would get snowed in and freeze to death. Then, as abruptly as it had begun, the snowstorm stopped, and he was standing hard by the forest, blinking in a wash of stingingly bright winter sunlight.

"Thought I might lose you in that," said somebody close at hand. It was a man's voice.

Davy was almost not surprised. He turned to see a man of medium-height, his bearded face uncovered beneath a beanie-hat, itself topped with a disc of snow like cake-icing. He had a large pack on his back and his clothes were old-looking and patched.

"If you've come to kidnap me," said Davy, surprising himself with how steady his voice held, "then you'll have to join the end of the queue."

The man did something unexpected. He smiled. "Davy, isn't it? My name is Daniel."

"Daniel," said Davy.

"I was told that you had a speech impediment," said Daniel. "But I have to say: it's really not so bad."

"You're clearly a master of the compliment," said Davy. He had been raised by an unusually fierce Ma to be respectful to his elders at all times, but—well, he'd been through a lot. He was shivering with the cold, and bitter and angry and sorrowful. So he added, "I've a compliment of my own. Fuck off, big nose."

At this Daniel actually laughed aloud. "It's genuinely good to meet you Davy. And I haven't come to kidnap you. If you want me to fuck off, then off is precisely where I shall fuck. Before I do so, though, I might offer you one piece of advice."

Davy's heart had sped up with the thrill of his own transgression. Now he flushed with embarrassment. *Fuck off big nose!* Was that really the best he could do? "What advice?"

"Don't issue the off-fuck order. Rather, keep me the fuck with you."

"What?"

Daniel nodded, as if agreeing that he hadn't expressed himself very well. "You want to get across the river. That's your home, isn't it?" He tipped his chin at the westward hills.

"Have you been there?"

"I've been all over," said Daniel. "So I probably have. But if you are asking, have I specifically been to your home? No, I don't think so. Nor do I plan to. You want to get home, of course you do. I can help you. I know you went right down to

57

the river to see if you could cross and decided, wisely I might add, not to try swimming it. Really, you'd be dead in seconds if you went in that water. So you thought: I'll go south because there's a ferry at Goring."

"Big-nosed *and* a mind-reader," said Davy, his heart rate pumping up a second time. "What a rare fellow you are." This speaking-to-shock business was exhilarating.

"See," said Daniel, shaking his head, "that wasn't funny. It's not the content, it's the delivery. And knowing not to overegg it. Not that I hold it against you. Davy, my friend, there are people very keen to find you and take you away. They have their reasons, and those reasons don't require that you be comfortable, or happy, or even alive—at least not for very long. You don't want to fall back into the hands of those people, trust me."

Davy now felt embarrassed at what he had said. "I'm sorry, sir," he tried. "I don't mean to be rude. I don't know what came over me." He was shivering so hard with the cold that it added vibrato to his voice.

"Ditch the sir," Daniel advised. "Leave it alone, let it lie fallow and we'll come back to it next season when it looks more fertile. For now what you have to do is: think. You reckon your only practical option is Goring. If that's the way your reckoning is going, then the people who are after you will think that too. They will be heading there right now. And if they don't apprehend you on the way—which, incidentally, they *will* if you just go stumbling down the *rive gauche* of the river the way you have been—why, then they'll pick you up neatly in Goring town itself."

"Reeve goes?" Davy queried.

"So he does. You need to find another way across," said Daniel. "Is my point. You need not to go the way you've been planning on going, and more to the point you need to start thinking seriously about things, risk-analysis-wise."

"You shot Steph."

Briefly a look passed over Daniel's haggard face as if he was rolling back through a long scroll on which were written the names of everyone he had ever shot, looking for and failing to find the entry for 'Steph'. Then he said, "The woman back at Benson?"

"Why does everybody keep shortening that name?"

"That was me, yes. I did shoot her."

"Is she...?" Davy was going to say *dead*, but the word refused to come out.

"Is she what?" Daniel returned, although he clearly understood what was being asked.

A few, slow-zigzagging snowflakes were falling again, and the light had diminished to suggest that many more were on their way. Davy was shaking all over with the cold.

"Is she...?" Davy tried again.

"What you need to understand," Daniel told him, "is that she's not alone. She is very much not alone. And the others from her community are as single-minded as she."

"Who are they a-wuh-wuh..." He was shivering so hard he couldn't properly articulate his words. "Who. Are they. *Anyway?*"

"Davy my friend, they are alarming people. I'm happy to tell you more, but you need to make a decision. If truly you wish me to fuck off then that I shall take your words as an actual command. But *if* that's what you want then say so right now, because whilst we stand around here jaw-jawing I'm freezing my metallic and simian testicles *off*."

"I'm also cold," shuddered Davy. His teeth added a Morse-code underclack to his speech. "Is there sasa somewhere war warm weaker we can get to?"

"Warm*er*, certainly. I have a tent, and a stove. It's not a large tent, and you'd have to be OK getting inside it with me, but considering the alternative is probably freezing to death, I might suggest it's worth your while to trust me."

"All right," said Davy.

"You're rescinding the off-fuck command? Excellent. Come on, my boy. I'll pitch a tent, and we can get warm, rest assured. Although I'm just not pitching the tent out here where everybody can see us."

He pulled two sticks from his backpack—for a startling moment Davy thought they were rifles and that Daniel was going to shoot him, but they were skinny metal walking-sticks—and started walking. He was heading north, back along the direction Davy had just come, and the snow was starting to fall more thickly now. But the thought of being alone again filled Davy with a terror, so he trotted after him.

Movement took the edge from the cold, but Davy was horribly uncomfortable. His feet were nothing and his fingers were going, but his face felt as though acid were eating into it, and breathing hurt him way down his throat and into his chest cavity. It was growing swiftly darker too. It was partly the snowstorm; and also the sun was starting to set. If this Daniel man kept up this pace there was a good chance Davy would fall behind and lose track of him in the murk. Away to his left, the river hissed and cracked its knuckles. Some snaps were large enough to sound like detonations—very large pieces of ice breaking away. It occurred to Davy that this was only making the body of water he had to cross wider.

Then he walked into a large bush. It loomed up suddenly and the next thing he knew its branches were scratching his face. He danced back, yelping, and then looked around. The snow coming down was grey against the darker sky. The bushes and shrubs were wraiths disappearing into darkness. Daniel was nowhere to be seen.

Panic seeped up Davy's spine. What was he going to do now? He called out, "Hello? Hello!" Thought he saw movement away to his left and set off in that direction at a pace. The hill-line across the water was black now against a deep-blueing sky; the land to the east was already nighttime. Fear made his head tingle, and the high dark purple began to shimmer with other colours—cyan, mauve, an infrared glow. Sparks in everything. The very atoms out of which the universe is built sparking. His breathing was hard, fast, reaching that point where the tipping would lurch him into somewhere else. The river was humming a gigantic *om* as it flowed down the trench of the world.

It was only when he slipped that he realised he was actually out on the ice. Down onto his front, face banging on the cold floor: an effective smack in the chops. The colours shrunk back into their shells, his head focussed back down onto the simplicity of pain. What was he doing? Running wildly at the Thames—if he went into the water he'd die and his body would never be found.

And his new sobriety had taken shape, and it was a man grabbing him by the sleeve and pulling him upright. "Good job you're wearing a light-coloured coat," Daniel said, "or I wouldn't have seen you dancing away like a giddy goat. What got into you?"

"I thought I'd lost you," Davy gasped. "I thought I was lagging behind. I figured I saw you and came over here."

"If I were a superstitious man," said Daniel, "I'd say a river siren was beckoning you. Attractive was she, this person you saw? Nice hair? Plump? Good tits?"

Davy had a flash of Gal, on all fours, cleaning the floor, her round belly swinging gently with the counter-motion of her scrubbing. This in turn provoked a spike of something that felt very like shame, or perhaps embarrassment. That in turn pushed him into rudeness. "Better looking than you, at any rate."

"That's the spirit. Let's get off this ice."

Daniel lead Davy back to the frozen-marsh margins of the river, and as the world went out around them like a guttering candle they marched a few hundred yards further north. This time Daniel made sure to keep a grip on Davy's sleeve. "I'm only half joking, you know," he said.

"About the river spirit?"

"I've heard things about you, Davy."

"Things? Why is everyone so interested in me? I'm honestly a nuh-nuh-nuh... Honestly I'm a nobody."

Crunch crunch crunch went their footsteps. "There's a lot of old, old superstition about epilepsy," Daniel said shortly. "Now I'm generally a science-and-rationality kind of guy. That's the governing philosophy of my town, you could say. Nonetheless, there are people pretty convinced that what we're dealing with, where your abnormal brain chemistry is concerned, is something more than just the old falling sickness. Something more, what's the word? Visionary."

"Senses working overtime," said Davy.

"Say what?"

"It's what my Da calls it. When I have one of my turns." He was shivering, and miserable, and exhausted and he would quite literally have given his left hand to be home, and warm, and in bed.

"Maybe that's part of the pathology. Tuning you in to— something. We all know the deeper history, don't we? Humankind exploited nature for thousands of years. Then came the Sisters, and after that nature has been getting her own back. You can't travel around the countryside for as long as I have and not get a sense of that. The hostility. The stubbornness. It teeters on the edge of being personal, you know? And maybe there's a part of your mind, sensitised by the epilepsy, that tunes in, like a radio, to that? Or maybe," Daniel added, in a different tone, "that's just bollocks. Let's get my tent out before the last shreds of light disappear completely."

A long grey wall glimmered in front of them: the side of a house, roofless of course, and the windows unglassed, and bindweed growing in darker patches all over it. Daniel took

Davy in through an opening and then groped in the shadows, assembling a tent by, it seemed, touch alone.

Finally he lit a tiny portable stove: a compact metal dome that, at Daniel's prompting, put out a claw of blue-purple flame. "I try to husband this," he said, "but needs must. I've only the one blanket, and it's antique thinsulate, which is all a bit shit. But it's better than nothing." He wrapped this around Davy's shoulders and then, by the uncanny blue light, he made first one and then two cups of tea. The shadows loomed and writhed around the two them. There was just enough light for Davy to be able to see that they were in the ruins of a house, tucked into the corner of one of the old rooms under the last remnant of roofing. Then Daniel turned off the stove and darkness swallowed them both.

Five seconds of clutching this tin mug in his gloved hands and sipping the hot fluid were sheerest bliss: the worst of the cold receding. Then there were several minutes of intense discomfort as sensation returned to his hands and face—it boiled and stung and he couldn't stop tears of suffering leaking from his eyes. Eventually sensation returned to his fingers, and they felt less like they were being flayed with a potato-peeler. Ten minutes and he almost felt normal again.

Daniel may have been going through a similar experience. At any rate the old guy sat cradling his own mug and staring into darkness.

"You can explain all this?" Davy asked.

"I can explain some of it," Daniel replied, in a tired voice. "Tomorrow. Now we need to sleep."

Davy had never agreed with anything so vehemently in all his life.

CHAPTER SIX

TWO DAYS AFTER Hat's boat sank the Monsoon came and everything and everyone battened down for the duration. Aggie's tavern was full for the inundation, but she took pity on Hat and let him make up a little bed in amongst the barrels of one of her two store-rooms. Since all his money was on the wreck, he had to agree terms of credit, and here she was less pitying and more hard-nosed. Not that Hat had any option. He ate stew, had a beer, smoked a herbal cigarette and listened to people alternate consolation with theories as to who or what had blown up his boat. Coal dust was the dominant theory, although some blamed Guz—they'd been shaking up the Downs for over a year, a light but unmistakeably military force that didn't seem inclined to pull out. They weren't levying any tax, and weren't interfering in day-to-day life too egregiously, so people didn't object with any great vehemence. Still they were the closest the North Wessex Downs had to strangers, so naturally they came under suspicion. Hat nursed his pint and had no opinion on Guz.

"So what do *you* think happened to your boat, Hat? Who do you think is behind it?"

Hat ran his thumbnail vertically up and down his bearded chin cleft.

"What will you do now? What line of work, do you reckon?"

Hat took a sip from his pint. Shook his head, slowly.

Eventually people went to their rooms, or else left the tavern, in ones and twos, into the hard falling rain, until only Agnieszka and Hat were left in the bar, with only the red light of the dying fire for illumination. "What *will* you do?" Agnieszka asked. "You got to find a new way of making a living, I guess."

Hat stared into the fire for a long time before he said, "Sheets."

"Textiles?"

"Plastic."

"Plastic sheets?" Surprise verily oozed from Agnieszka's voice. "Are you very for-real serious? But where will you get your stock? I mean plastic's useful an all, but most of the land round here has long since been picked clean of it. And you couldn't go into business here, anyway not on this side of the Downs. Bert has all *that* kind of business sewn up."

"Bert Rand," said Hat, nodding. "I'll have to go see him tomorrow."

"Partnership, you mean? He won't be interested in that. Why would he? He's doing fine as he is."

Hat nodded slowly.

Next morning he went anyway. Rand sold his plastic out of a big shed, a half hour's walk west out of Goring. Perhaps it had once been a barn, or a storage facility; but now it was piled high with a sterile rainbow of plastic sheets and bags, thousands and thousands of old supermarket bags, binbags, old sheets. Rand told the sodden Hat that immediately *before* the Monsoon was his busiest time of year. People getting ready with as much waterproof material as they can afford and such. There wasn't much stock left.

Hat explained what he wanted and gave Agnieszka's name as a guarantor on credit. Rand was a lugubrious elderly gentleman, skinny and possessed of a long thin nose with a large bulb of flesh at the end, like a clove of garlic. "If you'd come last month," he said, "I'd have told you to fuck off down the hill to the river and jump in. That much plastic? Still, still. As it is, nobody will be buying now until the farmers come in the spring. So how much you offering me?"

Hat named a price.

"Fuck off halfway down the hill and jump in a hedge," advised Plastic Bert.

Hat suggested a slightly higher price.

"Fuck off about ten yards, just enough to take you outside," said Rand, "and wait there until you're wet right through."

"I'm already wet right through," Hat pointed out.

"I'm charging a damages fee for any rips," Bert said. And that was that. To seal the deal he took Hat into a small room heated with a black iron stove and they toasted one another in potato vodka. Then Bert selected a range of larger sheets from the supply. Some were clear plastic, some blue and one was a kind of shimmering black-green, and twice as thick as the others. These Hat folded as best he could, tied them, and balanced the resulting parcel on his head as he went down the hill.

Agnieszka was puzzled. "That's not enough stock to start a shop," she pointed out. "And ordinary people don't want big sheets like that. They want small bags and so on to make waterproofs. And farmers aren't in the market for plastic during the Monsoon. Still, I suppose you know what you're doing, Mr Hat."

Hat doffed his hat. Water dribbled off the rim when he did so.

There wasn't anywhere in the tavern spacious enough to spread the sheets out, so he had to work on small sections at a time, with the rest folded underneath, which made the whole job much harder than it would otherwise have been. And Agnieszka kept coming through to see what the stench was—"Foulest smell known to mankind, burning plastic. Unless burning hair is worse."

"Burning hair," Hat agreed, "is a bad smell."

"What are you doing?"

"Melting it along lines," Hat said, scratching his beard.

"If you want to get warm, then come in the saloon bar. I'll shoo the regulars away from the fire—for five minutes at least."

"Much obliged, Agnieszka," said Hat. But he didn't come through.

The next day Hat went out to a specialist dealer he knew north of Goring, and bought some actual-to-God nicotine cigarettes. They cost almost as much as the plastic, but he no longer cared. He'd been smoking herbals for so long he has forgotten what actual cigarettes were like, and now that his boat was on the bottom of the river he wasn't going to postpone any longer. He folded the six cigarettes in paper, and wrapped the paper in plastic, and tucked them in a pocket, and came back through the rain to the tavern. Agnieszka's theme for the evening was: "you can't stay here forever you know, Hat." He nodded, and nodded again, because, after all, it was true. "It's not that I dislike you or anything—you're a harmless old boy, I know. But this isn't your home."

"I know it's not, Agnieszka," he agreed.

"I know you're paying me, but you need to make other plans, and sooner rather than later. Don't get too comfortable here."

"I won't, Agnieszka."

The day after that the rain was falling as heavily as ever, and nobody was outdoors. Streams ran down the middle of all the riverward roads, and the roofs were furred with spray. Hat took his parcel of plastic down to the river and sat for a while on a log on the bank under trees that acted as only partial cover. There was no point in putting it off any longer, but some part of him was reluctant to take the inevitable next step. Of course there was no alternative. Where was this reluctance coming from anyway?

He told himself to get a grip. Always a useful asset, a grip.

So he took off his coat and his trousers, and then, as a final gesture, he took off his hat. All three items were sodden with rainwater anyway, but he folded them and put them under a bush. Then, clutching the weighty heft of folded plastic to his chest, he walked to the river, jumped in and sank straight down.

The mid-morning sky was murky and grey-black with rain and cloud, and the light underwater was much dimmer. But the submerged boat was more or less impossible to miss, and to say Hat knew every single inch of it intimately stem to stern, inside and out, was no exaggeration. He pulled himself along and through the main hatch, inside. There he stowed the plastic, yanked himself down and through to a particular yellow-painted box. Then he was up and to the surface where the raindrops patted him on the head as if congratulating him on a job well done.

The water was cold. Not unbearably so, but Hat was not a young man, and had no desire to stay longer down there than he needed to. He swam to the bank and tossed the yellow box on the side. Then he took a couple of deep breaths and ducked down again; hauled himself through the hatch and began unfurling the plastic. It was much harder to do than he had anticipated—almost complete darkness, and the plastic reluctant to move in the water, liable to get tangled in itself, and just as he thought he was starting to make progress he had to swim back to the surface to breathe. After four or five dives that accomplished very little, Hat took a rest on the bank, sitting in the constant rain, shivering a little, and thinking about things. The next dive he swam to a stow-hole and pulled out an old plastic hose, once stiff but now malleable with age. Back above water he tried to rig it as a breathing tube. But it didn't work: even when he tied one end to a buoy, so that it floated, and swam down with the other: the effort of hauling air so far down hurt his lung muscles, and resulted in not enough air; and what little made it down was flecked with rainwater that had got in and made him choke and cough. So he gave up on that idea and simply did what he could in the dive-times he was able to squeeze out of his increasingly weary body.

By mid-afternoon he'd more or less unfolded the plastic inside the sunk boat. The innards of the craft were divided by a bulwark about two thirds of the way down—if Hat had had the foresight to shut the door tight on the fateful day of the explosion then he wouldn't have as great a labour as now faced him. But it couldn't be helped. The front two thirds were the important bit.

Hat dressed himself in his soaked clothes, reverse-peeling the sopping fabric over his wet and exhausted flesh. Then he trudged up the hill to the tavern. The saloon was crammed with people, and he couldn't get anywhere near the fire. Agnieszka was in an angry mood, shouting at people that they couldn't take advantage of her shelter and her heat if they weren't even going to buy her fucking drinks, and that if they *weren't* even going to buy her drinks they could fuck off into the rain. Hat slipped through to the store-room where he was staying, stripped off and dried himself as well he could with one of his two blankets; then he sat wearing nothing at all wrapped in the other. Wearing nothing at all except, of course, his hat.

The following morning his clothes were still damp, and the fire was long dead in the saloon.

The peculiar yuckiness of getting dressed in wet clothing.

Hat went out once again in the relentless Monsoon downpour. Again there was nobody about, and again he was absolutely soaked almost as soon as he stepped outside. But his heart was lighter. Down at the riverside he partially undressed as he had done the previous day. Then he dived into the body of the sunken boat and fitted the pump's hose to the nozzle sealed into the plastic inside. Hauling himself onto dry land, shivering in the rain, getting back into his soaked clothes, still shivering.

A good bout of exercise would warm him, he told himself. And so he set to work.

The pump was one with two rotating handles, one on either side—an ancient but still perfectly functional artefact. Usually Hat employed it to clear the bilge, but it could be switched about to push air into, rather than sucking water out of, whatever it was attached to. So he began turning the handle, as the rain splashed and splattered and gusted around him. Some ducks drifted up to watch him, perhaps intrigued by the bird-tweet squeak with which the right handle sang; but when he didn't feed them they grew bored and drifted away.

The cranking was hard work, but a decade of winching his boat up and down the Thames had strengthened his muscles.

To begin with he could feel the pressure building as resistance to his strokes, and for an hour or so he pumped assiduously away. There may have been rearrangements of the wreck, bubbles coming to the surface and so on: it was hard to tell, in amongst all the rain. But some way into the second hour, as Hat's old arms burned with fatigue, he sensed a slackening of the pressure, somehow. The handles kept turning, but it felt as though he was pushing air out through an unattached tube rather than filling a balloon. So he stopped, stripped off again, and went back in the Thames.

He wondered if the nozzle had become loose, which would have been easy to fix, but he soon located it and it was still fitted snugly onto the inlet. So he came to the surface and took a breath and went back down. The first exploratory dive was fruitless, but the second located the problem—the expanding bag had snagged on a coign of the interior space and ripped. A gash big enough to get his hand in, vomiting enough bubbles to make the texture of the water fluffy. A third dive and he effected a basic repair, clipping the rip shut. It didn't have to be perfect; it just had to hold enough in for the rest of the bag to inflate— once it was pressed against the inside of the hull it would seal itself. Close enough, at any rate, for government work.

Hat came back out, scrambled up on to the dank grass and lay on his back until he got his breath back. The rain eased off, and for a while it even looked as though the clouds might break and some sun might come down. But then a drizzle started up again, and soon enough it was back to full Monsoon downpour.

Hat resumed turning the handles and felt the gratifying resistance again in the action. He cranked and cranked, and after another hour or so he began to sense something was happening. The surface of the river still bristled like a hog's back with droplet splashback, but now there was something else—a push from beneath, a set of eddies or currents. Then, as he ignored his complaining muscles and increased the rate of cranking, he saw the top of the bridge push through the meniscus and slowly lift clear of the water. Hat pumped on, and the bridge rose, wobbled, tipped forward slightly and then leaned back as the bow came up.

The rain died away for a time, and Hat pumped on, his heart filled with a fierce sort of joy, unusual for him. The boat rose and rose, its flooded stern almost entirely underwater but its bow lifting up like a swan. In time it came all the way up. It was a beautiful sight indeed, sitting on the surface once again, with water draining off in a dozen little curving sheets and mini-overflows, and the myriad raindrop splashes covering the whole like glitter. Exertion-panting, Hat jumped onto the angled deck, slipped and fell, picked himself up. The clouds had thinned, and the quality of the light was brighter, as he got to the prow and peered over. There was the hole that had sunk her: a ragged oval, with splinters small and large, and one half-broken plank, all pointing outwards. A blast from inside the boat, then. Leaning himself over the gunwale, he could reach the largest outward-bent plank, and lever it back, roughly, into place.

The plastic bag was not, of course, a perfect airtight whole. Hat could even hear the hissing of its deflation, and as he moved about on the deck he felt the whole craft shuffle uneasily beneath him. He needed to act fast. He managed to get one of the two deck-lockers open—water slurped out and poured away across the deck—and retrieved a tarp and some kit. Then he dangled himself over the gunwale again, and quickly tacked the top of the cloth over the hole. To fix the bottom he had to go back in the river again—he was thoroughly wet anyway, and he didn't need the manoeuvrability required when he'd been swimming through the submerged innards, so he didn't bother undressing. The bottom of the tarp was fixed and he smeared some putty around the edge.

The sun came out for about ten minutes and the whole wet world sparkled. After that the clouds closed again, and soon enough the drizzle built from downward mist to distinct droplets and on to the harder rain. It was still the Monsoon , after all. Hat didn't care. He retrieved the pump from the bank, swapped its function about and used it to pump water out of the rear compartment, into which the plastic float had been unable to expand because of the compartment wall. The plastic bag was deflating now, but it had done its job.

The sun was going down. Exhausted as he was, Hat would have preferred to get down inside and start proper repairs to the breach in the hull straight away. But he needed light, and both his boat's oil-lamps would be sodden and useless. And perhaps it would be best, just for his own sake, to wait until the morning. He needed to rest.

His last task of the day was the most surreal of all. He needed to retrieve one of his lamps, to take it to the tavern and dry it out, but that meant going belowdecks and wrestling with the soggy, bulging body of the mostly-inflated bag—like fighting a blind slug the size of a dragon—to squeeze round between bladder and the inside of the hull, groping his way in darkness to where he knew the lamps were stowed. It took him a while, and began to assume the lineaments of nightmare, but he found the lamp, and got out again and back onto the bank, and at last was able to trudge up the hill though the rain and back to the tavern.

"Where have you been all day?" Agnieszka asked him.

"I needed to get this lamp," said Hat. He held up the lamp. "May I put it close to the fire, to dry out the wick?"

"Where did you get that old thing? It's filthy. Did O'Connor sell you that? I hope he didn't charge you too much."

"I found it in the river," said Hat.

"Maybe you can rub it and get a genie out of it." But she permitted him to place it near the fire, and even cleared away the scrum of her regulars to let him dry out his clothes. They didn't get completely dry, of course, but as he sat there wrapped in a blanket, drinking a beer, he felt some small sense of satisfaction. "If you don't mind, Agnieszka," he said, "I'll smoke a cigarette."

"Be my guest."

The whole room went quiet when he lit up the fag—the authentic aroma, the ancient scent of it. Men and women stood there drawing his second-hand smoke with their nostrils. The whole room seemed to relax. The mood lifted.

"There's a genie, after all," said Agnieszka. "You know, you'd dry your hat quicker if you took it off and put it by the fire with the rest of your clothes."

"I prefer to wear it," said Hat.

The next morning he was up early and down at his boat. The temporary seal had held, and the boat was still floating—much lower in the water than Hat would have liked, but still. He had his lamp and tinder in a bag. The Monsoon rain was light but steady, and there was a greenish-blueish quality to the daylight.

First order of business was to get the big, improvised plastic bladder out of the way. This took longer than he had anticipated. The whole structure had deflated by two thirds overnight, and was floppy inside the hold. But getting the last of the air out proved an onerous business. It would have been simplest just to rip the whole thing with a knife, but Hat had promised Plastic Bert that he would get the fabric back to him with as little damage as possible—it had been that, or else actually buy the whole lot outright, which was much more than Hat could afford, credit or otherwise. So he was reduced to massaging the whole dying slug, squeezing out air in a series of gushy puffs and oofs and farting sounds. Eventually he got the whole thing bundled up into a more or less portable roll, and pulled it onto the deck. It was filthy with river mud and crap, but that didn't matter. Hat had become mired with the same substances as he wrestled with it. The least of his concerns.

With the plastic out of the way, Hat got his lamp out of its bag, lit it and hung it from the ceiling. The inside of the boat was a mess. Of course he had expected this, but it was still a shock to see how badly things had been shaken up.

He was standing in a foot-or-so of water. A great quantity of mud had come in through the breach when the boat was on the river-bed, and all sorts of objects were scattered everywhere.

The first order of business was to mend the breach. That meant carpentry, and it took Hat ten minutes to locate all the tools—they'd somehow ended up in the rear compartment. It also meant cannibalising some of the boat's own wood. Hat had previously decided that the door to the rear compartment might as well go: he could get a new door when he was up and running again. So he unscrewed the portal from its hinges, broke it into component planks with a chisel and set to work sawing, fitting, and nailing. He got one layer in, behind the tarp, using a file to make the fit with the ragged edges as close as possible. Then he painted a great quantity of waterproof putty into the joins—a homemade concoction, this, rendered from bone glue, plastic fibres and tree resin, and very much a temporary solution to any given leak. He needed to leave this to set, and anyway it was lunchtime. His larder had remained closed the whole time, and although water had, obviously, got in there, the cured meats still seemed edible. He ate and drank and finished off his small store of soggy nuts, since he couldn't realistically dry them out and if he didn't eat them they would go bad.

Then it was back to the breach, and a second layer of wood carpented into the hole.

It took him almost all day, but he finished. The boat was still leaning forward, its stern a foot or so higher than its bow, because of the weight of the mud and the way the water naturally lay deeper at the front of the slope than the back. He could pump the front compartment clean tomorrow, and begin the tedious and doubtless drawn-out job of scooping the mud out then too. It was enough for today.

It was only as he stood there at the end of that long day's work, looking forward to appraising the sheer mess that he would have to deal with that he noticed for the first time something that shouldn't have been there. A shoulder.

It was unmistakeably a naked shoulder, rising about the flat murky layer of water like a dolphin's back.

The first thing that occurred to Hat was: I had been working in this space all day, inches from a dead body, and I never even noticed. He was cold and wet, but the shiver that trembled through his body had nothing to do with either of those facts.

He went over and touched the shoulder. It turned under his pressure, and the body went onto its back. The front was covered in mud and grime, but a number of things were easy enough to see as the face came up through the water. It was a young person. It was female. It was naked. It was dead.

CHAPTER SEVEN

DANIELS'S TENT WAS a small tent, and that meant he and Davy were forced into a physical proximity awkward for two males who hardly knew one another. On the upside this arrangement had the advantage of sharing body heat. Davy had not had the chance to get dry after being snowed on for so long, but his thin blanket did help, and though he didn't feel exactly warm at least he didn't feel too debilitatingly cold. Besides, he was utterly exhausted, Davy finally fell asleep.

When he woke he was alone in the little tent. He knew straight away where he was, and what was happening, and the knowledge filled him with despair. He was separated from his home. The night before he had thrown his lot in with a stranger. He had been desperate, but it was foolish to trust strangers.

He lay under the flimsy blanket trying to work out what he was going to do. But, absent the prompt of the sheer exhaustion that had overwhelmed him the previous night, it wasn't very comfortable. His coat was still damp, and that had transferred to his inner clothes.

He dragged himself out of the tent.

Daniel had started a small fire in the very corner of the dilapidated room. Scraps of old wallpaper isolated schematic red-blue flowers against an otherwise rough-surface façade of concrete scabbed with patches of plaster. Daniel had cleared detritus from a patch of floor, and managed to coax fire from a heap of twigs, though they spat and hissed as they expelled what had once been frost, and the flames were very pale in the morning light. But it was heat, and Davy huddled as close as he could.

"First things first," Daniel announced. "Shoes and socks off. Let's dry what we can. No point in getting trench foot."

He had salvaged a strange little structure made of plastic-covered wire from somewhere, a kind of frame a foot high. Davy peeled his damp socks off and draped them over this, as near the fire as possible. Then there was a quantity of tricky manoeuvring of his feet so as to soak up at least some of the warmth. It was far from being a fierce fire, but it was certainly better than nothing.

Daniel made some more tea and shared a little bread. The little was not as much as Davy could have eaten.

"Sleep all right?"

"I slept," said Davy. Close up, and in full light, he could see how exhausted-looking the older man was.

"You were pretty blotto," Daniel agreed. "Last night you were so exhausted you almost zombie-walked into the river. That would have been the end of *you*."

"Where are we, anyway?"

"There was a town here, pre-Sisters. Big expensive houses on the banks of the river—they're all under water now, of course. Some of the properties further from the river's edge are still standing, more or less, and that's where we are. I don't propose staying here very long, though. I don't propose staying anywhere very long."

"They'll be coming after me," said Davy.

"The new reality of your life has finally sunk in, I see."

"Why?"

"They consider you a valuable asset. So do we, evidently, or I wouldn't be here."

Davy took a deep breath. "Who are *they*? And who are *you*? And what on earth is going *on*?"

"Let's take those in order, shall we? They first. They are a powerful group, or tribe, who work out of Wycombe. It's a female collective. But of course you know of them. You live hard by their back garden. They don't trust men, is their premise. Can't say I blame them, as far as that goes. We don't have much of a record, do we? Men, I mean."

"I know about them," said Davy. "I mean, everybody knows them. They keep themselves to themselves, and Wycombe's a long way east of here."

"No such a long way, really. And their days of keeping themselves to themselves are at an end, I fear. They've been bounced out of that by, well, events. The bigger picture. But the thing to bear in mind about them is that they're a Power. The story is that the name Wycombe is short for *Women, come*. I don't know if that's where the name actually comes from. I daresay it's an ancient name and originally had nothing to do with women. But that's what it means now. Wycombe has become more than a refuge. It's become a force in the land. They have numbers, and they have good land and some useful infrastructure and tech. They've got a *real* steep hill—I've seen it, it's practically a cliff-face—which makes defence that much easier. And most of all they have a unity ethos. An ideology. Something that motivates them, that makes individuals prepared to sacrifice themselves for the greater good. That's rare in this dog-eat-dog world. Most local warlords have to enforce loyalty by terror and punishment, which is a fragile sort of discipline. But Wycombe is different."

"What's a *thos*?"

"Not thos, ethos. An ethos. It's a, you know..."

"I don't know. Is why I asked."

"Well it's sort of a shared, a shared set of beliefs and values."

"But why do they want *me*? These women?"

"Well that's an interesting question. We're not sure. I say we and I mean my bosses, and if I'm honest I'm not privy to their strategy meetings. But they say come and I come, and say go and I go, and right now they reckon Wycombe are up to something. They're not *exactly* sure, although we have a pretty good sense. A pretty good sense of the larger motives. If my supervisors were better at keeping me in the loop I could tell you more. At any rate, we know they consider you a valuable asset, worth taking a risk to obtain."

"You're not explaining very well. When you say bosses what do you mean?"

"I'm from a town west of here, called Guz. A port. That's us, that's we."

"Port means it's on the coast, yeah?"

"That's it. South coast, couple of weeks' travel west of here. A few summer weeks' travel, rather more winter weeks' travel."

"So you're even further from home than I am."

Daniel's beard spread and his teeth flashed in the midst of all the hair. "You're not wrong there, my boy."

"So what's *your* thos? You people from Guz, I mean?"

"Our thos is—it's complicated, actually. I'd like to say: civilization. I'd like to say: bringing order and decency and humanity and all that back to this benighted kingdom. Davy, trust me when I say I believe it. I really do. It's just that if we break down civilization into order and decency and humanity, the first of those three terms rather overwhelms the other two. In practice, I mean. Turns out we can't do anything without establishing order, and that establishing order can be a bit... violent, really. Still. That doesn't make doing nothing an option."

"Doesn't explain why you're so far from home."

"Oh I go all over, believe me. Davy, listen. It's over a century since the Sisters. Then the long autumn. For decades people clung on to existence, the barest minimum of survival. I mean, most people didn't even manage that, but it was week-by-week precarious for even the most fortunate. I'm not pretending that it's milk and honey now, but things are better. We've settled, adjusted to living in this new world. Various communities are managing it, though of course there are plenty of desperate people, plenty of starving folk and refugees. But there are centres, now, where life is more stable. Guz is one such. The Parish and the Hill—your neck of the woods, I mean, over the river. It's small-beer, but it's doing OK. I mean, no offence, you know? But it's stable. Otherwise there's Southampton down south, and Oxford up north, although people tend to overplay the strength of that town. Wycombe is a citadel. Each of them puts out their own money, tokens—a lot of it is pre-Sisters coinage filed and restamped, but still."

"We don't have a lot of use for money on my hill," said Davy. "We baa."

Daniel put his head to one side. "Like sheep?"

"I'm forgetting the word. You know what I mean—we swap things for things, we keep a mental tally of who owes what. You know the word."

"I know the word," Daniel agreed. "But you on all fours bleating strikes me as a better system still. And you do know what money is—barter's less effective at a trading point like Goring, or Henley, and so there are tokens. But you're distracting me from my main point. Us: Southampton, which is a failing state actually. Oxford. Wycombe. All right, what happens next? What do *you* think? You think that people will happily co-exist, rub along, concentrate on their crops and their livestock, do a little trading on the side?"

"Why not, though?" Davy asked, ingenuously.

"Why not indeed," said Daniel, and stared at the fire in silence for a while. "So, yes. War. That's mostly how the land is parcelled up. Local warlords here, local warlords there."

"Guz too?"

Daniel peered at him. "You're shrewder than you appear, my boy."

"Hadn't you heard, I'm a visionary? They call it epilepsy but it's actually telepathic powers. See the future, read minds."

"Read my mind right now," said Daniel, "and learn a new range of swearwords, all of them deployed with reference to you."

"You got anything else to eat?"

"I have, but we need to ration it. So here we are, you and me. And all around us things are arranging and rearranging. Two kinds of warlords, at root. The impatient warlords strike too soon, are defeated and killed and ploughed into the general mulch of history, to be forgotten. So that just leaves the patient warlords. Those are the ones we're dealing with now. The ones Guz like to think they're playing seven dimensional chess with."

"I don't understand that reference at all."

Daniel nodded. Then he turned Davy's socks on their broken-down little frame. "Patient warlords," he said, "wait until they have overwhelming force, so they can be sure of victory. They pick their battles carefully, and slowly augment their territory. The patient warlord doesn't think of the glory he can accrue, but rather the empire he can bequeath his children. Power. That's what you find when you dig down, past the immediate appetites for food and shelter and warmth, down past them to the need for sex and children and meaning and religion and love, right down, keep on going. That's the granite bedrock of humankind. Power."

"Don't take this the wrong way, Mr Daniel," said Davy, "but you're kind of pompous sometimes, you know?"

Daniel gave him a hard stare. "Anyway," he said. "Guz is

strong, compared to lots of other places. We used to be a naval shipyard, back before the Sisters. Boats are still our *forte*."

"That *is* a lot of boats," agreed Davy.

Daniel gave him another hard stare. "You know your history, do you lad? You know how the military of this country of ours used to be disposed?"

"Not only don't I know that," said Davy, looking serious, "I don't even know what *disposed* means."

"There were three branches. There was an army, a navy and an air force. The army is soldiers, boots on the ground, guns and massed charges, snipers and bayonets, but also tanks and cannons and men on horseback covering the ground real quick. The navy is boats and ships and also this clever kind of boat that goes underneath the sea. Submarines they were called; sub which means under and marine which means the sea."

"Under the sea? Isn't that the seabed, that's under the sea? Do they burrow through the seabed, these submarines?"

"Beginning to see why these groups want you dead."

"I'm only being logical. If they go completely under the sea they ought to be tunnelling through the seabed. If they just go through the water they should be called sub-the-waves. Or... something."

"Navy," said Davy, firmly. "Army for land battles, navy for sea battles and also for delivering army soldiers to different coastlines for different land battles. Guz is the closest thing anybody in this country has to a navy, nowadays. I mean, in that proper, old sense. Then there's the army. And in amongst the various small-time bandit chiefs and petty warlords, there are a few larger scale, more dangerous armies being mustered. One operates out the south-east, down Kent way. The man in charge suffered a setback, but he's recovered from that."

"Was it you who set him back?"

"Hah! I wish. Anyway, most of Kent is his now, and that's a pretty tidy base from which to operate. Kent is—I don't know if you know your geography. It's like a peninsula, which is a word you don't know the meaning of, I'm guessing?"

"You're good at guessing!" said Davy brightly.

"Peninsula is a prong of land that sticks out into the sea. Kent is like that. I mean it's a big chunk of territory, but it's basically that shape. So King Frank is surrounded on three sides by water, like a moat around a castle. He's been pushing solidly west for a while now. He's one worry, because he has an army."

"But no navy."

"No, indeed. Then there's the north. I've been up north, and it's hard country. But what we're hearing now is that something is gathering up there, and probably for a large scale assault. You ever heard of Father John?"

"*My* father is called John."

"Not him."

"Well," said Davy, reasonably, "I daresay a lot of fathers are called John. It's quite a common name."

"I hate to say I liked you better when you were freezing and weeping," said Daniel. "But it's becoming increasingly hard to avoid the truth of that. Father John is real, though enough legends have accrued around him to suggest that he's done a good job generating a cult of personality. He's very dangerous, and from what my superiors at Guz can glean, he's pulling together a very large army. You don't do that unless you intend to use it."

"Maybe he wants it for parades and such?"

"John's focus has been to his north for a long time, but what we're hearing is that he's sorted all that out now. Which means his attention is liable to be redirected south. Which is bad news for everybody in this territory."

"Guz, the navy. John, the army."

"There's also Wycombe. Plenty of people have underestimated those women to their cost. Picture the whole island. There's us tucked away in the bottom left. Then, from the bottom right, through the middle and up to the top, in amongst the many smaller groups and militias, are three more considerable armed forces, all with their own ambitions and plans. Kent, Wycombe and John in the north."

"Mother Patel has a big atlas-book at her house," said Davy. "I used to go and look at it, to work out where the Hill was in relation to the rest of the country. I spent a lot of time exploring the land with my mind, wandering up and down rivers. But it turned out I was looking at a map of Italy."

"Didn't the fact that it said ITALY give it away?"

"Oh I can't read," said Davy, matter-of-factly. "Ma concentrated her energies on teaching my sisters, obviously."

"Obviously?"

"Well, they're older, and they're not brain-sick like me. Julia and Sue. Ma said she didn't see much point in teaching me after them. Too busy. Sue, my next-up sister, says she'll try and learn me some proper reader when she gets a bit of time. I know some of the letters. But I figured England began with an I, and saw the I at the start of ITALY and then made the rest of the map fit what I thought it should look like."

"*Moving*," Daniel said, blinking, "right along, and before I degenerate into a gibbering loon: we come to the reason why you're in such high demand, my boy."

"At last!"

"England, you see. This is a difficult territory to fight over. It's difficult even to travel across in the most basic sense. Before the Sisters there were roads and cars and rail lines, the whole country threaded together. But the roads and the rails are almost all gone, and the few cars we still maintain are pretty useless without roads to run on. Before the Sisters I could've travelled from Guz to, let's say, *here* in a few hours. Now it's weeks."

"This doesn't explain why I'm in such high demand *at all*," complained Davy. "I'm starting to think you don't know."

"Be patient. I'm getting to that. We talked of the two oldest branches of the military-as-was: army and navy. But there was also an air force."

"Up in the air. Flying soldiers? Men with wings?"

"Men inside machines with wings. A few of those machines still exist of course, but flying them is not like driving a car, and nobody really knows how to do it any more. Besides which, they use a lot of fuel. I mean, an insane amount of fuel. And it's a slow, slow business distilling that much ethanol. That's even assuming we can get these flying machines to work. Guz knows more about these old kinds of aircraft than anybody, because we have a ship called an aircraft carrier *stuffed* with them."

"Wow," said Davy.

"So here's the thing. One point the old histories of war—I mean, pre-Sisters war—all agree on—to win the war you needed to control the skies. And that makes sense. You might have a great big, well-trained army on the ground, but it would be an easy matter for a war-plane to fly over and bomb your men to little, squelchy-red pieces."

"Ugh."

"Ugh is the whole of war in one handy syllable, my lad. And there are other advantages. If the roads were open, and the bridges still standing, and if I had a car and a full tank, I could drive you to Guz in a number of hours. But if I had a fuelled-up plane, I could fly you to Guz in minutes—and without any regard to whether or not there were roads, bridges or thick thick *jungle* beneath me. Having access to the air would completely revolutionise travel."

"So, all this—me being kidnapped, Wycombe, the man in the leather coat—this is about machines that can fly in the air?"

"Bingo, my boy. Bingo."

"I still don't understand."

"I have bosses, in Guz. They have their contacts all around the country, some of whom stay in touch via radio. They also send people out. People like me. We've been scouting, recruiting, checking on things, a little bit of firefighting here and there, and piecing together a bigger picture. But over the last year we've been hearing rumours, and from several different sources. Rumours of something big. Something to do with aircraft."

"Are they true, these rumours?"

"Well that's the million dolorous-dollars question, isn't it? The way Guz figures it, I suppose: it's not something that can be ignored. It's not outside the bounds of possibility that Father John has some aircraft. Maybe he's got crew who have studied them, read the handbooks, put time and resources into maintaining them. Maybe he can even spare the fuel to fly them, train pilots and so on. But it's going to be few, and it's going to be limited. Make a sort of statement at a big battle maybe. Try and intimidate the more easily scared members of your enemy's army. But hardly an air *force*. Because the old aircraft were not fundamentally different to the old planes and trains. Same sorts of engines, just put to a different use. Same fuel needful. And nobody's putting pipes into the ground to suck any more of that stuff out any more, so it's little copper stills and ethanol and drip-drip-drip. It's never enough. It's a cul-de-sac. You don't know what cul-de-sac means."

"Testicle?" Davy guessed.

"Close enough. But then these rumours started. Rumours of different tech. Just before the Sisters struck there had been breakthroughs in energy generation and new kinds of motors were developed. Still experimental, not yet put into mass production. But a motor that didn't need constant refuelling. A special kind of flying engine. You must have electricity, on your hill?"

"Mother Patel had an electricity generator. She ran it on pigshit," said Davy, eager to show off. "And it lit two lights inside her house when it got dark."

"Evidently your Mama Patel is quite the village tech-geek."

"But the lights were these wallets of glass, with little stamens inside, like the insides of flowers."

"Bulbs," said Daniel.

"No, not like tubers or seeds. Like the *insides* of a flowering plant, you know? These little twisted-around strands that got hot and bright when the electricity went into them."

"Filaments. I know about the technology. The whole thing is called a bulb."

"No," said Davy, confidently. "Anyway they were made all of glass, these lights, hundred-year-old glass. And then one broke. And then the other one broke. No way to get any more. One time a tinker came to her door, she told us, and promised he could get her a working one from Oxford, but he wanted a whole pig in payment. A whole pig! *And* some other stuff. She told him to go fish in the river for whole pigs, called him a cheeky *mah-der-chod*. That's what's she called him."

"What does that mean?"

"No idea. So, anyway, he went off. And after all, lamps and candles are just as good at shining out light, and not nearly so easy to break."

"So what did your Mama Patel do with her electrical generator after that?"

"She ran a tub with it that shook water around and made washing easier. But then the motor on that broke and she sold the generator to a man from Moreton. He came up with a horse and cart and took it away."

"The point is: you know the basics."

"Electricity," agreed Davy, in a knowledgeable voice.

"Once upon a time, electricity was *everything*. In the old world, I mean. Whole palaces were built in stone with no other purpose than making it. The towers you can see, looking towards Didcot? Poking out of the flood? They're all that remains of a huge castle that did nothing except make electricity. And the old world could store it too, in batteries. Now we can make batteries, but they're big boxes that dribble out only a small charge and don't hold it for very long. Pre-Sisters, people carried devices powered by batteries smaller than your fingernail that lasted days, or weeks. So anyway, the rumours—the rumours are that a new kind of charge-device, or motor, or something, had been developed, back then. Who knows? Davy my boy I'm going to show you something."

He rummaged in the front pocket of his bag and brought out a coin, tainted almost to coal-black by age and use. Davy had often seen old coinage from the pre-Sisters world tainted as black, and had even been amazed when Mary had polished one up to reveal a bright, bright silver artefact beneath all the grime. Daniel held this one up for Davy to see, and what he saw were numbers and incomprehensible sigils shining, a faint red, on its surface. The numbers changed, and Davy realised that the thing wasn't a coin at all but some kind of old-world device. The blackness was not any kind of taint but was rather the colour of the substance out of which it had been originally made. "What is that?"

"We're not entirely sure," Daniel conceded. "More than a clock, at any rate, although clock is partly what it is. That's not the amazing thing. The amazing thing is that it is still working. It must be one hundred and ten years old at the very least. What kind of battery could last so long?"

"Open it and find out," Davy suggested.

Daniel tucked the magic coin away, as if he feared Davy was about to bash it with a rock. "That's been done. The devices are sealed in, so we have to break them to open them, and then they don't work any more, and we're none the wiser. Anyway. The reason I'm showing you that is because it stands as evidence, howsoever small, that there may be something in these rumours."

"It's so small!"

"Small things can have big implications. This small thing is why I've been sent so very far from my home and comfy bed, for one thing. And I will take any wager you care to offer that it, or something like it, is why so many people are after you, and willing to risk killing and dying, and enduring this foul weather too."

"It is a strange fate," said Davy "that we should suffer so much fear and doubt over so small a thing."

Daniel looked at him oddly for a moment, and then said, "The rumours are about various places, but there's a particularly persistent one to do with Benson."

"Where the strange man took me."

"The strange man was called Steven Harding, and he was a nasty piece of work."

"You knew him?"

"For my sins."

"He was a *priest*?"

"What? No. Jesus, Davy, are you doing this on purpose? Knock-off the dum-dum act and try to pay attention."

"It's not an act," said Davy, in a small voice.

"I mean that he and I had crossed paths a few times in the past. He was a ruthless man, and a traveller and a warrior when he had to be, and a torturer even when he didn't. You were very unlucky to fall into his clutches, and lucky to have been freed from them."

"Why did he take me?"

"Near as I can figure it, he was hired by Wycombe. The women paid him to snatch you and bring you over to them. But he'd got wind of enough of the stories about Benson, and he was greedy enough, to think he might cut out the middle-… eh, the middle-woman. Go directly to the site. But the folk at Wycombe are not fools, and they had him shadowed. Well, either that or else they had someone at the Benson compound. Maybe they keep somebody, or somebodies, there all year. It would make sense to guard it, if the rumours about it are true."

"And what are the rumours about it?"

"In the old days Benson belonged to the British military. They flew flying machines from there, and serviced other flying machines. The rumours are that they developed new kinds of flying machines there too. I don't know how they started, these rumours, and I certainly don't know if they're true or not. But like everyone else, Guz has to take them seriously. Because if they are true then the whole balance of power shifts, and whoever can open the storehouses at that place can start making serious plans to roll through the whole kingdom like floodwater and set up their empire on whatever terms they choose."

"Storehouses?"

"You saw the compound. You were *at* the compound. It's all old buildings, all more or less tumbledown as all the regular buildings from the old-days are. If nobody tends them, houses fall down. But according to rumour there are also *underground* storage spaces, and that's where the new tech was developed and stored. According to rumour. The story is that the power for that part of the facility was not wired in from the electricity generating facilities like everyone else's. That it was the tech itself." Daniel shrugged. "Who knows? Where we are, at the moment, is: it doesn't matter if it's true. It doesn't even matter whether we believe it or not. The crucial thing is: we know *other* people believe it, and are acting on that belief, and this is destabilising the delicate socio-political balance of the whole area." He chuckled, as if he had said something funny. "So we have to act."

"Of course," Davy suggested, "what you've just said might be what all the *others* believe—if you see what I mean. Not that this magic machinery really exists, but that others believe it does. Maybe nobody actually believes this stuff exists, but everybody believes everybody *else* believes it."

"When I suggested earlier that you were a dum-dum, I may have spoken too soon. That's very astute. You should join the strategic team at Guz."

"I have to get home," Davy blurted, immediately. Then, after a breath, "I mean, it's very kind of you to offer, sir, I'm sure. But I need to get back to my Ma. And my Da, obviously."

"Calm down lad. I didn't mean straight away. But maybe think about it, longer term. Unless you're really happy working a smallholding for the rest of your natural?"

"It's home."

"Of course it is," said Daniel, with a sigh, as if the very concept was becoming a remoteness to him. "Of course it is."

"And—what I don't understand, still, what I still don't understand," Davy said, pushing his knuckles into his gut to try and relieve the hunger pangs a little, "is why *me*?"

"Why you indeed. That's the real puzzler. Here we enter into the land of Speculation. What's clear, or clear-ish, is that Wycombe think you can open the vaults under Benson. Who knows why they think that, but they evidently do. I figure that Steven Hardman believed he might be able simply to take you to Benson and then—well, you tell me. What did he ask you to do?"

"I don't remember."

"You don't remember anything?"

"I had a seizure, on the Hill," Davy said, looking through one of the glass-free windows, beyond the turbulent winter river at the distant uplands. "Next thing I knew I was waking up there."

"Who knows what he planned? It didn't work, at any rate. The question is: *would* it have worked, if he hadn't been, eh, interrupted by an emissary from Wycombe? Which is related to the question of what it is about you that makes people think they can use you to unlock these vaults. I don't suppose you've any inkling?"

"How should I know?"

"How?" Daniel seemed surprised by this answer. "You are *you*, aren't you?"

"But I'm nobody! Sir, believe me. I'm the runt of my family's litter. I herd the cows and do my chores and that's it. I'm an epileptic scrap of a boy."

"Or a visionary," said Daniel, rousing himself. "At any rate, we don't want to dally. I'm sorry breakfast wasn't more filling. Put your socks on, and we'll head north."

"North? Where—Oxford?"

"Not so far as that."

"It'll take weeks to work round Oxford and come back down!"

"Trust me, my lad. North is our best option. Put your socks back on."

Trust me was the sort of thing bad people said. Trust, Davy knew, was a quality to be earned, not something a sensible individual gave away free. But when he eased his now dry, warm socks back over his chilled naked feet the sensation was so exquisite—such an intensity of local, physical pleasure—that it quite drove suspicion from his mind.

"Boots on," said Daniel, getting to his feet. "Let's yomp."

CHAPTER EIGHT

HAT PULLED THE body out of the water and wrapped it, for want
of a better shroud, in some of Bert Rand's plastic. Then he sat
down in his boat and had a bit of a think. He wasn't a heartless
person, but it did cross his mind to push the corpse over the side
and get on with reclaiming his boat. But he didn't think he'd feel
clean, in himself, doing that. And anyway, he wanted to know
what the girl had been doing on his boat in the first place. And
what the person, or the people, who killed her had been doing
on his boat. Presumably they had blown up his boat to hide the
body. Or perhaps to punish him. Or maybe to do both at once.

Hat pulled away the plastic to take one last look at her face,
and wiped the unresisting, uncaring features with a rag to
scrape away as much mud as possible. It wasn't, it seemed, the
same girl as the one who had stowed away, those many weeks
earlier. He looked for a long time, but he was pretty sure it
wasn't her. Though it looked a little like her. But this individual
had a longer nose; and her skin was a little darker, when you'd
expect death to send the body's colour in the other direction.
And Amber—the stowaway girl—had not had a mole on the

side of her brow. Hat was pretty much certain of that. "Mole? Beauty spot," he said aloud, "I mean to say." As if the corpse cared!

He covered her again and clambered up onto deck. The rain had stopped, at any rate, and he made his way up into town.

There was no mayor, of course; no police, no courts, nothing like that. But on occasion an informal council of a dozen or so of the wealthier inhabitants might gather together, to organise tribute for a particularly pushy warlord, to keep things like the ferry chain in good order, or add fencing to the bits-and-pieces defensive boundary of the town itself. That sort of thing. Hat figured something like this dead body fell under their purview. If the girl were the daughter of a local notable, then they'd surely want to track down the killer. Of course, if the girl were a stranger or an unknown the whole town might, as it were, shrug its collective shoulders. Either way, Hat felt he had to do something. To stave off his future conscience.

He stopped by the tavern, got a little drier by the fire, and told his landlady that he'd be sleeping on his boat from now on.

"You bought a boat?"

Hat pondered this for a moment, and scraped the skin of his chin through his beard-hair. "No," he said. "I managed to raise my boat from the riverbed."

Agnieszka goggled at him. "You *did*? Clever Mr Hat."

"I am," said Hat, slowly, "both pleased and disturbed."

"Pleased!"

"To get my boat back."

"Of course. Disturbed?"

"When I raised my boat from the river bank," he said, and paused. Everybody in the saloon was paying the minutest attention to his words, now. You could have heard a flea cough. "There was a dead body inside it. The dead body is still inside it, actually, although I have wrapped the body in a makeship shroud."

"Makeship?" queried Agnieszka

"Makeshift, I mean. Excuse I, but I'm quite tired."

"Male or female dead body?" asked somebody—it was Sylvia the Wool, over by the door.

"A female dead body. A young, female, dead body."

"Whose?"

"I," said Hat, "did not recognise her."

"What was she doing on your boat? Did she drown when it went down?"

"I don't know."

"Did she die when it exploded?"

"I don't know."

"What was she even doing on your boat?"

A shrug.

"*Clothed*?" asked a man in the far corner, in a deeply resonant voice.

Hat shook his head.

That tripped the whole saloon into a collective conversational buzz. This was something. People peeled away and ran over the still-damp streets to pass the news about. Hat, accompanied by half a dozen people, returned to his boat, and explained half a dozen times, to half a dozen different people, how he had raised it from the riverbed. People clonked onto the boat and bashed about belowdecks and Hat didn't like it at all.

The initial question was whether anybody recognised her. Nobody did. So that took some of the urgency out of the situation. People crowding the bank absorbed this news. The phrase "Does anyone know who she is?" became replaced with "Does anybody know who it is?

Hat was able to persuade two Goringers—merchants both, prominent in the town, one woman one man—to take the body out of his boat and find a place for it on land. A group pushed the body up to the hatch and a second group grabbed it from on-deck and pulled it through. As it came the rain started again, and the plastic sheet covering the corpse slipped free. The crowd oo'd like a theatre audience: a naked girl! Careless who saw her! The new rain made her slippy, and she twisted and fell to the deck with a clunk.

Hat was finally able to shoo all the people off his boat. One of the last to leave was Sylvia Carr, Sylvia the Wool, who came close and cupped Hat's elbow in one of her hands. "We'd like to have a talk with you about this bad business," she said. There was a rather fierce expression on her face. It jolted Hat out of his usual placidity.

"It *is* a bad business," he said scratching his beard with his unencumbered hand. "I was very sorry to have found her, in my boat. I could have just pitched her over the side, you know."

Sylvia looked closely at him. "You did the right thing," she said, in what was perhaps an attempt at a softened tone of voice. "I'll send one of my lads to escort you tomorrow, Mr Hat. We'd just like to chat."

As far as Hat knew, they put the body in a mushroom shed in the east of the city. He was just pleased, to begin with, that he was finally alone again. He made one more trip: up to Bert's Plastic Emporium to return the fabric, and then looping via the tavern to pick up his things, and then he got onto his boat and began the business of cleaning up.

Sylvia Carr's 'lads' didn't come the following day, and Hat was content not to be compelled to leave the boat so soon. There was a lot to do. He began by pumping out all the remaining water, scooping most of the mud out with a small shovel and cleaning up the rest as best he could. He tidied up all the bit and pieces that the sinking had tossed about, and discovered, in amongst his things, a set of clothes that, he had to assume, had belonged to the dead girl. He put these, sodden as they were, in a bag.

This all took a day, and the inside of the boat reeked of decay and riverbed and damp. There wasn't anything Hat could do about that as yet, and he slept an uncomfortable, fitful night in his damp clothes. The rain kept raining, off and on, all night, and all the next day.

In the morning he found a pool of water by the repaired section of the hull, and he went over the inside with putty and treated the outsides again too, even though the rain was constant. Since this necessitated his going back in the river to reach the lower parts of the repair, it was not comfortable. The putty was a temporary solution. What he needed was tar, and for that he needed a heat-source.

So Hat spent much of the rest of the day trying to get a fire going in his stove, a frustratingly awkward process.

The stove was an antique black iron structure, built well before the Sisters came—possibly hundreds of years before. It was of course damp inside and out, and all his firewood, carefully collected and chopped up with Hat's little axe, was soaked through with water. Hat dried out individual shards of wood over the flame of his oil lamp, and when they were dry enough to light he stacked them in the stove and set them going. He had to do this three times: the first two lots fizzled and died in moments. The third burned, though, and Hat kept feeding in large splinters and twiggy-chunks of wood until the interior of the stove dried out. Then he cleared it out, and set a fourth fire, bigger than the rest, and carefully, one by one, handed through extra chips and portions. When the fire was properly raging and nicely hot, he fed it one of the damp chunks from his reassembled woodpile. This block hissed and smoked and generally made a racket, and although Hat wondered if it might catch in the end it simply smothered the original fire. So he took this log out and carefully reset the fire with shards warmed over the oil lamp. A second time, and with the same log, the fire bedded in properly.

For long minutes Hat huddled in front of the stove in almost a fugue state, letting the heat reach his flesh. But he couldn't afford to waste time. He split a large log, did his best to dry it out in front of the fire, turning it as though cooking it, and as the original fire turned the corner from peak brightness and began dying down he fed one of these in. Again there was a great deal of spitting and hissing, but although the flame dimmed very low, in didn't go out, and soon the fire was as bright and hot as before. He did the same thing with the second half of the split log, and within five minutes the stove was stonking hot.

Hat shut the stove's front door and piled as much wet wood on top as he could. Then he spent an hour or so going through the whole of the belowdecks, tidying away everything else that was amiss, wiping as much dirt and mud off as possible and throwing out the strands of weed. Some of the food in his larder was already going off. He threw away the clearly dangerous stuff, ate the stuff that was just on the turn—hoping for the best—and arrayed the remains out near the stove to try and dry them a little.

The heat of the little stove was already drawing the worst smells from the damp wood and a kind of misty fug filled the interior. It wasn't pleasant, but it was bearable. Some of the wood on the top was dry enough now to feed to the fire, and to do so with only minimal hissing. He restocked the top with wet wood, curled up on the floor in front of it—like an old dog—and fell asleep.

He didn't sleep long, conscious that he didn't want to let the fire burn out. Nonetheless he woke feeling more refreshed than he had for a long time. It was easy, now, to feed stove-dried wood into the fire, and to stack more damp logs on top to dry; and he piled the rest of his wood supply behind the stove. Then he tidied up some more, and spent a tiresome but worthwhile hour wiping away the last of the interior mud with two rags, which he rinsed in rainwater on the deck. He spent another hour scraping mud out of the seams between the planks and regrouting where he needed to. Then he laid out all the various bits and pieces of carpets he had acquired over the years on the deck to wash clean in the rainfall.

By now, the working stove was creating a virtuous circle of heating and drying. The wet was being driven out of the walls and floor—more slowly than it would have been in summer, of course, because it couldn't simply be ventilated. But for the first time in several days Hat felt his body relax into the warmth. If anything, in fact, it began to feel too warm belowdecks. That couldn't be helped either.

He went through a few of his belongings to determine whether the water had damaged them beyond use. He had three treasured books, the pages transformed from tight-bound neat rectangles into crazily contoured and blotched rhubarb leaves. There seemed little point in keeping them to read, although he stood them up on the opened V of their spine and fanned the damp paper out in front of the stove to dry them. They'd be good as kindling. An old clockwork clock seemed, still, to work, and his spare clothes would dry OK.

He had one last task to do before he could call it a day. He retrieved an old screw-top tin, and put it on the top of the stove. Tar.

He went up on deck. The rain had eased off for a while. The only sound the xylophonic dripping from the trees into the puddles below. He wiped a bench dry-ish and sat down, looking around him. The air smelt clean. He retrieved a second precious cigarette. For a while he simply looked at it and put it to his nostrils to sniff it. Finally he lit it up, and sat smoking it for as long as it took to smoke. Three dark birds, possibly rooks, took advantage of the absence of rainfall to scutter into the air and flap away south. Eastward, over the hump of the rising Chiltern hills, Hat saw a brief flicker of light, as if the sky god was trying, and failing, to kindle a fire. He counted one, good-and-ready, two, good-and-ready... and had got to ten before the crunching rumble of the thunder swelled into audibility. What was that? Two miles away?

What had the girl been doing on his boat? He didn't know.

Why had she taken off her clothes? Maybe she had she set the explosion, and maybe had accidentally died in it? Her skull broken by the blast, or herself drowning before she could escape the sinking boat?

More likely: somebody else had killed her and sunk the boat to hide the corpse.

He didn't know.

The sky overhead was cauliflowered with grey-white clouds, but there were enough breaks over the brown of the westward hills to let in tints of egg-yolk yellow and low red light. The sun setting, as it always did.

Hat went back belowdecks. It reeked down there, and was far too hot. The tar was liquid now, bubbling with slow-popping black blisters. The smell of it was very strong. Hat wrapped his left hand in an old rag, lifted the tar from the stove and took it to the repaired breach. He didn't have a proper brush, so he used a rusty old spatula, and spread the steaming black goo into the seams and cracks of his repair. He put the tin away, scraped the spatula clean, had a little more to eat and went to sleep.

Three days later Sylvia's lads finally came to escort him up the hill to the Carr house. "Just a little chat," said the eldest. "Nothing to be afeared of." Hat hadn't been particularly scared until the fellow said that.

They let him into the big house and left him waiting in the downstairs hall—a tall, whitewashed space with many pictures hanging on the wall and clusters of mildew spotting the edges and corners. There were two wall-mounted radiators facing one another on opposite walls, and an electric light dangling ostentatiously from the ceiling. Privileges of wealth: heat and light at the press of a button. She must have a generator out back. Or in the basement.

Eventually Hat was ushered through to a chill room containing a heavily scratched and revarnished dining table. Across this sat Sylvia. Her eldest son sat on her left—a man called Don, Hat thought, or maybe Ron—and a man Hat didn't recognise on her right. She didn't introduce anybody.

"Mr Hat," she said, "We want you to tell us everything about this dead girl."

Hat scratched his chin, and then smoothed his beard-hair back into place. "I don't know everything about her."

"Tell us what you know."

"I don't know anything about her."

"Don't play games with us, Hat," said the grizzled stranger on Sylvia's right.

Hat thought about this. "I'm not playing games," he said.

"Tell us," Sylvia tried, "how you found her."

So Hat told that story. It wasn't much of a story. "I didn't recognise her. I gave a lift to a girl a month or more ago. Perhaps two months. I took her up from Henley to Pangbourne, and that's where she got off. For a while I thought the dead girl was her, but she looked," Hat crunched up his brow, and ran his thumbnail over the left and then the right flank of his moustache. "Different," he concluded.

"Who was this girl, the one you gave a lift to?" demanded the gruff stranger. "Were you sleeping with her?"

"No," said Hat, mildly. He rather wished, now, that he hadn't mentioned the other girl.

"I'm trying to see the relevance of that little story," said Sylvia, in her stern voice. "Were you also giving the dead girl a lift on your boat? Is that why she was on board?"

"No," said Hat. "I never saw the dead girl before. The first thing I saw of her was her shoulder, when the rest of her was submerged. Then I saw all of her when I pulled her out of the water. That was the first time I ever saw her."

"How do we know *you* didn't kill her?" squeaked Sylvia's son.

"Hush Ron," said Sylvia, scowling at him. "Hush now." She turned to face Hat. "How *do* we know you didn't kill her?"

"I didn't," said Hat.

Oddly, they seemed to take this as tantamount to proof of his innocence. They all nodded.

"We've spoken to people who were in Agnieszka Lis's tavern," said Sylvia. "They confirm you were there all morning."

"They *confirm* it," agreed the cross-faced man on Sylvia's right.

"So you can't have killed her."

"*Can't!*" repeated the cross-faced man, as if the word were an accusation.

"The girl—we don't know her name—"

"We haven't," the cross-faced man broke in, glaring at Hat as if this were somehow his fault, "been able to discover what her name *was*."

"—the girl was tortured."

"Oh dear," said Hat in a voice so low it was almost a whisper.

"There were marks on her wrists to suggest she'd been tied. There were signs that sharp objects, needles maybe, had been driven under her fingernails and also her toenails. You didn't see the marks of this when you recovered her body?"

"I didn't look too closely. It didn't seem," said Hat, his mouth dry and his voice low and hoarse, "decent to ogle her."

"Somebody wanted to hurt her," said Sylvia. "Either to get something from her, information maybe. Or else just for the pleasure of hurting her."

Hat stared at the table top. Most of the scratches on it were shallow, and most ran parallel to the rim of the table. But there were one or two deeper scrapes and gouges that ran from the outside in towards the centre. He couldn't imagine how they'd come about. They looked as though somebody had set out to damage the table on purpose.

"Horrible," he said, eventually.

"It would help us if we knew who this girl was," Sylvia said. "But you don't know."

"I don't."

"See yourself out, Hat, won't you?" Sylvia said, and it was so abrupt that it took Hat a moment to realise that he was being dismissed. Belatedly he stood up, and turned, and went out.

It was raining again.

He walked back down the hill in a low mood—his old mum, decades dead, used to divide sadness into three categories: the blues, the purples and the blacks. His heart was edging blue into the mauve end of purple. That poor lass!

Back at the boat: he'd left the stove on, and belowdecks was stifling and hot, with a strange pong of wood-resin and river-algae and staleness and tar. One object that had survived the sinking and raising of the vessel without harm was a small jar of apple whisky, stoppered with a plastic cork. He took three sips of this sharply burning liquid, recorked the jar and stowed it again. Time to sleep. It was so hot belowdecks that he stripped entirely naked, lay under a blanket in his bunk and tried to turn off his brain. The thought that he was sleeping within yards of the place where the nameless girl had been tortured and killed kept him awake for a long time.

Eventually he drifted off, only to wake—moments later he thought, but it was actually hours—because somebody was knocking on his deck. Banging a fist or kicking a heel on his deck. The cheek!

He got his hat, draped the blanket over his shoulders and popped up through the hatch and jumped fairly nimbly, given his age, onto the deck.

There was no rain, and the full moon was shining through a gap in the clouds making everything shine as if glazed: the wood of the deck; the river flowing past, mere yards away, in undulating crescents and *tilde*s and snakes; the mud and grass on the bank; all of it. The air smelt fresh.

A tall figure in a long coat was standing on deck, a few yards from the hatch. Standing on his deck!

"Good evening, Madam," said the stranger, gravely.

Hat said nothing. Adjusted his cloak of blanket more tightly about him.

"You'll pardon me for stomping about on your boat, Madam," the stranger went on, in a voice much closer to gloating than apology. "It's just that I was surprised to find it afloat. I'd heard that it was sunk."

"It was," said Hat.

A quizzical expression perhaps passed over the stranger's face. It was hard to tell in the dimness. He took a step forward, and then continued. "I was quite prepared to believe the stories about the boat being sunk, Madam," he said, "seeing as how I sunk it."

"You're the one who killed the girl."

Again, a pause, as if puzzled by the timbre of Hat's voice. Then, "She held out longer than I thought she would do. You can be proud of her. On the topic of whereabouts on the barge you keep your records she gave nothing away at all. I don't suppose you'd care to enlighten me on that one? I looked pretty thoroughly, but you can understand that I was in a hurry at the time."

Hat said nothing. The stranger stepped forward again and lifted something out of the shadows of his coat. It looked like a handgun. Hat registered this, and then thought about it. In his experience, guns were more likely to misfire during Monsoon season than at other times of year. Damp getting into the ammo. Then again, the probability of a misfire was not the sort of chance it was worth literally risking your life on.

"No?" said the stranger. "Well, I'm not surprised. You realise, of course, that the alternative to me *having* it is me putting it out of the way of everybody else, yes? Can't see that stuff falling into just anybody's hands, can we? I suspect your bosses would even *agree* with me, on that score."

Hat said nothing. The stranger leaned a little closer, as if trying to get a clearer view of Hat's face under the shadow-hung rim of his hat.

"Madam," he said, "do we *know* one another?"

"Don't believe so."

The stranger peered down through the hatch, although the gun was still trained on Hat. "You can feel the warmth," he said. "You've been drying the old boat out, I see."

Hat said nothing. He was sizing his opponent up. That sizing was not a reassuring process. The stranger was at least six inches taller than him, and bulkier, and younger. Presumably he was more experienced when it came to fighting. Evidently he had no qualms about hurting and killing people.

"Good idea," the stranger was saying. "And handy for me. You can imagine the sort of accident that might befall you—falling asleep before the fire. A lady of a certain age, liable to nodding off, drowsy with the fumes of the stove. And then—*pouf*, up in flames. The weather probably won't hold for very long, but a good chunk of the boat might burn before the next bout of rainfall. And that would serve my purposes perfectly adequately."

Hat pondered this. "Most," he offered, "of the timber is still damp."

"You're probably right. Still, *you* needn't worry, Madam: it won't be your problem. You'll be past caring." With his free hand the man was fumbling something out of his left coat pocket. A snake, or a belt, or a rope. Hat dropped his chin, half a nod of understanding—the stranger was going to throttle him, and burn his corpse, and try to burn his boat, for whatever incomprehensible reasons had led him to killing the girl and sinking the boat. Strangled, cremated, forgotten.

It was, all things considered, an undesirable turn of events.

"Your second-mate," said the stranger, and then stopped again. He seemed again to be peering in a puzzled way at

Hat. "Is that the correct nautical term? I'm no expert in these matters."

Hat looked up. "Say?"

"Your sailor-ward did give me the name of the *place*. Eventually, she gave up that information. Benson, she said. Good news for you, since otherwise I'd have to go to work on you to extract the name. I don't mind saying: in my experience women crack more easily than men, and old women crack more easily than young ones. It's exactly what you'd expect. One might think that a counter-intuitive state of play where the old hold out longer than the young, and women have steel in them that men lack—think childbirth, think period pains. But what it is, I think, is that pain fires up male testosterone and makes them more stubborn." He was saying all this, Hat figured, to give himself time to arrange the cord in his left hand—a process that was taking him longer than it otherwise would, because he was still aiming the pistol with his right.

"Benson," repeated Hat.

"Indeed. Your people haven't played it very well, I must say. It hasn't been too difficult for me to put together the magic boy and the place, has it?" A cloud shunted in front of the moon, and the already dim light thickened and dimmed further.

"The magic boy?"

"You do understand, my dear," said the stranger, coming another step closer, "that I have to cover my traces. It's nothing personal. I can't have your people coming after me, to punish me, as they surely would if they knew what I had done. But I am no sadist. I can make it as quick and painless as can be imagined, as a courtesy to you, ma'am. I assume you have some inkling of what he will unlock, at Benson? I can be honest, in the circumstances, and confess I don't. Perhaps you could even tell me?"

"Honestly?" said Hat, "I haven't the first fucking clue what you're even on about, mate."

The moon emerged from the clouds, and the deck gleamed with faint white light. Hat whipped his blanket off with his right hand and twirled it round into a ropey tangle of cloth. The action made his cods jiggle in the moonlight.

This disrobing seemed to freeze the stranger to the spot. Presumably, having believed he was in conversation with a rather gruff-voiced and elderly woman, it took him a moment to readjust his understanding of the situation. And, a fraction before his mind clicked into a proper sense of what was going on, Hat had whipped the blanket round and smacked him in the face.

The stranger flinched back from the blow. His foot slipped on the wet deck and his other leg kicked up like a dancer's. He almost fell right over, but with a lurching hop on his one leg he managed—just—to stay upright.

Hat wasn't about to stick around. Clouds veiled the moon again, and everything was suddenly dark. But Hat knew his boat. He ducked, turned, and ran past the length and round the bridge. This structure was not tall, too stumpy to give him any cover, but the stranger couldn't see very clearly. A slit in the cloud let a single shaft of moonlight down, and Hat's nakedness shone like a ghost in the night.

There was an intensely loud noise, like the whole boat snapping sharply in two. Hat was already bent over, but he ducked a little lower and heard a two-tone sound somewhere to this right, a whizz so high-pitched it was almost into dog territory shifting marginally down in register after passing him. Then his bare foot was where the gunwale should be—and it was—and he was leaping from the boat onto the shore.

He jinked to the right, and ran as fast as he could to get behind the trees he knew grew that way. But everything was dark and he didn't know the bankside like he knew his own boat, so he misjudged this. As he thought he was approaching the tree he was actually at the tree, and a painful jarring collision of shoulder against bark informed him of that fact. He reeled, slipped on the wet grass and went down. But he was up again, and running.

The night was so quiet he could hear the footsteps of his pursuer. But he was on the main street now, climbing away from the river, and already there was a light in at one of the windows. That gunshot would have awoken many. If the stranger fired again it would bring the whole town out of bed, which could only be good for Hat. Assuming a second shot didn't kill him.

From behind the stranger bellowed something weird, "I thought you a pretty strange looking woman," he called. "But now I'm wondering—are you *Henry himself*?"

Henry, thought Hat. *Henry*? And he sprinted on, his cock slapping left and right on his thighs like a hard-swimming fish's tail.

Given that his life was at stake, there seemed little point in reticence. "Haloo!" Hat yelled, as he ran naked up the high street, his blanket, still clutched in his right hand, flapping behind him like a great flag, his hat firmly on his head. "Haloo! Haloo!"

Soon enough the whole town was up. People picked up crossbows and guns and went down to Hat's boat. The stranger had returned to it andhad attempted to set it alight, but although there was some scorching belowdecks the timbers were too wet to catch fire—exactly as Hat had said.

Hat spent some time warming his frozen feet at Agnieszka's fire, the blanket around his shoulders again and tucked between his legs to preserve his modesty. She gave him a glass of mulled cider, and he thanked her. Sylvia Carr emerged, looking cross at having been woken, but she was efficient: organised a posse that went round Goring and found nothing. The ferry was safe, the fire on Hat's boat had been put out, the stranger appeared to have vanished into the countryside.

"He'll be back, I suppose," said Agnieszka. "To finish the job."

Hat couldn't disagree with her. That is to say: he had no idea why the stranger had killed that girl and sunk his boat, or why he had assumed Hat was a woman, and threatened and cajoled him to give up some secret before killing him and sinking his boat again. All that was a perfect blank to him. He didn't even know why the dead girl, whoever she was, had been on his boat in the first place. But the stranger's murderous animosity didn't need to be comprehended to be understood.

By the time he emerged from the tavern, walking barefoot down the chilly road to his boat, dawn was making the rim of the eastern hills glow ruddy and pink. He readied himself for disaster, but actually the inside of his boat was not as disarranged as he feared. The stranger had banged about, knocked stuff over, and started a fire with some of his kindling. The fire hadn't taken, and the stranger had, clearly, run off as the town began to wake and shout and run around. Hat got dressed, cleared up the downbelow, and went up on deck to sit and watch the sunrise take proper possession of the eastern sky.

He had nearly died, he thought. He had nearly been killed, which would have left him with four tobacco cigarettes unsmoked. That eventuality would have been almost a bigger tragedy than his actual death. Then again, he was still alive, and that was something. So he lit one of the remaining fags and smoked it slowly, and the daylight swelled and filled the east.

The clouds were few and scattered. It looked like the Monsoon was drawing to a close. And even if it wasn't, it would make sense to move on, put distance between himself and whoever it was who wanted—for whatever crazy reason—to kill him.

He didn't want to give the people of Goring the impression that he was absconding, so he stayed another day. He spoke again to Sylvia, and thanked her. But she was distracted—news of the commotion had reached the ears of the consignment of soldiers from Guz, and some were coming to check things out, a state of affairs that evidently preyed on Sylvia's mind rather more than Hat's being alive or being murdered. Hat gave Agnieszka a formal IOU, and said his goodbyes. Then he got back on his boat, and started the precarious business of navigating it down the Monsoon-swollen Thames.

The next day the temperature dropped sharply. Ice began to form on the edges of the river's flow. One day more and ice was floating past him as he moved. He put all his clothes on, two pairs of gloves, and kept the stove on all day and all night. He made it over the flooded remains of Reading and had almost got to Shiplake when the whole river froze solid, clasping the boat tight as a corpse bride holds her lover, and taking the decision of where to stop out of his hands. Hat stomped up and down the deck. It was a lonely sort of place, which was worrying—what if the stranger were tracking him with intent to finish what he'd started? But then again, maybe the stranger had gone further north—he'd mentioned Benson, hadn't he? Wasn't that an old town, long swallowed by the Thames? The benefit of Hat's present location was that there were many trees round and about: harder to cut off branches and boughs, now that they were all frozen, but still a source of fuel. He would wait out the deep chill until the river thawed, and then go on down to Henley. Stay there until spring and the warmer weather.

He was, Hat reflected as he fetched his axe, lucky to be alive. So maybe luck was with him after all.

SOME NIGHTS, WHEN he sat in his snug, the stove on, the freezing world outside, uneasy thoughts came to him. He couldn't help imagining what it had been like for that poor girl, hurt and then killed, in this very space. These curving wooden walls the last things her mortal eyes saw, some horror of a man, tall and pitiless, pressing her into pain and death and not letting her ever return from that place. Hat wasn't a man given much to dreaming, but he sometimes woke up in the night feeling sick and scared, and remembering what had happened.

He hoarded his last remaining tobacco. It had cost him dearly, after all. Indeed, together with the debts he had incurred in Goring it would take him most of the spring and summer to get his head back above water, financially. So he went back on his herbal smokes, and he made the best of the situation. Sitting on his deck, swaddled up with as many items of clothing as he could fit in, smoking and looking around the frozen world.

It all had something to do with Wycombe, of course. He wasn't stupid. He could figure that much out. Content as he was to keep his head down and just get on with his life, he was aware that Henry up in Wycombe had big strategic plans for the place. The poor lass killed must have been part of it. The killer thinking he—Hat the Boat, a most unfeminine individual—must have been a woman. That was because he assumed the boat was Wycombe's vessel, and that Wycombe's plans were hidden inside it somewhere, and that if he (the killer) couldn't find them it was better if it (the boat) was completely destroyed.

It was a mess, no question.

One day, some weeks later, Hat went out on the frozen river, a dozen yards from his boat, and cut an oval in the ice (he was aiming for a circle, but the shape got away from him as he laboured). He dangled a line in the water. He sat on a little stool and looked at the birds flying over the gleaming white sky above. And then he looked at the perfectly silent, trees, all wrapped in the suede of their frost. And here, coming through the trees, was a stranger.

Naturally Hat was apprehensive. But as the figure came closer he saw that he knew her. It was Eva, from Wycombe, the person who had given him the docket that had originally taken him up who had given him the docket that had originally taken him up to Pangbourne, the voyage on which the other girl, Amber, had tried to stow away. Eva, whose previous arrival had more or less kickstarted this whole turn of events.

"Hello Eva," he called.

She stepped from the bank onto the ice, and carried on walking towards him, stepping less steadily on that more treacherous surface.

"Hello Hat," she said. "Any luck, with the fish?"

"Not yet," he said.

She reached him, and stood next to him, her breath coming out in ferny clouds. "Hat," she said, when she had got her breath back. "I've been looking for you."

He nodded slowly, as if he expected nothing less.

"We heard about all the business in Goring," she said. "Somebody tried to sink your boat."

"Somebody succeeded in sinking my boat," said Hat.

"We're sorry."

"I got it back up."

"And you found a dead body on board, I hear?"

He nodded.

"Hat," said Eva. "I'd like it very much if you could tell me all about the whole thing."

And so he did.

CHAPTER NINE

DAVY TRUDGED BEHIND Daniel as they walked north-west, following their own hazy shadows over crunchy ground. Every now and again Daniel would get spooked, and usher Davy into some cover or other—behind a clutch of trees, or into the ruins of an old house. They would sit there for a while as Daniel surveilled the landscape with an unhurried eye. Davy couldn't see anything, or anyone, but Daniel insisted his sixth sense had saved his life on more than one previous occasion.

Eventually they resumed their trek.

To their left the river widened and slowed, until it was a cold lake stretching almost to the horizon. The surface had a mauve-black quality, speckled with patches of paler ice, and the far bank was softly occluded by a low-lying mist. Every now and again they would see the steeple of an old church lifting Excalibur-like from the water's surface, or the vegetation clogged roofs of taller buildings. Far away, just visible in amongst the cold haze, were the bin-shaped tops of the old Didcot power generating chimneys. Nobody had ever explained to Davy how chimneys could make electricity, but everybody knew that once upon a time they had done precisely that. Aunt Eley had an elephant-leg basket in which she kept umbrellas: a real elephant leg, she insisted, cut off hundreds of years before and hollowed out and embalmed. That's what the distant power chimneys looked like to Davy.

They clambered up onto slightly higher ground, which made Daniel nervous because they were more exposed. Then they descended the other side into a maze of young trees, none of them taller than Davy was himself. They passed an overgrown children's play-area, climbing bars a solid wall of ivy, a tree bursting through the roof of the play house, and Davy saw movement out of the corner of his eye. He looked again: far away, through the trees, he saw a skinny, hunched-over figure darting from trunk to trunk, the saplings not quite fat enough yet to hide him.

Davy caught up with Daniel and grabbed his arm. "There's somebody there."

"I know," said Daniel, without looking round. "He's been following us for a while. He's been following *me* for much longer."

"Is he one of yours? From Guz?"

Daniel laughed a brief and humour-denuded laugh. "No. He's more by way of being my Gollum."

"Your Gollum?"

"You know that story? People still tell it, I think. He's in one of his harmless phases. Far as I can tell. I mean, he cycles through—up and down, dangerous and harmless. But I don't think we need to worry about him at the moment."

"You don't *think* we do?" Davy repeated. "That's not a very reassuring thing to say."

Daniel looked round at him. "It's not far now."

"You have a particular destination in mind, then."

"Indeed I do."

They picked their way through undergrowth and back down

towards the edge of the water. The river at this point stretched away almost out of sight, to where the hill lifted its shoulder over the horizon. Another wilderness of sedge, yellow as cream, brittle and sharp-edged as upended icicles. The clouds were breaking up overhead, like ice on the pond of the sky, blue starting to show through. The mist thinned the distance into unreality.

They turned proper north and went on half a mile or so. At one point they crossed an old road, its surface somehow not overgrown or broken up by time: it ran straight into the river, like a boat launch track. They waded through. Then, on the far side, they came upon a ruined farmhouse and beyond that a large copse of trees.

Daniel went into the copse and Davy followed. An ancient, torn-up tarpaulin was snagged on the lower branches of one of the trees: blue old-world waterproof fabric stained brown with age and old leaves. "Shit," said Daniel.

"Shit?"

"Shit."

"Are you using the word as an invitation?" Davy asked. "Or an expression of exasperation?"

"There was supposed to be a punt under that tarp."

"What's a punt?"

"It's a kind of flat bottomed boat. You pole it along. I was going to use it to take us both over the water, and get you home."

"Oh," said Davy.

"The annoying thing," Daniel said, poking the ruined tarpaulin with his foot, "is that they left the tarp. I mean, it's a bit ragged, but it's a perfectly good piece of tarp. Steal my boat, steal my pole, but leave the tarp? I mean, what were they *thinking*?"

"What," agreed Davy. "Also, another what: what are we going to do?"

For about a minute Davy stood staring into space. Small waves were patting the edge of the land a few yards away, and making a soothing kind of sound. Davy listened. It sounded like a dog drinking from a bowl. The faintest of winter breezes made the bare twigs shiver. "Plan B," said Daniel, eventually. "I have a friend at Chalgrove. It's further east than I'd have liked to go, but I should be able to borrow a boat from her. I mean, I say friend. Friend might overstate things a little. But I'm fairly confident she won't actually kill me and sell you to Wycombe."

"Fairly sure?"

"Yep," said Daniel.

"Not," Davy pressed, "wholly sure?"

"Nope."

"Fairly is the best you can manage, sureness-wise?"

"I mean," Daniel said, kicking the tarp again, "I did think about maybe locking it up. But how does one even lock up a punt?"

They headed off. The copse was too dense, and the undergrowth too brambly, for them to pass through, so they had to come back out and go round. Then they pushed across a field hip-deep in grass and up a slope into more scrubland. Davy caught one more glimpse of Daniel's Gollum, whatever that name meant, hanging back at the copse they had just left, seemingly reluctant to come any further. They marched on and left him behind.

They passed a tractor, its body all rust, shreds of long perished rubber hanging from its wheel-hubs like meat on old bones. Somehow its front windshield was still intact, after all these years. It made Davy want to stop—that transparent rectangle would be a valuable thing to bring back to the Hill. Make a nice window, or an element in a greenhouse. But of course he was carrying no tools with which to extract it, and even if he had been there was no way to port it across country. He felt a twinge of desolation, a more-than-ordinary sadness, as he hurried on to catch up with Daniel. Such a waste!

Waste was the worst thing. The unfairness of it. The wealth of the world poured away into the dirt.

They passed through more woodland: an older, more passable stretch of forest, mostly house-tall conifers. Then across a field dominated by gigantic ferns, like something out of the Jurassic period, each one electroplated by the frost. They passed a wide cove in the lake, all iced over and glistening the sun like a tearful eye. "Looks like your Gollum has finally given up following us," Davy remarked, in passing.

This made Daniel stop. He looked around. "You're sure?"

"I think so. After we left that copse, where you'd left the punt so carelessly unlocked, he crossed over to it. But then I think he stopped there."

"I mean, don't get me wrong, he *is* insane," said Daniel, turning a slow three-sixty and surveying the whole landscape, "but he has a pretty healthy sense of self-preservation. That makes me wonder if he saw something."

For a minute or so the two of them stood in silence. The wind was picking up. Away to the north Davy could see a misty scrabbling in the zone between the ground and the low-running black clouds. It looked like sleet, rather than snow, or maybe just heavy winter rainfall. It would presumably roll down here eventually. "Maybe we should get under cover?" he suggested to Daniel. "Put the tent up?"

But Daniel was peering in a different direction—away to the east, with his hand to his brow like he was saluting. "Now that's the kind of thing that makes a fellow say," he said, "bollocksy bollocks and a second helping of big bollocks."

"What?" But Davy could see them too: half a dozen riders, coming down the lower slopes of the Chiltern Hills on horseback.

"They might not have seen us?" Davy offered.

"They've seen us."

"They can't know who we are!"

"They know who we are. We have to go, Davy my friend, and neither dilly nor dally." Daniel turned abruptly and set off jogging due west. Davy hurried after him. They got to the edge of the field and in amongst a stretch of bushes and junior trees, and then Daniel ducked down. He was breathing hard.

"If they saw us, they're going to know we're in here," Davy pointed out.

"They will indeed. I'm trying to weigh up options. I've half a mind to plunge into the river."

"I thought you said it was so cold it would kill us in moments!"

"It is, and it probably would. Which would mean you'd have to be insane to follow us, right? But there are two difficulties with that plan. One is that the river here is just too wide. If we were back beneath Benson it might be different. But that's not where we are. Two is that they're on horses, and horses can swim. So they'd probably just follow us in anyway."

"You're forgetting three," Davy added. "Which is that it would kill us within moments."

"There's too many of them for us to have any luck with a defensive redoubt, or to try to stage an ambush. Oh Fuckton-on-*Thames* this is unlucky. I tell you one thing—whoever half-inched my punt has a *lot* to answer for."

"We can't just crouch here all day."

"No, Davy my mucker, we can't. I'm going to break a resolution I've held to for many years and try to get to Oxford. Upriver, I'm afraid. And we're both going to get a lot hungrier than I initially thought we would. But I can't see what our alternatives are. Stick close to the river's edge, because the horses won't like that terrain. Take as much cover in woodland as possible. Who knows, maybe we'll get lucky and find a boat?"

"Or a magic flying machine?"

"Laughing in the face of terror, Davy. I approve. At any rate, we'll have to go into the storm. That storm, there, on the horizon. It'll be harder for them to track us though that. At least, I really hope it will. Though it'll mean we get wet, I'm afraid. Wet and cold. I'm sorry about that. Come on."

They kept low and managed an uncomfortable crouching half-run through the shrubs. Then they dropped down a slope nearer the water where they could stand up. They jogged alongside the wide expanse of slow-flowing water as it turned the corner from south-east to south, the river moving like an immense millstone under an equally impassive, similarly coloured sky. The raincloud was certainly coming closer. The wind was getting up. "We stand a better chance in that weather," Daniel called over, "though it won't be pleasant. But it will be better than the alternative."

"We can't run all the way to Oxford!" Davy called back. He had a stitch.

"There's a causeway about half a mile. If we can cross north over it our options increase—places to hide on the far side. Woodland, farmhouses. Might even be possible to steal a horse. But there's nothing for us on this side."

They jogged on, until Davy couldn't jog any further and stopped. Daniel noticed and doubled back for him. "Come on, my lad. Trees, up ahead. We'll stop in there."

So Davy stumbled on, his flank singing with an almost musical note of pain, until they came into a thicket of oak and birch trees. Three egrets, tall as children, stood knee-deep in the water staring at them: bright white and solemn, like priests. The wind chuffed up the edges of the feathers on their backs. Davy leaned against a tree trunk and tried to get his breath back. Daniel went further into the wood and returned a moment later with a broken bough, twigs and dry leaves rattling where the separation of the larger branch had robbed them of the instinct to fall. They looked like they had been stamped out of bronze foil.

"What's that for?"

"I was thinking cover," said Daniel, looking dubiously at his own find. "But maybe—I don't know, a weapon?"

"You have a crossbow."

"I was thinking more for you."

"What am I supposed to do with that?" Davy demanded. "Fan them?"

"Come on."

They pushed through the trees and out the far side. Here at last was the causeway—an old railway bank, raised against the flood-prone flatlands. The rails had long since rusted, or else been removed by enterprising locals to be melted down and repurposed. But the hefty concrete sleepers remained.

As soon as Davy had clambered up the bank he felt ridiculously exposed. Maybe Daniel's portable bush wasn't such a bad idea, after all. There wasn't any other cover up here, beyond weeds and binding creepers.

The extreme straightness of the causeway's line, out across the cold water, looked uncanny, even unpleasant, after so much natural variety. But it meant they could pass over rather than through the water, moving directly north-north-west, instead of having to detour miles round the marshy bank. Daniel looked back, grimaced, and beckoned Davy on. Davy thought about looking behind him, but decided he'd rather not know how close the pursuers were.

"If we're lucky their horses will be spooked by this strange spit."

"And if we're unlucky?"

"If we're unlucky they'll run us down like hounds chasing foxes. Come on."

At first they made good progress. The line of falling sleet was getting appreciably closer, and the colder wind from its stormfront pushed at Davy's face and body. But then fate gave them a hint as to whether luck or unluck was going to characterise their efforts: Daniel, stepping on a sleeper, dislodged a chunk of ancient concrete from its set, and did something horrible to his ankle—bent a knight's-move shape out of his leg and foot. He went straight down, and sat there cursing inventively, clutching his lower leg.

Davy crouched beside him, but there was nothing he could do. Three times the older man gathered himself, somehow, into an upright position, but each time he could sustain no weight at all upon the injured joint. "I'm sorry my forktongue boy," he said, through gritted teeth, "but I'm going to have to lean on you."

"OK," said Davy, uncertainly.

Daniel abandoned the birch bough, shouldered his pack and tried to use Davy as a crutch. It didn't work, though. The lad was too short, and did not have the necessary strength to keep him up. "We're wasting time," Daniel snarled, from the ground.

"Leave the backpack, maybe?"

"Not on your nelly."

"My what?"

"Christ alive. Nelly, nelly, nelly. Come *on*, we have to *go*."

Davy looked around. On either side the flat expanse of cold water stretched away; slushy ice moving queasily against the banks of the causeway. To his left chunks of larger ice bobbed and lolled as the flow carried them south. Up ahead the storm was much closer. Behind them, the riders had made it onto the old rail track, and were trotting towards them with an insolent leisureliness. It was horses they were riding, not donkeys; and nothing in the horses' demeanour suggested they were in the least spooked about the track they now traversed. Davy could see the riders were all armed, some with rifles, some with crossbows.

"Come on," said Daniel. He had retrieved the broken bough and was trying to fit his shoulder in amongst the dry leaves and smaller branches, to be able to use the broken end of the branch itself as the base of an impromptu crutch. He had his pack over his other shoulder and managed a few stumpy strides, before he went down again. He struggled up once more, and Davy tried to help him, and the cliff-wall of sleety rain curtained the whole land before them, mauve and black and flecked with shadowed blue-white. It was suddenly much colder, and Davy's hair was alive and struggling as if it wanted to leave his scalp. The stormfront was almost upon them.

Where the rain struck the surface of the water it sent up a mighty hissing sound like something cooking in a vast frying pan. But their pursuers had finally caught up.

"The end of the line," shouted one of the riders, drawing her horse up. She balanced a rifle across her forearm.

Daniel struggled upright yet again. "Abigail," he yelled, over the sound of the sleet *ss*-ing into the water behind him. "What a delightful surprise."

The other riders brought their horses up behind the first woman. All had rifles and crossbows and all of these were aimed at Daniel.

"You shot Steph through the *hand* with a crossbow bolt."

"Yes. Sorry about that. That was the friendliest option available to me at the time. She all right?"

"You know you half-choked her when you tied her to that rail, yeah? I mean, you know that, right?"

"Yeah, sorry about that too. But I knew you'd come get her. And look at it this way: you got a free length of rope out of the deal. That's not to be sniffed at."

"Nobody's laughing, Daniel. You're deep in the shit."

"Did you call me deep and a shit? Because, you know, half of that is actually a compliment."

"You heard what I said."

"It's just," he shouted, "it's pretty hard to hear you, over the noise of this storm."

Davy looked behind him. The first few bulletheaded drops of freezing rain were arriving, banging the ground like a drum, pulling tall nipple-shaped splashes out of the surrounding water.

Then the storm was on them. There was a sound like a gigantic sigh, uttered by the whole of the air around them, and suddenly everybody was wet. Thick threads of water were everywhere, spinal plummets of freezing drenching rain. The horses didn't like it, shook and jerked their heads. All at once the storm swallowed them. Everything was rain: cold drops hard as shot pummelled him from above. Everything went murky and indistinct, and the level of noise magnified. Davy was soaked in a moment, and shivering with cold in another.

"End of the line, Daniel," called Abigail, again.

"Don't," he said, the expression on his face visibly slackening, "don't hurt the boy. All right? He's a good kid." Davy looked at him and felt a queasy sensation in his gut.

"That's out of your hands now, Daniel," said Abigail, shaking her head. She lifted the rifle a fraction and put her free hand down to her horse's neck, to calm it before the startlement of the gun's discharge. The intensity of the hard rain was increasing. She may have said something else. Davy couldn't be sure. His ears were filled with the percussion of the whole sky, and it was hard to make out anything through the rainfall.

Davy's panic swelled. "Wait," he called, but his voice sounded thin and reedy. He put a hand to his face to wipe the water away. It felt like total immersion, and the water was as cold as if it had fallen all the way from outer space. On either side of him the Thames, insofar as it could be seen at all through the torn-up, blurry air, was fizzingly spiky and white and lively.

Abigail *was* saying something else, but though Davy could see her mouth moving, and could hear a sort of human-sounding *wah-wah* in amongst the crashing and flushing of the rainfall, he couldn't make out any words. Daniel was staring up at her.

She lifted her rifle a fraction more, aiming it with one hand, and pulled the trigger.

Nothing. Either the round was a dud already, or else the sudden rain had seeped in and soddened it. And Daniel was suddenly in motion. He lurched forward, his mouth wide open, possibly yelling—it was impossible to hear over the noise of the storm. But it was surely a yell, for he had put his bad foot forward, and surely that hurt like hell. His motion brought him close enough to swing the bough at the snout of Abigail horse, and the beast didn't like that—flinched back, danced several hoofsteps in reverse, pressed its rump into the face of the horse behind. Abigail was shouting something, and one of the riders behind got a shot off—even in amongst the huge sound of the storm Davy heard the detonation clearly and saw the briefly shining tassel of discharging gunpowder leaving the end of the barrel.

Even as the charge was exiting the gun, Daniel was ducking down; or not ducking, so much as falling forward, unable to bear any weight on his bad ankle. But it was a strategic tumble. He bent both knees, hit the sodden ground, and slid on his belly away to the left.

A second rider, further back, fired her rifle too, and a moment later something flickered through, glinting in the scrabbled light. It might have been a crossbow bolt.

Daniel was no longer on the causeway.

Abigail swung herself into an athletic dismount, put her jammed rifle into its saddle holster and pulled out a crossbow of her own. She stepped over a sleeper, knelt down and aimed the weapon into the water. She was only a few feet from Davy, and it occurred to him that she was presenting him with a target. He could tackle her, push her, fight. But of course he didn't do that. Of course he did nothing.

She was trying to see through the scratched-up rainy view, to pick out Daniel's form in the frothing water. Or, maybe, to check that he had gone under and wasn't coming back up. One of the other women shouted something from her horse. Davy couldn't make out what, but he heard Abigail's reply. "He's gone."

The hammering din of the rain, everywhere, all around, all encompassing. Water streaming into his eyes.

It felt as though some entity inside Davy's gut reached up and clutched hard at his heart.

Abigail stood up, wiping her face clear of water, scanning the scene.

Then there was another shot. Not from the causeway this time. Abigail's horse snorted a great puff of steam from its nostrils and made a noise somewhere between a cough and a groan, loud enough to be heard over the sound of the storm. A fat black fly had landed on its big horse face, just behind its left eye. But this fly didn't rest there. Nor did it fly away. Instead, freakishly, the fly dissolved and spread. It began generating matter out of its deliquescing body, and this became a trickle and then a constant flow, spurting down the beast's broad cheek and dripping off it to fall, with the rain, to the ground. The horse coughed again, and then knelt on its two forelegs, with a clunk and a shudder of its harness. Then the beast rolled onto its side and put its head on one of the crumbling railway sleepers as a pillow, and lay still.

Abigail watched this, her mouth an O. Then she turned and lifted her crossbow and aimed—shifted her aim and tried again—and aimed a third time. Didn't pull the trigger. She could see nothing to shoot, and there was no point in wasting a crossbow bolt.

Davy stared at the dead horse. Rain pounded it and fizzed a kind of halo over the curve of its body. It was so bulky. So much weight and heft, and yet it was dead. It had possessed life in its enormous frame, and now it possessed none at all. The sheer weight of the corpse made it seem, somehow, more dead than it otherwise would.

But his eye was distracted by Abigail in motion. It took him a moment to understand what she was doing. She was dancing—leaping in a pure frenzy of frustration. And she was screaming at the frantic water, yelling through the endless rain, "Daniel you'll pay for that—I'll *make* you pay for that—I'll *personally* make you pay for that!"

Soon enough she got it out of her system. The rage dance ceased. The rain continued falling, and the women gathered to strip the body of the horse of its trappings, and redistribute them to the other mounts. Finally they came for Davy, with a hood for his head and a set of old metal handcuffs for his wrists, and then he was hauled up, sightless, onto a horse behind one of the women, and away they went.

INTERVAL

The Borough

HENRY WAS SHORT for Henrietta. She had heard the joke about her name many times, and from all sorts of people—had, indeed, heard it reinvented from scratch by a whole new generation who thought they were being clever and unique. When she was a girl it would be:

"Hey, I'm looking for my sister."

"Henrietta?"

"He *did*? That's terrible!"

And when she was an old woman it would be:

"Say, what's the deal with that old woman up on Stately, with the goats?"

"Henrietta?"

"Did he?"

"Hungry times, I guess."

When she was a child she would smile along with the joke, not because she found it amusing, but because people liked jokes, and there was no harm in indulging them. But the older she got the less patience she had with people and their foolishnesses. As if this was an epoch for *jokes*!

Then again, if her long life had taught her anything it was that jokes contained a pip of truth inside them, and that this truth was always uncomfortable. Take Punch and Judy, popular with travelling puppet-men. Itinerants entertaining villages for a heel of bread and a cup of beer—what was funny about Punch and Judy if not our fear of being beaten, or our deeper fear at how much we would enjoy beating others? And what did that say about us?

One time, Father John's people hanged a man for stealing sheep. They threw the rope over a tree bough, and as they fitted the condemned man's head into the noose he said, "This is a strange necktie, my friends, it floats up instead of hanging down." And everybody laughed! The whole crowd gathered to see it *laughed*. Then the hangman said, no need to worry there, my friend, when we tighten this knot your tongue will come out and hang all the way down to your balls, and the crowd had laughed even harder. Henry had been there, an old woman by this time, and she had seen it with her own eyes. Why were they laughing? And the most remarkable thing was: the condemned man had laughed harder at the hangman's joke than anybody else! What was *he* laughing at, except his own death? And why else was he laughing, except that the alternative was to weep and howl and despair?

So, the people who made fun of young Henry's name died, and Henry survived, and Henry was not devoured by death. Lady Death in her black silk dress.

On the contrary, it was Henry who did the devouring.

That's how it turned out in the end, anyway.

Somehow, as all the people she knew and loved fell away, Henry stayed alive, such that she eventually became very old. Too old to know precisely how old she was.

She was long-lived enough, in fact, to have a kind of personal connection with the catastrophe that had redefined the whole world. Her grandmother had witnessed it, or so she claimed, when she had been a young girl. She had seen the Sisters with her own eyes, she said. They'd been living in Milton Keynes, and her great grandmother had worked with 'computers', those magic boxes that had powered so much of pre-disaster life. Gran had been at school, the day it happened. Or so she said. Henry's mother used to warn her, "Don't take everything granny says literally. These sorts of stories get built up, over time. A pinch of salt," she used to say, "is needful for the listening. I think she probably heard the story from *her* mum, and has appropriated it as her own" And Henry could believe it. Still, granny was as vivid as a poet: she was only six years old, she said, and at a primary school, and they'd all been out in the schoolyard playing at breaktime when there was a great shining dazzle in the sky. It illuminated the whole west of the sky so violently that the horizon was swallowed in light, and the trees outside the school were silhouetted so blackly that for three days afterwards they appeared on your inside-eyelids every time you closed your eyes! All the kids in the playground had stared, and then a couple of the younger ones had started crying. Granny said she hadn't cried herself, not at first. The brightness faded, and everyone was blinking—all the teachers had come outside to stare up at the sky. After that, Granny said, there was another set of blue-white flickers, from way over the horizon. Everybody started crying then, even some of the teachers, Granny said. Then, after the light, came the noise—a great tidal wave of rumbling and grinding, loud enough to hurt your ears. And a great wind. And then: panic.

Great-Grandmother used to have family in Nottingham, and in the first weeks of the chaos she had taken her family up there; but the city back then was a mess, riots and fires and destruction, and granny's two brothers had died. After a period—Granny was hazy about the length of this period, and the specifics—they'd ended up in Bicester, but then there was some kind of explosion and fire in Banbury that took down most of the town, and a bunch of refugees came south to Bicester, and life in the town grew uncomfortable. So Granny moved out, and somehow got hold of some land to the east, here in the Borough. By the time Great-Granny died, long before Henry's own birth, they owned a smallholding. Granny had married and bore many children, including (she claimed) six sons. When Henry asked her mother, "So I have six uncles?" Mammy would shake her head sadly. The details never got unpacked or laid out, because they were too painful, or perhaps because they were too muddled in Granny's head. She was a very old woman by the time Henry was old enough to pay her any attention, and would ramble, and repeat herself. Maybe her uncles had gone off to fight for some warlord or other and had got killed. Maybe they just got sick and died. Happened a lot.

Still, Granny Taylor had lived through the worst times and come out the other side. That was something. And if some of her children had not, then at any rate Henry's mother, Georgina, had not only survived but prospered. Everybody was raising livestock. The new climate made arable farming tricky. The year was punctuated by a lengthy monsoon, weeks and week— months, some years—of crop-rotting rain. Winters tended to dip into shocking cold, and the summers were short. And yet somehow Mammy had got into a rhythm of growing wheat and corn, such that she had a surplus harvested and stored-away come the rains, and that made her rich. She had married, and Henry's Dadda had built a barn, and the two of them had had four children, of which brood Henry was the youngest daughter. But Dadda had died when Henry was a baby. He got stones in his bladder, Mammy said, and they grew so agonising and stopped his pissing and his legs swelled and the whole thing became impossible. So he had arranged for a doctor to come up from Oxford, because Oxford people knew about these things. The doctor was paid to cut the stones out, but the operation didn't go well. Dadda had bled a lot, and kept seeping blood,

Mammy said, and his operation cut had never healed properly, and soon enough it went black and bad and he'd got so hot he yelled he was being roasted on a fire, and then he had died.

"You were sad," Henry said.

She must have been—who knows? Five years old, six maybe, when she first heard this tale. She had noticed that the other kids had fathers and asked why she didn't, and Mammy had laid the whole story out. It meant little to her.

"I *was* sad," Mammy confirmed. "Everyone was sad for years and years."

Still, Mammy's oldest child was twelve when Dadda died, and old enough to help; and over the following years all four kids were recruited into the running of the farm. It was a fine art, timing the crops, Mammy used to say, and some years it didn't work out. Some years the Monsoon came early, or the rain stopped altogether and parched the wheat. But other years they were able to grow and harvest a barnful of grain, and people came from all over—came from as far as Aylesbury and Winslow to buy their grain. People love bread. That's how people are.

They also kept pigs, of course, for the scraps, and a couple of goats and some chickens. In lean years they'd eat most of these, and in fat years they'd buy more. After Dadda's death Mammy took another man, Jim, but he was a wastrel and got drunk and she kicked him out. He came back from time to time, yelling, and the two of them would fight. One time he hit her so hard she dropped down—dead, Henry thought, running to her and crying and hugging her, but she was all right. She got back up after five minutes, groggy and complaining, but still alive. The side of her forehead went a queer shape for a week or two, but then settled back to normal. Two weeks after that Jim came back to live with them, and never mentioned it. And Mammy asked him to leave, and he didn't. So she yelled at him to leave, and he threatened her with his fists until she stopped yelling, and then he got drunk on the last of their beer. The next morning he wasn't breathing, and Mammy got Ted—Henry's older brother—to help her dig a grave. "The booze takes some men that way," Mammy said. "They tope too much, and the next thing their lungs stop. It's sad but it's sometimes what happens, and we'd best be quiet about it." Some years later Ted told his sister, "We didn't bury him, you know, Henry. The pigs ate him. The pigs ate him up." "Good," was what Henry said to that.

After that was Uncle Sunil, and he was a much nicer person. A little lazy, when it came to helping out, but good-natured and a born storyteller—fantastical stories with no basis in reality, about things like flying cows and strange monsters and treasure hidden in caves. And life was not bad for a while. They got on well with their neighbours, and all went to church in Bicester most Easters and Christmases, and when bandits came rattling through young Ted joined the posse to scare them away. Later they ended up paying their tithe for protection—to Father John's predecessor, a Scotsman with the unusual name of Wod. Soon enough, though, and with what looked in retrospect like inevitability, Father John took over the whole landscape north of Oxford and they ended up paying their tithe to his men instead. John's ascendancy at least reduced the incursions by bandits, though it did little to stop individual thieves.

Mammy Taylor put up a big wire fence all round the farm, with some old rusty barbed wire along the top. This wasn't much of a deterrent to pilferers and trespassers but it was better than nothing. Over the years she supervised the bolstering of this boundary with wooden posts, and pieces of salvaged infrastructure from the old world, and that was much better. But having walls alone was not enough: the key was having people to guard the walls. And although Mammy took on extra workers at harvest there wasn't enough to do in the farm most of the year to enable her to build up the community enough to protect it properly. So things were always a little precarious: some years good, and some bad. One year a group of lads were tearing up the countryside—originally from Cambridge way, the rumour was—and they abducted Henry's older sister Jenny. She was gone for three weeks, and bad things happened to her. Eventually she came home, because Wod's men had hanged all the Cambridge boys and let her go. But she was never the same: didn't want to talk about it, couldn't get back into the rhythm of farm life. Soon after that she told Mammy she was going, and not reasoning, not begging, not tears could persuade her otherwise. She took some supplies and went south.

Henry never saw her again. She got on with life. She brewed the beer, because that was one of her chores. Beer was safer to drink than water. She tidied and cleaned. She fed the goats and the chickens. She grew up from childhood into adulthood.

Wild pigs got established in the woodland east of the farm, and Ted used to go out hunting them with a group of his friends. It made a pleasant change to eat the gamey pork of these beasts, and when the hunters came home successful it was an excuse for festivity: a big fire and as much meat as anyone could eat, songs and stories. One year, though, Ted shot a big boar with his crossbow without killing it, and the creature ran him down, and trampled his face. The pig's trotter put out one of Ted's eyes, and scarred up his face pretty badly, and his good temper deserted him after that. One glimpse in a mirror, and he would grow sullen and angry. He married, eventually, and Henry hoped that his wife would restore him to the easy-going brother he had been before, but it didn't work out that way. Then Uncle Sunil died of asthma. And then there were several hard years, when somebody from somewhere—who knew the details?—tried to topple Wod and seize his kingdom. It was open war in the summer, and winters of sniping and guerrilla raids, and life grew pinched and untrusting. But they lived through it, and whatever was going on in the larger world resolved itself, and the fat years returned.

When she was of age Henry married a boy called Dick from Fringford, and they had two children. She left home to live with him in a house near his family and swapped-out farming for armoury work. Dick's father made bullets in a big shed in their garden: difficult, pernickerty work that left him exhausted at the day's end. Dick helped him. "It's the danger," he told Henry. "It's a constant worry. The whole place could explode—any time." Sourcing the raw materials was also tricky, and expensive. But it was lucrative work, because everybody wanted ammo, and Wod's people favoured Dick senior since his rounds had a lower failure rate than many others. So Dick lived pretty well, and for a time Henry had so much leisure time she grew bored. "Just care for the kids," Dick said, but that hardly occupied her whole day. When she travelled home for a visit Mammy scolded her preciousness, "Nothing to do all day? You should relish it!"

Henry's kids were Owl and Crow—Oliver and Charles, really, but Owl and Crow to everyone. Bright, curious kids full of laughter. And they grew strong and tall, and Henry, who knew how to read, taught them their letters. Then at the age of eleven Owl fell out of a tree and broke his thigh, and though a doctor reset it something wasn't right about the fracture, and the leg swelled big as a sack of gloop and went black and in a week Owl was dead. Crow died the following winter of a fever that came out of nowhere and from which he seemed to get better. But even though he seemed to get better he still died. Dick never got over this double blow. He withdrew into himself, and he and Henry stopped having sex, and eventually she left him, just walked away and returned to her Mammy. She later heard that Dick had been press-ganged into Wod's army, when Father John made his play for power, and that he had died at the Battle of

Little Tew. She also heard that Dick senior went on making bullets for Father John, just as he had done for Wod before him. For what else would he do?

The early years of Father John's rule were not easy, because John at that time was young and ruthless and wanted to stamp his authority on the land. Many people got hanged. Some of these danglers were thieves and troublemakers, who deserved it; and some were cranky people who did nothing worse than call John names or mumble in the tavern. Three years of bad harvests made things worse, because everybody was hungry and restless and that only made John and his lieutenants more paranoid and so more ruthless. But then the weather improved and there were half a dozen years of plenty and life settled down into more bearable rhythms.

It was during this time that Henry got together with a man called Rossi. They weren't church-married, but it was a to-all-intents-and-purposes union. He was sweet, and physically demonstrative, and good-looking; although he was also weak and dreamy and almost wholly lacking in initiative. But she let him stay, because it was better than being alone. And in a little while they had a daughter. Henry called her Rosie, because Henry thought that went cutely with the name Rossi.

Four years went by with nothing but the usual ups and downs.

Henry had acquired a reputation amongst the youngsters of the Borough as a humourless old bag. It was true she rarely laughed—but then again, what was there to laugh about? It didn't help that she was with a man nobody respected. Teens would yell jokes at her, "Did you hear about the woman so stupid she had a man's name?" And once, when she was waiting on a fishing line by the pond, and couldn't just move away, three youngsters came up and told her a story about the stupid woman who married Rossi.

"How stupid was she?"

"She was so stupid that one day she came home and found

her husband cheating on her with another woman—a redhead, it was."

"So what did the stupid woman do?"

"What did she do? She pulled out a gun and held it to her own head, to pull the trigger. And when Rossi leapt up and said, stop, what are you doing? she said, 'Shut up, I'm shooting you next.'"

Jokes weren't funny. Best to just ignore them.

One day in the summer Henry was coming back from Bicester where she had done a bit of trading, and settled a few promissaries, and stayed overnight. In the morning, she'd had breakfast and headed home with nothing in her backpack, and accordingly no real fear of being robbed. But a mile or so from home two teenage lads had jumped her, dragged her into the trees and bundled on top of her. She struggled, but they were stronger than she was. For a while they felt her up, and excitedly called out all the obscene things they planned to do with her, and how much she would love it all. She knew who they were, of course: one was Hal, Old Denny's youngest son from Oakmanor farm, and the other was one of the Stringley boys. So she kept her head, and tried rebuking them in as stern a voice as she could manage. Told them to stop. Warned them that their actions would come back to punish them, that she would tell their parents. They laughed at her, and pulled her top off, and tried to get her trousers off. This proved a harder task than they had anticipated, and after a little more struggling they suddenly gave up and ran away. Henry sat in amongst the trees, gathering herself and putting on her clothes again. She could hear their laughter receding into the distance.

She went straight home and told everybody what had happened to her. Her brother Ted was furious; and Rossi looked pained and distant. Mammy counselled caution, and there was a big row about the whole thing. "We can't afford a war with Old Denny," she said. "He's much richer than us. He outnumbers us in friends and allies. We'd lose, and that's that." But the next morning Ted had borrowed two horses from Carrie, two farms down, because (he said) riding on horseback made it harder for other people to ignore the three of them. Then he had ridden one horse, and Rossi and Henry had shared the other, and they all made their way to Old Denny's place. The old man was expecting them, of course, and opened his gate and came out to speak with them alone. He was carrying a rifle, and his people shut the gate behind him.

"I know what happened," he said, without preliminary, "and I'm sorry. I've thrashed my boy. I can't speak for that Mam Stringley, or what she'll do to hers, but mine's been punished."

"We're not happy about it," said Ted.

"Won't happen again," said Old Denny.

Rossi said nothing. He was staring away to the left, like a mooncalf, distracted by some birds in the trees.

"It's a bad business," said Ted.

"I can offer you two piglets," said Old Denny. "I can't speak for Mam Stringley, but she'll surely have something to offer you too."

"Well all right then," said Ted, shifting in his saddle. "Two, is it? Well all right."

"I don't want piglets," said Henry, speaking loud enough for everyone in Old Denny's compound to hear. "I'm the one was wronged, and I don't want piglets."

"What do you want then?" asked Old Denny, his features taking on the familiar lineament of his bargaining face.

"I want to thrash the boy myself."

Nobody was expecting this answer. Old Denny stared up at her, and then said, "I've already whipped him. He's had his thrashing."

"Not at my hands, he hasn't. I'm the one he wronged."

"Being thrashed twice for…" Old Denny began, and stopped with a growl. He changed his tack. "They're just kids, and they was just mucking about. There was no—" but he couldn't maintain eye contact with Henry for this next word, "rape performed." He faced Ted again, and addressed him directly, "Two piglets is more than fair."

"We can always find room for pigs, sis," said Ted.

"Rape was what they were planning," said Henry.

"They were just mucking about," Old Denny repeated. "Having some fun."

"Wasn't fun for me."

"Well," said Old Denny, shifting his rifle from one hand to another, and still looking at Ted, "I've made my offer."

"Sis?" urged Ted.

"Keep your piglets, Denny," said Henry. "Let's go home."

"I already thrashed him, like I said," Denny called after them, as they rode away. "He's learned his lesson—I *made* my offer. You all heard it."

Back home there was another row. Henry used the J word, but Mammy laughed in her face. "How do you get *justice* by picking a fight with Old Denny? If you beat Hal he'll come wanting restitution from us, and it won't only be a couple of piglets he demands. You'll just have to let it go." Everybody had an opinion. Sally said she'd always hated Hal, and that he'd once pushed her against a wall in Bicester and put his hands in her pants. Ted said they'd lost face by not taking the piglets and now they had nothing and would get nothing.

"I'm going to see Mam Stringley," said Henry.

"In that case I'm coming with you," said Ted.

"You can come if you keep your mouth shut," said Henry.

So they rode off together, just brother and sister, this time with Henry leading the way on her borrowed horse, and Ted checking his gun over and over.

Mam Stringley didn't even come out of her compound. She leaned from a first floor window and demanded to know why she was being bothered at all.

"You know why I'm here," Henry said. "You know what your boy did."

"High spirits," said Mam Stringley.

"Bring him out, and I'll show him some high spirits of my own," said Henry. "I have a crop here."

"A what?"

"A riding crop. Send your boy out."

"He won't be coming out to be whupped by you, Henrietta. He is not going to be whupped by no-one, I say. What did he even do wrong? Whupped, for a little kiss and a cuddle?"

"A kiss, a cuddle and an attempted rape."

"Who cares, Henrietta? I heared what passed at Old Denny's. Such airs, you have! *You're* no thirteen-year-old virgin, that we should get upset you get fucked by strangers. You're old. If you ever were anything save an old boot to look at, I'm surprised to learn it. You ought to be grateful for the attention."

"You a woman," said Henry, calmly enough. "You, to speak such."

"Fuck off Henrietta Taylor, and don't bother us no more."

"Mam Stringley look me once in the face, just one time, and then you can go your way. Look me right in the face, one woman to another."

"One mother to another," said Mam Stringley, meeting Henry's gaze, "boys is boys."

This, Henry reflected afterwards, was when the softer tissues of her heart crystallised into a more pitiless substance. It took all her self-control not to yell back at Mam Stringley that Owl and Crow had been *good* boys, and brought up in the ways of respect, and would never do what the Stringley brat had done. But her beautiful lads were dead and Stringley's were, however worthlessly, alive. And Stringley only said what she said to get a reaction. So Henry kept her lid down, and smiled and said, "You let yours run wild the way they are, they'll be hanging from one of Father John's ropes, Mam Stringley."

"Nasty woman," said Mam Stringley, laughing. "They should have fucked you proper, my dearie, and maybe you'd be happy instead of so cranky."

"That's uncalled for, Mam Stringley," yelled Ted, suddenly. He was, Henry realised belatedly, very angry. That explained his uncharacteristic silence. "You ought to be ashamed, saying such a thing to my sister's face."

"Oh," returned Mam Stringley, pleased (Henry could see) to be given a reason to lose her own temper, "and her telling me my own boys will be hanged by Father John is *not* shameful, is that it? Shame on the whole withered Taylor clan, I say. You're all cursed in the heart, and none of you will prosper." And she drew herself in and shut her wooden shutters and that was the end of their conversation.

The following weeks were pretty uncomfortable, but things settled down eventually. Settled down everywhere except inside Henry's heart. But for the time being she had to put up with Hal swaggering about, and gurning at her insolently every time he saw her, and had to put up with young Tor Stringley spreading rumours that she'd been the one to initiate the whole encounter—she'd waylaid them on the path, he was telling people, and begged them to take her into the forest and do her. They'd only held back out of respect for Rossi, Tor said. That last bit was a particularly risible touch, for nobody in the district had any respect for dreamy, quiet-headed Rossi.

There was nothing she could do. It would have been a simple matter to ambush either boy and punish them—beat them, slice their nostril, drill a hole in some extremity. But everybody from Bicester to Buckingham, more or less, knew the story, so straightforward revenge would come straight back and bite her. The general opinion in the Borough was that she'd been stuck-up and stubborn-headed to turn down Old Den's offer of two piglets. It wasn't that people necessarily believed Tor's malicious stories. They knew what those boys were capable of. But that didn't mean they had much sympathy to spare for Henry. Any punishment she herself meted out, directly, would have consequences. In all likelihood it would lead to open war—a bad idea on any terms, Mammy pointed out, not least in the likelihood that a squad of Father John's enforcers would ride down to restore the peace, and hang up half a dozen people picked at random to encourage the others—by their thumbs if John was in a good mood, by their necks if he wasn't. So Henry just had to endure it.

Autumn passed, and the shame of the assault died down. But at Christmas Old Den made a big deal of sending round a young suckling pig, cooked with wild onions and tied up with a thick strand of string. Just string, said Mammy, but Henry knew perfectly well it was supposed to represent a whip. A peace offering, the lad who handed it over said. A peace offering. But it wasn't. It was a foot on Henry's neck. And everybody was talking about the gift, and at chapel Old Den was there staring pointedly at the altar, but his sons couldn't hold back from peering at her and grinning.

By that stage, though, she had hardened her heart.

Still she was invested, as the phrase goes, in keeping the momentum of everyday life going, and her daughter was a comfort. Rose was a withdrawn, rather serious child, who took after her father more than her mother. But she was affectionate—as was he—and seemed healthy.

One day, in mushroom season, Henry was picking fungi in the forests north of the compound when Tor Stringley—a young man now, and considerably stronger than she was—came at her from, it seemed, nowhere. He must (she reasoned afterwards) have been watching her movements, and have followed her. At any rate, he grabbed her by the neck. He banged her against the trunk of a tree, and threw her on the ground. Then he pulled her trousers down to her thighs, just enough to humiliate her, and sneered, "I wouldn't if you was the only woman in the Borough.

I wouldn't if you was twenty years younger and twenty billion times as pretty. I'm going with Laurie from Mayfield now, and she and I do things you wouldn't credit, old woman." And he left her.

There was nothing she could do about this incident.

The next thing to happen was that Rossi went off with a cult, and took Rose with him. This was a blow made harder to bear by its unexpectedness. A wandering band of religious loonies came through the district and stayed for a few weeks in tents by the Common Pond, until they were chased away. They worshipped not the One God, or Big Christ, or any of the regular things. They didn't even observe Christmas. *They* worshipped the Sisters, they said. According to them the Sisters were goddesses who lived in heaven, and they were displeased with humankind for the way men had made war on women. Women were the sacred principle, they said, and the planet Venus was the true centre of the solar system and a mother-goddess in her own right. The sun was a male deity who had elbowed himself aggressively close to the Earth, and the effect of his rays was to make men violent and red-raging and burnt up with lustful fires. But a true worship of the Sisters, the triple goddess in the form of maiden, mother and crone, would restore harmony and fertility to the world. There was a lot more in this vein. It didn't surprise Henry that Rossi drank it in like a thirsty man at an oasis. A lazy, randy fellow who had spent his life drawn to stronger, older women, it chimed perfectly with the masculine passivity of his worldview. But Henry didn't quite realise how deep this new gospel had sunk into him. He spent all day with the Sisterhood, and when he came back to the farm he attempted to convert Henry to their views. "Bollocks to that," she told him. "You know how many bonkers religions have sprung up in this benighted country? They're a cult, leave them be." He tried three nights running, and by the third night she was so pissed off with his unusual persistence she smacked him right in the face. He took this rebuke meekly. Indeed, it wasn't as if she'd hit him very hard. His beard took the brunt, so she didn't even leave a red mark. But two days later the Church of the Sisters packed up their tents and left, and Rossi went with them. He took Rose because, it turned out, the Church valued virgin girls above all other kinds of human being. Indeed, there were rumours that the real purpose of these missionary treks around the countryside was to pick up as many pre-pubescent girls as possible, with their parents if the parents could be persuaded, by straight abduction if not. These girls were taken to be priestesses of the Sisters in some great holy chateaux in the north—at York, some said. On a platform in the Eastern Sea, said others. Others even suggested the palace was located on the moon, and that the girls taken there would never grow up but would spend eternity dancing in complex circular patterns and singing songs to the Sisters to avert a renewed tragedy.

It was all bollocks, of course it was. But although Henry wept and raged, and ranged about the countryside looking for them, they were gone. Nobody would help. Nobody would lend her a horse; nobody would even rent her one, and she couldn't afford to buy one. Carrie told her to her face, "You'll be riding off up and down the county trying to find your girl, and wearing my nag out, and if you did find her there'd be a firefight and my nag would get hurt. No, Henry, not with my horses you don't." Ted said he would help, but he also said he was glad to see the back of Rossi, who had never been a proper man, and whom he'd never much liked. But Mammy was not who she had been, and Ted was kept very busy running the farm. So in the end it came down to Henry filling a pack with supplies and taking a walking stick out into the countryside, trying to track the group. It was fruitless, though it took her two weeks to accept that fact.

She lived another four years in that place, as her Mammy grew vaguer and vaguer in her mind. Eventually Mammy Taylor became a sort of elaborate walking-talking-pissing life-size toy version of a human being. Ted took over official ownership of the farm, and it stung Henry that he didn't even discuss it with her first. Mammy took to absconding at night, when everybody was asleep, and wandering the woodlands naked, calling some man's name over and over—not Dadda's name. Some prior lover, to whom her ruined brain now returned. It didn't matter in the summer, but when the colder weather did not deter her they began locking her in her bedroom. Eventually she stopped eating, and they had to tip mugs of broth in her mouth to keep her alive. But then she stopped drinking, kept her lips stubbornly sealed, and that led quickly enough to her death.

Henry was an old woman now, by the standards of her community. She was reduced to a condition of effectual childlessness, and uncourted even by the single men in the area, and now Ted ran the farm. He was not so skilled at getting the wheat and corn to grow as Mammy had been, but he did what he could, and he enjoyed enough success to maintain his reputation. Ted had his wife, Angelica, and his own kids living on the farm: six kids, all told. One died in the first few days and another died of sepsis at eight. But the remaining four were growing, and working the farm. Henry felt increasingly marginalised by this new centre of gravity.

One fine spring morning Father John sent a man down to live on the farm. He had heard such good things about the way they eased crops out before Monsoon, and grain was so valuable, the fellow said, Father John took a personal interest in it. Barry Winstanley was this man's name, but he insisted that his friends called him Stan. He was a tall, skinny fellow of middle age with three long scars running down the side of his face and neck—from fighting at Father John's right hand, he said. There was a nasty glint in his eye. Henry knew better than to trust any man who had got so used to getting his own way.

It was a dangerous time, they all knew. It would be so easy for Stan to report back to Father John that they were not cooperating, or that they were enemies, or spies. It would be a simple matter for Stan to have Ted and Henry expelled from the farm, or to have them killed, if the whim took him that way. Henry thought, in her heart, that the main reason he didn't was that he was too lazy to want to manage things on his own. But Angie was fearful of her place, and did what she could to placate the new man, and Ted talked him through all the strategies they had developed to coax up their crops. Henry understood that she was the unpredictable element, the one person liable to say something untoward and jeopardise the new state of play. For a month she was able to keep a lid on her feelings, but then Stan started casting unmistakeable glances at Ted's oldest daughter Carol, and Henry felt her anger settle into dangerously sharp and stable shapes in her chest.

She could kill him easily enough. Ted had made a still out of an old metal tank salvaged from a wreck on the M40, with the rust carefully sanded off, its iron body heated in a fire to bend it and to melt new seams. It was not perfect, but it distilled a drinkable barley-gin, and there was a surplus of this for valuable trade. Stan liked to finish his days with a tipple, and often snored the night through dead drunk. It would be easy to polish him off then. Henry thought back to that time her Mammy had been unable to get rid of fist-happy Jim, and had, she assumed, squashed out his life with a pillow one night. But if Stan died, even if it looked like natural causes, Father John would make an exhibition of punishing them, just for the strength-show of it.

She could strike back against these men, and could even get away, but by striking she would bring terror down upon the people she left behind.

It was frustrating. Soon enough Stan began fucking young Carol, and though it was clear that Carol wasn't happy about it, she put on a brave enough face. What were the alternatives, after all? One night Angie confided to Henry that she'd personally schooled her daughter in strategies that would sexually pleasure Father John's man without penetration and the resulting risk of pregnancy, and that if none of those held him off she was to use a vinegar pessary she had given her in a small clay bottle. That was the moment Henry realised she couldn't stay on the farm. Not stay *and* keep her mouth shut, at any rate. Sooner or later she was going to say something that would have deleterious repercussions for the whole family.

Rather than risk it she took herself off.

There was a tiny smallholding on a low hill, sarcastically known as Stately. Until recently it had been occupied by an elderly couple called the Chans. They'd barely subsisted and had for several years depended on charity top-ups from the rest of the Borough, but eventually Mrs Chan died, and a week later Mr Chan died too. Old Denny, the closest the Borough had to a recognised deputy of Father John, had appropriated the moveables and the few chickens, but nobody much wanted the hut. So Henry moved into it, re-thatched the roof, cleared out the soot-clogged stove, and using her brother's name as credit purchased two goats and half a dozen chickens. And that was where she lived for the next three years, summer and winter; keeping herself to herself, perfectly well aware that the rest of the community regarded her as a crazy old crone. She lived on goat's cheese, eggs, nettle-soup and nuts, and she grew small squares of grasswheat that she hand-ground into flour in a stone bowl. Sometimes she visited the various farms and compounds, or went as far afield as Bicester, and she acquired a reputation for medical expertise based on nothing more than the fact that she could read the surviving medical textbooks. But it meant that she had a place in the community; some bare bones status and role. There were some farms she never visited, of course. Old Denny's and Mam Stringley's for example.

She dreamed of her daughter Rose often, and wondered where she was now, and if she was still alive. And once she dreamed of her long lost sister Jenny, who had shouldered a pack and walked south and had never been heard from again. "*Come south*," said dream-Jenny. "*Your destiny is not there, it is down here.*"

One thing Henry had never believed in was *destiny*. And she couldn't go anywhere. She couldn't leave.

Or, she couldn't yet.

She visited Ted often, and for a while it was pleasant to come home, but Ted himself was growing angrier and more bitter, and during one visit it became clear that Stan was augmenting his pleasure with young Carol by, from time to time, fucking Angie as well. Nobody told Henry this: of course not Ted, and certainly not Angie herself, but Henry could see it in the way people related to one another. She could read the day-to-day despair, the sheer ghastly nothing-to-be-done-ness of it all. So she withdrew to her small hill, and sat there day by day, like the fool in the old song people still sometimes sang, and didn't go back to the farm for a long time.

Stan was gathering a full one-third tax of all the farm's produce and sending it directly back to Father John by cart. The reason for the extra tax became clear soon enough: Father John was going to war, and a big war too. This was not a defensive fight against possible conquerors. This, the Borough gossip said, was a war of conquest. He was striking north, to secure his borders and expand his territories. The stories were mostly about faraway battles and rumour distorted by distance and what they call the 'Chiltern whispers' whereby stories mutated when passed from mouth to mouth. But there were aspects of it that were real enough to Henry's community. All farms now had to cough up a huge portion of their produce, carted away to feed the soldiers. And it wasn't just provisions: Father John's recruiting squads visited each town in turn, went from farm to farm, and when they rode away they took sons and brothers with them. One recruiting officer said, "You should be happy, you lot. Father John is securing the future. One less mouth for you to feed, and when he comes back he'll have a whole new set of skills. You'll thank John, one of these days, when the whole land is peaceful and we can all get on with life."

Securing the future was the slogan. Old Bill, known locally as 'Gerontius', although nobody could say why, laughed about this one evening in the tavern. "Securing the future? Ah, but why should I put myself out for the future? What has the future ever done for me?" This was accounted a notable *bon mot*, and went all round the Borough. Inevitably it made its way back to Father John's men, and they did not view it with amusement. Instead they dragged Gerontius out of the cottage he shared with his daughter and grandchildren and hanged him from the tree by the Common Pond. People stopped making jokes about the war after that.

Jokes, thought Henry. *They're nothing but trouble.*

For half a year the war was the only thing anybody talked about. There was no official news, and the only rumour came from unreliable sources—tinkers and tramps passing through, who would say anything for a bowl of soup or a pint of beer. But families were desperate to know how their menfolk were doing, and seized on the slightest hint.

There was still no official news. And then one day Ping Flannegan from Marsh Gibbon farm, a buck eighteen years old and handsome-of-face, came hopalong into a Bicester tavern with one leg missing and a crutch under his armpit. He'd lost his pin in the fighting, he said; and as people clustered around him in the bar and supplied him with drinks, he talked about where he'd been, and what he'd seen. In the event it transpired that he hadn't seen very much: mostly, he said warmaking is a lot of walking, and sleeping rough, and going hungry, and getting bored; and then it's five minutes of terror and excitement and concentration all tangled around one another as guns go off and people yell and you run towards, or run away. At any rate, he'd lost a leg when a mechanical slingshot had broken from its place and crushed his knee. And he spoke of other losses too. He'd seen young Tor Stringley get shot in the face, a quarter of his jaw knocked clean away by the bullet, and red flesh and white bone revealed to the universe, and you could even see the honeycomb of the inside of the cheekbone and the way the roots of the teeth fitted in their little cubicles. Tor and he had been brothers in arms on account of having come from the same neck of the woods, and he—Ping—had been right next to him when he'd been shot. He'd taken three full days to die, and hadn't stopped screaming that whole time. He'd even screamed when he slept, or, if not screamed, then made this sleep-wail, or moan, or noise at any rate. Finally he'd died and would somebody go tell Mam Stringley please? Because he—Ping—wasn't up to that task.

The news about young Tor's death reached Henry of course, soon enough. She felt nothing. She thought about this as she chewed on some wild onion. She might have felt satisfaction at the sense of karmic retribution, or she might have felt sorrow for the young life thrown away, but actually she felt neither. She imagined people in the town bringing her into the story.

"Wasn't there some story about him, Tor, and that crone who lives up on the Stately? What's her name? Whatever happened to her?"

"Henrietta?"

"Did he? What a horrible thing to happen to an old woman!"

But of course nobody was talking about her, or connecting her life to young dead Tor's. Nobody paid her the slightest mind.

The next thing to happen, though, was a surprise: Old Denny himself, riding a donkey, bringing a sack full of goods as gifts straight to Henry's door.

"Long time since you and I had any kind of chat, Den," said Henry, coming out of her front door.

"I've come to talk," said Old Denny, "and offer you some

good things to eat and keep. I don't expect to be welcomed with open arms, of course."

"I've turned Jew, and won't eat pork," Henry told him. But he had no idea what Jew meant. He couldn't read and had little curiosity about things outside his immediate day-to-day. So he only gawped in incomprehension at her statement. "Sit down there," she told him, "and talk."

"I'll not small the talk. I'll come to the point," said the old man, "and you'll do one of two things. You'll say yes, and then we'll be friends, and I'll have my people bring you quantities of good things often. Or you'll say no, and I'll leave you be, and you and I need never interact ever again. That's all: a simple yes or no."

"The older I get," said Henry, "the less I find simple yes or no ever truly addresses the complexities of things. It's always a mixture of the two, though, isn't it?"

"No games," said Old Denny. He looked drawn, older than his considerable age. His white hair was now thin and striped over his head like zebra stripes against his brown scalp. "I know you love your games. But. This is about my son."

"Hal," said Henry.

"I know he jumped you that time, when he was a kid, he and Tor Stringley who's dead now, in the wars. And I beat him, like I said. And did he ever do anything to you again?"

Henry thought of the years of insolent grins, and swaggering, and the way he would sometimes encounter her when he was with his friends and they would all immediately whisper together as soon as she had passed them. But she said, "No."

"So he learned. He was fucking stupid, of course he was. But he learned his lesson. Now, I don't expect you to love him. But I do expect you to understand that I *do* love him. You had a daughter with that lackwit fellow—dreamy man, don't remember his name."

"Me neither," Henry said, deadpan.

"I know he stole your daughter off, and I'm sorry for that. I daresay it hurt your heart. He was a no-good, that geezer. But here's the thing: my boy is married now, and a good husband. He has a kid of his own and he's a good father."

Henry didn't say anything to this. She waited for Denny to speak. Finally he did.

"People round here think I have the ear of Father John."

"I've heard as much," she said.

"Henrietta Taylor, believe me when I say I've never so much as *seen* Father John. I couldn't even tell you what he looked like."

"I understand he has a moustache," Henry said. "And an avuncular look."

"It's true," said Old Denny, scowling in puzzlement at this, but pushing on, "that I used to have an in with Maxim. You know Maxim? Who comes round the Borough from time to time, with Velma and Jonno and that other young guy, Pat? He calls himself Father John's number two, does Maxim. That probably isn't the truth, but he was high up, high enough up, in John's command I think. And he and I were friends. I did him some favours, and did what I could to keep the peace. For everybody benefits if we keep the peace, Henrietta, not just Father John."

"I know Max," said Henry. "He has a kind of hump, don't he?"

"He says it was a war wound, won honourable in battle, but it always looked like a hump to me. Still, when he was the overseer, and when I did what little I could to keep the peace for Father John, I was in his good books. When they came for fighting men last time I said to Max, 'My boy's soon to wed, don't take him,' and I gave him some money. And Max said, 'Plenty of other boys in the Borough.' And so he didn't take him."

"Lucky for Hal," said Henry. "Not so lucky for the other boys."

"I'm not in Max's good books any more."

"Why not?"

Old Denny sighed. "People in this Borough think I'm a canny politician, but I'm not. Not that I love Father John, you understand. Only that it's better to have order, better for everyone, and a strong chief ruling is more stable. So I helped, where I could, and took advantage for my family when I could. But that's all. I'm a simple man. Max thinks I'm a devious man, and he has grown more and more certain I'm seeking to replace him. I'm not, I'm truly not, but that's what he has come to believe. So now he won't listen to me."

"And you think he'll press your son into Father John's army."

"I believe and fear it."

"And you believe there's something I can do to stop that happening?"

"Stan lives with your brother. The whole Borough knows what's going on there. And, all credit *to* him, Ted has played it well—he ingratiated himself with Father John's man, and now Stan relies on him. If anybody has Father John's ear in this Borough it's your brother, now."

"So why not talk to him?"

"He hates me," Old Denny said.

"You think I don't?"

"I think you've maybe still a pond of resentment in your heart, over what Hal and the Stringley boy did to you. But I think something else about you, Henrietta Taylor. I think you've always cared about what's fair. And I think you know, deep and true, that I tried to do right by you, afterwards. I came out and met you when you and your brother and the dreamy man came to my farm. You could have shot me down, but I came out alone. And I apologised to you and told you I'd thrashed the lad—which I had—and offered payment. Now, it's true you were too pridebruised to take the payment, and I make no judgement on that. But you must accept I *tried* to treat you fair, by my own lights. And I know that fair matters to you."

"Maybe it does," Henry conceded.

"Now, I know you could tell me to fuck off, right here and now, and then my Hal would go to war, and probably get killed. That seems like a bankrupting price to pay for him grabbing you one summer in amongst the trees, all those years ago. And maybe you don't care about Hal, and I wouldn't blame you—you ain't seen how he's changed, how he's grown, how much better he is. But if that happens, it will break my heart, and I ask you, as one old person to another: help me."

Henry looked at him for a long time. Then she said, "Pond of resentment is a fancy image. In my heart, you said?"

Old Denny looked uncomfortable. "You know what I mean."

"I do. So shallow a pond could not endure, over all these years, without a stream to supply it."

"And there's been no such stream?" said Old Denny, hope starting in him.

"I would go to talk to my brother," said Henry. "Only it's a tiring long way for an old woman to walk, from the Stately, all the way down to his compound."

"My donkey can carry you," said Old Denny. "Take my donkey, with my blessing. Have him."

Henry nodded. "That's very kind of you, Denny. That's very kind. But still there's one more thing."

And at this, Old Denny's bargaining expression came over his face, and you could see that it made his heart glad. Now, for the first time in this awkward conversation, he knew where he stood. He was making a deal with Henry, just like he'd made a thousand deals in his life. The fact that Henry was bargaining with him meant that she was going to do what he asked of her, if only the price could be agreed.

"What one other thing, Henrietta Taylor?"

"I'd be afraid to go through these woods and over these fields riding so fine a donkey with nothing to protect myself with."

"You want a weapon?"

"Your family owns some of the finest crossbows in the Borough," Henry noted.

This was not mere flattery. Old Denny had several rifles, of course, but he didn't trust them; and he personally built and tooled a set of crossbows, with double-plated wire crossbow strings and a solid wind-up trigger. He had salvaged a set of brass rods from somewhere down near Didcot one summer, and these harder bolts combined with the stronger string, meant that his bows shot harder and penetrated deeper.

"Denny pulled his crossbow from his back. "It's yours," he said. "A woman needs protection going through the woods, no question."

She rather admired the straightforwardness with which he made this not-in-so-many-words acknowledgement. Henry drew out the moment a little longer. Holding the crossbow in one hand, she tried to lift it, and said, "It's very heavy, for an old woman to haul about."

"I have another," Denny said, pulling off his backpack and bringing out a handgun-sized half-bow.

"Then let us agree our deal," said Henry, smiling. "I will ride this fine donkey down to my brother's farm, carrying this beautifully constructed hand-bow with me for protection. And I will intercede on your behalf with my brother. With Stan. To ensure Hal's future."

"And the bag, here: it's full of good food. This is also part of the deal."

"I'm much obliged to you," Henry said. "I'm sure I'll be able to come by your place tomorrow, early, and let you know what's been agreed."

Old Denny didn't do gushing. That wasn't who he was. He nodded, once, firmly; and then he said, "Thank you, Henrietta Taylor," and walked away, leaving his donkey behind.

Henry sat for a while, watching the birds flipping out of the forest, up and up, and rolling through the air, and settling back into the foliage. Chaffinches, little brown heads, tan bellies and tar-and-cream striped wings, and every now and again a woodpecker.

It occurred to Henry that a third-party observer, if they had seen what had just transpired, would assume she and Denny had negotiated a simple exchange: he giving her some riches, she doing him a favour. Of course, Denny thought he was cleverer than the outside world. That he believed he was completing a deal begun many years before, when she had ridden to his compound and refused his piglets. He believed that time, and diminishment in the eyes of the community, had worn her down, filed away her stubbornness, and that finally she was willing to settle. To settle for more than two piglets, to be sure, but to settle nonetheless.

It occurred to her that Denny thought he had won.

That was what was so amazing to her. It was amazing to her that he could be so obtuse. Because he *had* taken the most important step, the one most people are unable to take—which is to say, he had realised that the fundamentals of human exchange are never about the actual things swapped and traded, and always about the power dynamic of the people doing the swapping and trading. That was a big insight, real wisdom. And yet, having opened that door, he somehow *still* couldn't see any further than what his own desires permitted him to see.

Was it because he was a man? Years later, when Henry and Amy were building the Wycombe community into something remarkable, they would sometimes discuss this particular question. Amy's view was that there simply was a narrowness in the way men saw the universe, and that the narrowness was to do with the one-dimensionality of their structuring appetites. Fuck this, punch that, win, dominate. All very up and down. Women on the other hand, said Amy, could think more widely, and hold more possibilities in their minds. Could understand that life was a web of connections, not a straight path. But Henry was not sure this was the actual reason. Amy, she thought, was too young to understand how old age disappears a person from the social view. People simply stop noticing you. You become a background figure, a three-legged-stool or an old jug. People see you're there when they want something of you, but otherwise you vanish from their minds. Looking back, Henry wondered if Old Denny simply couldn't conceive that this old woman was not finished with her life. As if he naturally assumed she believed she was at the end of her days, with nothing to win or lose but a few more undisturbed evenings nodding by the fire, and a slightly better stocked larder. Even though he was an old man himself, and didn't think of his *own* potential in so limited a way. Despite that, he had looked at her and seen only the fag-end of a life.

"So," Amy would say, "it *was* because he was a man after all—even if your theory is right. And either way it doesn't really matter."

"No," Henry would agree. "But it's good to understand how things work. What use is the past, if we can't learn from it?"

After Denny left, Henry examined the gifts she had received: the strong young donkey, and the useful little one-handed weapon for self-protection. She waited. She waited long enough to allow Old Denny to walk back to his own farm: an hour, more or less (she kept no clock). Then she made up a small pack and chucked the donkey's chin and patted him and got him used to her. Then she mounted up and rode the beast down the low slope of the Stately towards her brother's farm, the farm that had once been her Mammy's farm, that had once been *her* farm. She took it slow, and navigated the beast through the wide woods until she came to the back wall of the main compound. She had helped put posts up for this fence, with her own hands.

She tied the donkey to a bush, in reach of some edible vegetation to keep the beast quiet and peaceable. Then she climbed a tree and settled herself in amongst the leaves. She was old and the climb was not easy, but she was used to sitting still, and she had enormous reserves of patience. She had always had that.

From where she sat she could see over the fence into the courtyard easily enough. For a long time the scene was motionless. She saw Ted come out of the house and go over to the chicken hutch. He retrieved two eggs, and went back in the house. One of his kids—Rob, it was—came out and filled a bucket from the well, and went back in. There was a long pause, although little clues suggested movement in the main house. Henry didn't mind the delay. She could wait all day.

Finally Stan emerged from the main house, yawning and scratching himself. He wasn't coming out to do any chores, of course, because he didn't do chores. Instead he went to the outhouse, to use the jakes, and went inside and banged the door shut after him.

Quiet as a squirrel, Henry lowered her old body down the tree, and crept up to the back wall of the privy. Inside, separated from her by one layer of thin planks, Stan was humming to himself. She could smell his spoor. She stepped silently, as close as she could, lifted the crossbow, put the tip of its bolt in at a knothole in the wood, and squeezed the trigger. The shot went into the back of Stan's neck, tucking upwards just under his skull, with a sound like the bar of a lock clicking home.

Stan exhaled hard. It sounded *hah!*-like, as if he were half-laughing at a not-very-good joke. The only other sound was the knock of him slumping sideways and his head hitting the left side wall of the little hut.

Funny joke.

Henry slipped back into the trees, stowed the crossbow in her pack, checked that the donkey was tied securely enough that it would not yank itself free, and walked briskly through the undergrowth to her cottage. Then she made herself some nettle and springonion soup, which she ate with—since one of her hens had laid—a whole egg poached in it. Delicious. Then she napped. She wasn't a young girl any more, after all.

Her main precaution consisted in hiding the crossbow in a cache she had excavated out of the bricks of the kitchen wall. As well as that she separated out those elements of Denny's food-offerings that wouldn't look out of place with her stuff and put them in her larder. The rest she threw away in the forest. Then she went to bed and slept a deep and restful all-night sleep.

Eventually they came for her, of course. The whole Borough was in uproar. Stan's body had been taken to Bicester, and a rider had gone out to break the bad news to Father John's people—it had to be done, of course, for all that it would bring John's anger upon them. The Borough was too weak to make any kind of gesture of defiance. Everyone knew very well: it was going to cost everyone. So they took Ted into custody and they sent a posse to Old Denny's farm to ask him to give himself up. By all accounts, he acted surprised. "It was one of your bolts in Stan's head," Denny was told. "There's no mistaking it. And your donkey was tied up behind the outhouse, Denny."

"That's bollocks, that's all bollocks," Denny insisted.

"As may be," he was told. "Still, you've got to come along with us."

Denny wouldn't come out from behind his walls. Of course he told them that he had given both crossbow and donkey to Henry, and was at first believed to be joking, or trying to pass the blame for his obvious crime onto the least likely culprit. When he persevered with his story, four men rode up the Stately and shouted for Henry to come out.

She dialled up her old-woman act a little and took the trouble to appear more forgetful than she actually was. Two of the men, she knew, were old enough to remember her Mammy, and everyone knew the brain-rot that had taken her could pass down the family line. The trick, of course, was in not overacting the amnesia. No, no, she hadn't seen Old Denny, not since the Easter church service. No, no, though she saw him then, in church, she hadn't *spoken* to him then. She hadn't actually spoken to him in years. Come to her cottage? No, he hadn't done that. Why would he come to *her* cottage? What did she have, in her cottage, that would draw a man as wealthy as Old Denny? They left her alone, but told her to pack some supplies, because it was likely they'd all be trekking to Bicester. "Why?" she asked. "What's happening in Bicester?"

"Haven't you heard," said Leo. "Stan is dead. Some fucker shot him in the head with a crossbow."

Henry permitted herself a little flourish at hearing this news, and let her legs wobble, and plonked her arse down on the ground. "No," she said. "No, no. no. Oh, but Father John will punish us all for that. Oh, but that's terrible news. Where was he killed?"

"In your brother's farm, of course. Where else did he spend all his time?"

"Poor Ted," said Henry, staring at the grass. "This will go hard on him. That it happened in his farm is bad luck indeed. Terrible luck. Unless you think…? You think he…?"

"No," said Gonzo. "Christ knows he's stubborn, Ted, but he's not fucking *stupid*. Still, I wouldn't want to be in his shoes," Leo agreed. "Or Old Denny's either. It was his bolt that killed Stan."

"Denny's?" Henry repeated, adding in an extra dose of *shocked* to her voice.

"Yeah. Fucking hell, isn't it? I mean: Christ what was he thinking?"

"*That's* why you were asking about him. I see, I see. Should I come with you gentlemen?" Henry asked.

"You stay put, granny. Talk to you, is all we were ordered. So we've talked, haven't we? I'll go see what the word is. Though they'll probably want you to come down soon enough."

The four men rode off, and Henry decided the most likely

thing for her to do was put on a shawl and fill a pack with a few day's provisions and wait by her cottage door.

The first thing was that Max, who'd been (rumour was) supervising the building of a big flat-bottomed boat over Woodstock way, rode into the Borough with twenty men. Henry wondered if the show of force was his own initiative, or if he'd contacted Father John first to receive instructions. Presumably the former: he'd want his boss to believe he had control of the situation. Send a messenger north, and then ride straight in here and knock heads together. Pacify the place, find the culprit, present John with the whole problem solved even as he came tearing down here in force.

When people finally did come up the Stately to collect Henry, they were strangers. She went meekly along with them, nothing but a mild old woman. Max had ordered the whole Borough to meet by the Common Pond, near the church, and a good proportion of the locals were there. Not Old Denny, though. Ted was brought out, hands tied, and fixed by his wrists to a stump, where everybody could see him. The left side of his face was swollen, and there were little ruby lacerations on his cheek, chin and neck. He peeped at the gathered crowd out of his one eye.

"Old Denny refuses to leave his compound," Maxim said, in a clear voice. "Coward that he is. We'll smoke him out, or siege him to starvation, or maybe burn the whole place to the fucking ground. In the meantime we spoke to him, of course. Of course he denies the assassination. He says he gave the donkey to your sister."

"He's a fucking liar," Ted yelled. "I haven't seen my sister in two weeks."

"This looks bad for you Ted," Maxim declared. "At the very least you failed in your duty of protection to one of Father John's most trusted officers. At worse, you killed him."

"Why would I kill him? He and I were getting on fine. Ever

since he came to stay my standing in the Borough has growed, just as Old Denny's standing has dropped down, ever since..." and he craned his neck to look directly at Max, "... ever since he pissed *you* off. You think I wanted him dead? You think I couldn't have foreseen exactly what would happen if he died? All—all *this*?" He spat on the ground.

"You're saying Old Denny did it?"

"I don't know who did it. I only know that Stan's death is a fucking disaster for my family."

Maxim stared at Ted. "The failure in the duty of protection is serious enough," he said. "Henrietta, come over here."

Henry pattered across like a little old biddy. Maxim was a foot taller than she was, and he brought his hand round and down very slowly, so that everybody could see what he was doing, to grasp her by the back of her neck. It hurt, but she didn't flinch. "Denny says he came to talk to you."

"He's lying."

"Why would he lie?"

"Because that's what liars do."

"Says he gave you the donkey and a crossbow."

"Haha," she laughed. "Really? Why on earth would he do such a thing? Give me a *donkey*? The very idea."

"He says it was in return for you going down to intercede with Stan."

"What does intercede mean, dear?"

"It means to talk to Stan about Denny's boy. About him skiving his military service. Said you promised to get the boy off."

"That sort of thing is hardly in *my* power, dear. And why would he come to me? Why wouldn't he go to talk to my brother Ted, to ask him to talk to Stan? My brother at least has Stan's ear. I don't. *Had* Stan's ear, I should say."

"I suppose he figured Ted hates him."

"*Which* I do," barked the doubled-over Ted.

"I have more reason to hate Denny and his family than my brother does," Henry pointed out.

"That's the funny thing, though," Max agreed. "It's such a fucking bonkers story, it almost doesn't sound made-up. But that's not to say it com...," he coughed, hawked, spat, "*putes*. Fucking rotten mess, the whole thing. Why couldn't you people just play nice? Father John is going to be proper furious."

He released his grip on Henry's neck. She wobbled, kept her balance. Made sure her facial expression didn't alter.

"Whip him," Max told one of his people. "I want his back razored up good and gnarly, to make the point."

"Fucking hell," groaned Ted.

"Count yourself lucky I'm not hanging you by your neck. We're taking your farm, too. Of course we have to do that. You—Henrietta. Old girl, you can toddle off up there and tell Angie—is it?" He turned back to Ted. "Angie's your wife's name, yeah?"

"Fucking fucking hell," groaned Ted again.

"Tell her to pack up her shit and clear out. We'll give the farm to a loyalist. John will have a list of preferred candidates."

"You reckon you'll be able to grow wheat and barley without my help?" Ted called, struggling at the stump.

"I reckon I don't give a shit if we do or don't. I reckon this is a bigger fuck-up than any fucking arable crop is worth. Do him, make them all watch." Maxim mounted a horse and took two dozen men and rode off in the direction of Old Denny's compound.

Henry sat on the ground and watched as her brother had his shirt stripped off and his body lashed thirty times by two of Max's men, each taking turns whilst the other rested after five strokes a piece. At the beginning of this ordeal Ted howled like an animal, but by the twenty-fifth and twenty-sixth smites he was just sobbing and by the end he had passed out with the pain. They washed his back with pond-water, and that was the part of the whole thing that gave Henry the greatest cause for worry. That water really did not look clean, and the danger of sepsis was far and away the biggest risk of this entire undertaking. But, she thought to herself, there was a lot of salt in the farm's stores—one outward sign of Ted's recent accumulation of wealth. They'd be able to wash the wounds in brine up there, before they bandaged them. And there were old stores of paracetamol and some willow-leaf concoctions too, for the pain.

In the end, she didn't need to go over to the farm, because Angie got wind of the commotion and came down in a cart, arriving just as they unbuckled Ted from the stump. His hands were still roped together, but he rolled and lay on his side on the dirt. She would have been there earlier, but the cart—which, absent a horse, was being pulled by Rob and Xander—was a slow mode of transport. There were no histrionics from Angie or the two kids: the three went straight to Ted and helped him up as best they could. Henry offered her help, but she was not needed.

Just as they were settling a semiconscious Ted, groaning, onto a blanket on the back of the cart, Max and his men came galloping back up from Den's compound. "He has gone," he yelled, "fucking fucked the fuck *off*. Come *on*!" And all the other Father John irregulars saddled up, and they all charged away.

Evidently Denny had weighed the odds of being able to convince Max he had nothing to do with Stan's death and had decided they were as close to zero as made no difference. So he and his people had packed up in a hurry and ridden off.

Either that, or it was tantamount to an admission of guilt. Guilt was certainly how Max read it.

Henry went back to the farm in the cart, and helped tend Ted, and then helped pack stuff up. Since other people in the Borough were now wary of dealing with a family that had incurred Father

John's wrath, even indirectly, it wasn't easy buying a horse to pull the cart; but with Henry's help they eventually managed to get an older beast, at a ridiculously inflated price.

For a couple of weeks it looked as though they might not need to go. Father John mustered a whole troop of soldiers to hunt down Old Denny, with Maxim at their head, and the hunt took all his energies. This small army raged through the lands east of the Borough, generating enough unpleasantness to encourage the locals to give Denny up so as to get rid of them.

Angie began to speculate openly that Maxim had forgotten about them, and maybe they wouldn't have to leave after all. Henry knew that was foolish. Max might have had his hands full with a more pressing task, but he hadn't forgotten. He wasn't the sort to forget.

Gossip went round and round the Borough every day. The story now was: Den had killed his main rival Stan, and tried to pin the blame on another of his enemies with a crazy story. When it became obvious nobody believed his lie, he'd run.

When he was eventually caught it was because he'd tried to take too much stuff with him. Obviously he'd had to leave most of his wealth behind, but he should have filled his pockets and ridden his fastest horses and gone south. Instead he'd piled two cartloads with stuff and gone east, and soon got bogged in the flooded lands, and had to abandon the stuff anyway. Some said Father John's people had caught up with them in the ruins of Milton Keynes; some that he got as far as Bedford. The details were never resolved. What was inarguable was that one fine, clear autumn morning Max came trotting back into the Borough with Old Denny, handcuffed, his left leg broken, dragged behind a horse on a pallet, and Denny's son and grandson, rope-tied together and linked to Max's saddle pommel, running behind. The rest of the family—wife, daughters, son-in-law, daughter-in-law—were not brought back. Maybe they'd escaped altogether. Maybe they'd died or been killed already by John's men. Nobody knew, and Max wasn't about to go into all the details. Max looked, the whole Borough agreed, royally pissed off at the whole diversion.

Behind Max and his men was a large force of Father John's troopers. They had the appearance, Henry thought, of annoyed men; presumably because now they'd have to give up the relatively easy business of searching wild country and go back to the big war in the north. There was one thing to do before they left, though: to go from farm and farm, and compound to compound, and summon everybody to the Common Pond down by the church. Not everybody came, but the crowd was big enough to satisfy Max. He made a speech and hanged the three of them: the old man, the young man and the boy. The boy needed to have one of Max's men come and haul on his legs to kill him.

"Nobody touches these," Max ordered. "They're here until they rot. The crows eat these."

The very next day a dozen men, all of them new to the area, members of Father John's select and chosen people, rode up to the gates of Ted's farm and told everyone to clear off. Angie asked, "Can we stay in the Borough, once we've vacated this farm? Or do we have to leave the Borough as well?" The leader of the men replied, "*I* don't give a horseriding fuck. I don't care where you go, so long as you fuck off out of this farm."

The family had talked about it, obviously, before this moment arrived. Angie hadn't wanted to believe it would ever come to this, but of course they had to make plans. For Angie those plans were: go stay with her folks, in the Borough. Ted's oldest boy, Rob, wanted to leave the area entirely and start somewhere else completely new. Ted, still weak and in pain, said he had to go where his wife went. Something, Henry noted, dispassionately, had broken inside his spirit. The family bickered amongst itself, and nobody got around to asking Henry what she intended to do.

What she did was this: she went back to her tiny cottage on the Stately, amongst the weeds and the infertile soil. She stayed there three days, and on the fourth she packed a pack and walked away forever, heading south.

It had been clear to her for a long time that there was no future in the Borough so long as Father John was the overlord. And there was nothing she could do to unseat John, not sitting on her tiny eminence in the middle of that land. If that was what she wanted to do—and she did want to do it—then she would need a different vantage.

So she went to find one.

It was easier than she thought it was going to be. She knew enough to distinguish berries good to eat from berries she should avoid. She had a line in her pack with a hook that caught fish one time out of four. And when she came to settlements and farms she was often able to trade the fact that she could read and write for food and shelter. Sometimes this was a simple matter of writing letters, or reading them, or deciphering old instruction manuals whose pages were dissolving to dust at the edges. Sometimes it was more serious: a twentieth- or even a nineteenth-century medical book brought out, a child sick almost to death, anxious relatives urging her to read the cure out of the page. She did what she could.

Everywhere she went she met people who made the same mistake about her. People who believed her life was over because she was old, when in fact her greatest years were all before her. Who believed she was a harmless biddy when she was quite the reverse.

Nobody considered her a threat, because she was an old woman. That meant they let her into their compounds and houses, because they figured she couldn't do them any harm. That meant they chatted to her, and revealed confidences, and offered friendly advice.

"Don't go down Thames way," they said. "Monsters have

fenced themselves in there, cannibals. There's a war in the north," they said. "Monkeys have taken over Henley on Thames."

"Monkeys?" she asked, to check she'd heard correctly.

"Yes, yes, monkeys. There'd been a large private estate full of monkeys and after the Sisters the apes had all got out and prospered."

"I find that hard to believe."

"Yes, yes. Maybe it's just a story."

She skirted Aylesbury and came over the hill at Tring, and down into the flooded Colne valley, and that is where she first met Amy. At that time Amy was young and full of rage, and she and Henry clicked immediately over a shared distrust of men. Amy had energy and ideas, and Henry had strategic vision, and they worked together so naturally it was as if they'd been together for years.

What Amy was doing, in those early years, was salvaging the sort of pre-Sisters kit nobody else was interested in. "Everyone wants the big kit. The cars that still work. The tractors. Vats to distil ethanol. You can see why. But the real genius of the old world was the small stuff. Tiny things. And here, the whole of the Thames Valley was world-famous for its tiny technology. And that's what I retrieve."

It meant, often, going underwater into the Colne lake—right down, and into old buildings, with a helmet over her head and pulling stuff out of drawers and broken cupboards and old shop-buildings and even out of delivery vans and cars, all in the murk and dark and wet.

"There's a plane down there," she said, "an old-school plane long as a dinosaur, and full of the most amazing and baffling electronics."

"Full of dead bodies, too?" Henry asked.

Amy shrugged. "Sure. Or the coral bits that are left after fish ate all the soft stuff. You know—bones."

"I know bones," Henry confirmed.

Amy had rigged up a homemade aqualung, because she was super-clever with her hands that way. She was also, Henry realised the first night they bunked together, twitchy, unhappy, scared, damaged. She didn't want to talk about what had happened to her, she said, and Henry said she understood, and would never pry. And so they fell in together, and Henry persuaded her that there was no future on the lake—mostly frozen in the winter, and in the summer a place of malaria and constant bugs and bad smells. Toxins from the old world still leaked into the water from below, and the Thames flushed all the shit of middle England right through the heart of that place.

Of all the people Henry had met in her life, young Amy was the one who struck her as possessing the greatest potential. She was ingenious and inventive, found ways to work around problems. Quick witted and neurotic and a little paranoid— these last states of mind, once handicaps, positive survival traits in the modern world. For the first time in a long time Henry started to think it might be possible to accomplish something that she knew she wouldn't have been able to accomplish alone.

"We should go upland," Henry said. "There's a commune of women at Wycombe that would take us in. Nice people, but directionless. Within six months we could be running the joint."

"Sounds like a lot of work," said Amy.

"Sounds like a lot of power. The good thing about power is that you can use it to keep yourself safe, and also, if you want, to punish those who want to hurt you."

"I just want a place where I can tinker and build my machines," said Amy. "I just want a," and as the word occurred to her she began crying, such that her tears and the word came out at the same time, "sanctuary. I just want a sanctuary." Amy sobbed, and hugged Henry close to her. "I just want a place where I can feel safe."

"You want a shelter," said Henry.

"Yes. That's the word."

"Then let's make one," said Henry. "Together."

They spent their last night by the lake together, and Amy confessed that sometimes she cut herself with a penknife she carried in her pocket, and that sometimes she wished to die.

"The thing about *that* wish," Henry said, "is that it is the one single wish guaranteed to come true for every human, no exceptions. You just need to be patient."

"Patience," said Amy, as one might say *cockroach* or *faeces*.

"I'll tell you a joke," said Henry. "An old woman was walking by a lakeside one afternoon, and the sun was setting. It was such a beautiful sight, the orange-white-yellow flamelight from the sky shining on the oily surface of the water, that she sat on a fallen log to watch it. But there was somebody already on the log: a lady who would have been beautiful if she'd had any flesh on her white white face, or if she had been able to tuck her brilliant white teeth behind any lips. A lady dressed all in black with a black fur hood over her head, and in her left hand a great scythe. She had not been there on the log when the old woman had sat down, and the old woman had not heard her approach, and yet there she was. And as the sun sank, the old woman asked, 'Who are you?' And the fine lady replied, 'I am Death.' And the old woman nodded, and said, 'Oh I see,' and then she leaned a little closer-in and said," and Henry acted the motion, leaning in to Amy, speaking more slowly, more distinctly and with more volume, "'I said WHO ARE YOU?'"

"I don't get it," said Amy. Then she thought about it, and she said, "Oh I do get it. It's funny." She didn't laugh, because she never laughed. But saying so was praise enough.

"All humour is about death and pain and embarrassment," said Henry. "The trick is making sure it's somebody else's death and pain and embarrassment that you're laughing about."

In the morning they set off together, heading for the eminences of the Chilterns.

PART TWO

Learning to Read

CHAPTER TEN

FOR HALF A day Davy lived inside a bag. It might have been longer than half a day. Maybe not so long. It was hard to tell time. At one point he flopped out of consciousness altogether—the exhaustion, and hardship, not to mention the fear, provoking a seizure. But most of the time he was aware and conscious. It's just that the thing he was most conscious of was the canvas bag they had fitted over his head. The scratch of its weave. The smell of it. The way it amplified the sound of his breathing.

His hands were cuffed behind his back. At the beginning he'd been slumped over the saddle on his belly, like a sack, but this posture had not only been intensely uncomfortable, he had actually found it difficult to breathe. When the riders got off the causeway, and out of the rain, they stopped for a breather, and one of the women checked on him. "I don't like his colour," she said, and the others all gathered round. He was lifted down and propped against a moss-wet log. Finally he could catch his breath.

They gave him water, and a little flatbread to eat, this latter damp and flavourless. He looked around him, but with an anxious panicky crudeness of observation that registered very little except the wind-rumpled stretch of water in front of him and the general rain-sog of everything. The rain had stopped. The sun was low in the sky.

Then they put the hood back, hoisted him onto the saddle again, but in a proper upright position this time. They rode on. Sitting was easier on his lungs, and less painful; although the fact that he wasn't able to grasp the rider in front to steady himself meant that he kept swaying backwards, and feeling the dagger-panic that he was about to topple off. He was wet, and scared, and exhausted, and he was like that for a long time.

The next thing he knew his hands were cuffed in his lap, which meant he could tuck his fingers into the trouser-top of the rider in front of him. His back and shoulders felt sore. He flexed and stretched, and there was a palpable pain back there. Since he didn't recall being taken off the horse, having his hands untied, and retied in the front he reasoned that he had had a fit and fallen off the horse, and that the women had repositioned him when he was unconscious.

Senses working overtime.

They rode for an incalculable time. Finally they stopped, lifted Davy down and took off his hood. It was night. At least it wasn't raining any more. The sky was clear and cold, and the stars mingled with the prickles of light buzzing on the pricky surface of his own retinas. To his left and right profoundly purple-black columns blocked out tree-shapes against the starry sky. He was in some kind of open space, and the moon was shining. In the pale light it was hard to get a clear sense of the dimensions of where he was. Some of the women were setting up a fire. The horses were all standing in a pack, snorting and puffing, and one woman was going from hefty snout to hefty snout with a leather bucket. Did the horses miss their dead companion? Were they even aware that there had been another? Davy rubbed his eyes, and waited for them to adjust to the milky thin moonlight.

He was sitting on a hump of moss, and immediately to his right was an old tumbled-down trunk and bough, like a giant's discarded slingshot. Davy's senses were preternaturally aware. Even in so dim a light, he could make out a large spiderweb between trunk and bough, each line drily taut as if tensed for the terrifying inevitability of dew.

The moon looked like a still pond, very far away.

"Hungry?" One of the women was leaning over him.

"Did I fall off?"

"Did you fall *off*? Don't you remember?"

"I am subject to epileptic fits during which I lose consciousness."

The woman's face was a mask in the moonlight. She said nothing for several seconds. Then she said, "Gabbledy-gabbledy say what now?" She stood up. "Abigail?" she called. "I can't make head nor tail of this shitrabbit."

"He has a speech impediment," Abigail called back from the fire. They had just got the wood burning, and an orange gleam was peeking through the heaped sticks. Abigail was squatting down, trying to get at the warmth.

"Is he, like, a retard though?" the first woman called back.

"What would Henry want with a retard?" Abigail returned.

"Search me. What would Henry want with any fucking adolescent boy at all?"

"Maybe he's a savant. I don't know," said Abigail. "If you're looking for insight into Henry's mind, my Jo, then you're asking the wrong person." She turned back to the fire. The first woman bent down to Davy again.

"Maybe *you've* an inkling, though, babble-boy. What *does* Henry want with you anyway?"

"Henry," said Davy. "I thought you were taking me to Wycombe?"

"What? Speak slower!"

Davy concentrated, and tried again. "I thought you were taking me to Wycombe."

"Well aren't you just Professor of Bears-Shit-in-the-Woods-ology. Damn *right* we're taking you to Wycombe. That doesn't fucking answer my question."

"I thought Wycombe was a woman-only community?"

"Abigail?" the woman called, over her shoulder. "Do you want to see if this little shitpants wants a drink of water? If I have to keep talking to him much longer I'm going punch his nose so hard it'll relocate to the roof of his mouth."

Abigail got to her feet and came over, and the other woman took her place by the fire. It was burning quite heartily now. "Don't mind Jojo. Her bark is worse than her bite."

"I'm guessing her bite is still pretty bad, though," said Davy.

"Hah. Come on, lad. I'm going to uncuff your hands, and you're going to have a little drink, maybe a bit of food, get warm by the fire."

"Thank you," said Davy.

The cuffs snapped off, and Davy rubbed his wrists. "I don't even know why you've taken me," he complained, as Abigail handed him a water bottle. "I don't understand what's going on at all."

"No more do I, boyo," Abigail returned. "Henry wants you, that's all. It was supposed to be softly-softly—she hired that feller Hardman. He was supposed to grab you and bring you to Wycombe. Since you live in what amounts to Guz territory, we didn't want a big military ride-in-and-snaffle-you hoohah. Hardman was paid to slip in and bring you out. But he got ideas of his own. Bastard."

"He's dead," said Davy, the memory returning to him of Hardman's ice-furred corpse.

"He won't be mourned."

"That's sad."

"That he's dead? I don't think so."

"Sad that nobody will miss him, I mean."

"Yeah. Well. The world is full of sadness," agreed Abigail.

"But pity is a precious resource, in limited supply, and you'd be profligate to waste any on a bastard like Hardman. Here, have some jerky. We'll stop here a few hours and ride on at first light. You could sleep, you know."

Davy chewed on the leathery strip of flesh. He was, he realised, very hungry. "Did you kill Daniel?"

At this Abigail laughed a series of low, gurgling laughs, like a series of hiccoughs strung together. "I surely tried. If there's any justice, he's frozen to death in that water. But it wouldn't be the first time Daniel has evaded justice."

"He was my friend," said Davy, feeling tears swelling inside him.

"Did you mammy never tell you to beware of grown men who go about befriending twelve-year-old boys."

"I'm thirteen," said Davy.

Abigail was silent for a little time. When she next spoke her voice sounded almost offended, as though Davy had gone out of his way to insult her. "I'd keep that fact to yourself if I were you, boy," she said, and moved back to the fire.

Davy chewed the jerky, and looked at the brimming orange light. He was sitting a little apart from the rest of them. All the women were gathered around the fire, their faces given freakish gargoyle animation by the play of shadows and the movement of the light. One of them was heating coffee in a long-handled saucepan: Davy could smell it. It reminded him of home, because his mother always loved coffee, and that little pang of nostalgia brought the tears welling back. He had to struggle to contain himself. How dearly he wanted to be home!

From out of the distance came an elongated, shivery howl—a long, tubular, mournful noise. A wolf. Around the fire all the murmured conversation stopped, and every head turned in the direction of the noise.

"Aylesbury way," one of the women said.

"Lots of wolves Aylesbury-Hitchen area," agreed another.

"They keep trying to sneak up the hill. Bloody nuisance they are."

"Make," said Jojo brightly, "boffo *rugs* though."

"That's your real heroism, isn't it, Jojo," said Abigail. "Not the killing of wolves, so much as the haberdashery."

The distant wolf howled again, a great wailing leash of a sound, drifting out into the night air. It rang Davy's heart like a bell. One concept swelled inside him to possess him: home. He had to get out of this place. He simply had to go. Quietly he got to his feet and started walking—he didn't know where, except that it was away from the fire. Nobody seemed to notice. Shadows pulsed around him, hollows in the turf stretched by firelight and then snapped back to their original form, embers of fiery light floating past. Up ahead was a deeper dark that Davy thought might be a forest. Maybe if he could slip in there, whilst the women were all distracted by the firewarmth and wolfsong, maybe he could hide from them. And in the morning he would walk west—hop from ice-floe to ice-floe across the river—mount the hills on the farside and run down the lane to his own house.

The wolf's howl unspooled for a third time in the distance, and a human figure loomed up before Davy. It was Jojo. He opened his mouth to say something, to explain perhaps how very acutely he needed to be home right now, but before he could say anything her fist leapt at him and back again like an adder's strike. His forehead felt like he'd been hit by a slingshot stone—a burst of pressured pain right in the middle of his brow and an actual humming in his inner ear, and a follow-up thump across his back, and then he was staring at a mixture of white stars and red floating embers and the cold of the ground was starting to chill his shoulders and his bum and the backs of his legs. His skull curdled with pain. "Ow," he said.

"Where exactly were you sneaking off to, shitweasel?"

Davy's vision was starting to rotate, and the sparks at the back of his head were building in number.

The other women were standing over him now, but their voices swirled into an indistinct mess of human sound. Then something strange happened to Davy: something which hadn't happened to him before. He teetered on the edge of a seizure, and stayed there, teetering. He felt the inside of his head swell outward until its lip touched the lip of the sky, but it didn't dissolve into the cosmos and oblivion the way it usually did. The stars overhead were all snow, held in place because nobody had explained the law of gravity to them; and now and again they wriggled and dislodged and fell to the ground, and the rocks beneath the soil were creaking because they were being heated by the dawn and expanding, and it was this that generated the long, silver whistle of the wolves, and everything was held in an exact aeon-long tension with everything else.

He saw the Sisters with hallucinatory distinctness, the pack of them loping through the outer sky, wolves in search of prey. He saw them stretching their legs and opening their great mouths, fringed with stalactite and stalagmite fangs, as they zoomed down upon the world. Then: snap, and darkness, and the end of things that was also the beginning of things.

He expected to pass out, but instead the pain in his head focussed his thoughts back into the logic of consciousness. The stars shrank back into perceptual objects in the external world.

He was cold, because he was lying on the cold ground. His head was humming with pain. Hands were on him, lifting him upright.

"I was," he gasped, still a little dazzled, "I was going off to have a wee."

"What the fuck is this retard saying?" Jojo complained. "I swear I can't understand a blind word."

"I was going," Davy tried again, tucking his tongue down to make his articulation clearer. "Over there to have a wee."

"May," said Abigail. "Take him over there so he can relieve

himself. Jojo, stop hitting him. Henry will be most annoyed if we break him."

A tall woman put her hand on Davy's shoulder and lead him a little way from the fire. "Don't try to run off," she advised. Davy fumbled his little spigot out of his trousers and dribbled a little onto the grass. Then the two of them returned to the fire.

"My head hurts," he announced to the group.

"Good," said Jojo.

Several of the women unrolled blankets and stretched out. Davy didn't feel sleepy. The wolf appeared to have stopped its distant song.

CHAPTER ELEVEN

IN THE MORNING the women watered their horses and let them graze on the grass the fire had unlocked from frost. Then they packed up and mounted. The events of the night, which Davy might have expected to make the women more wary of him, in fact seemed to have made them more relaxed. They didn't bother cuffing him, and the woman he was riding with—her name was May—permitted him to hold round her round the waist. That made the ride much less uncomfortable. Indeed, and rather awkwardly, the fact that he was pressing his body intimately into the back of a full-grown woman had the effect—frankly—of arousing Davy. The motion of the horse, and the up-down rubbing that it provoked, made matters worse. Or better. It was more than just that he had a hard-on, although he had to do some shuffly rearrangement to ensure that fact wasn't made obvious to May. It was a whole-body suffusion of low-level excitement.

"We'll be in Wycombe before supper," Abigail said.

The hills were directly ahead, and the fields before them boiled with a chilly mist. Broken roofs rose from the white blur like aslant gravestones. The dark flakes that flew across the sky were high-up birds.

After an hour or so of riding the troop came down into a shallow valley. The mist was starting to thin. They stopped outside a row of old houses, now shells. Dismounted.

"Where's this?" Davy asked.

"Where?" replied Abigail. "Chinner, or thereabouts."

"You know what Henry says," put in one of the other women, whose name Davy did not know, "'I wouldn't loiter in the northlands for all the tea in Chinner.'"

"Henry certainly likes a joke," said Jojo.

"The worser the better."

"*Is* there tea here?" Davy asked. When the women laughed at him, he blushed, but added, with a little spark of spirit. "What? I'd like a cup of tea. Wouldn't you?"

Abigail went into one of the houses, and in amongst the rubble and broken wooden boards she revealed, like a prestidigitator, a metal box deliberately hidden under the junk. This opened to disclose a radio which, after a few tweety cranks of the handle, came to life. It was one of the kind that required Abigail to put on big headphones, and to speak into a little hand-held rectangular grill. Probably two hundred years old. Amazing that it still worked, really.

Abigail said little, and listened a lot, and after she had packed the radio away and hidden it again she announced a change in plan. "Detour."

Jojo groaned, but the others seemed unconcerned. Everyone got back on their horses and rode north-east, parallel to the bulk of the hills on their right. The land was littered with ponds and small lakes, all half-iced, and the going was slow. They crossed a road so clogged with rusting cars and trucks it was like a hedge of red-brown metal—the horses had to go single file between a lorry and a bus—and then trotted up a slope. Then they turned and rode north, with the hills shrinking down behind them.

In a debatable land, half scrub and half forest, they came across a pre-Sisters house. The tiles of its roof lay all around like discarded dragon scales, but somebody had gone to the bother of thatching the top, and inside was a fire and two more Wycombe women, and with them was the reason for Abigail's detour—a girl. She was sat on the floor with her back to the wall, and a very sour expression on her face. What Davy thought was a necklace was, he saw when he looked more closely, actually a rope, and, sitting beside her, he could see that it went down her back to where her hands were tied.

Abigail's crew greeted the two new women, and everybody had coffee and stood in front of the fire. Everyone except Davy. He went over to the wall.

"I'm Davy," Davy said to the girl. He figured she was a few years older than him. She turned her head very slowly, looked at him with scorn, and then turned back to stare straight ahead. Davy assumed she was going to give him the silent treatment, but instead she said, "My name is Amber. Do you want to do me a favour, Davy? Untie me. And then wrestle those women to the ground to give me time to escape."

"All of them?" said Davy.

Amber turned her head, again very slowly, and looked at Davy. "There's something not quite right with your speaking."

"I have a bit missing from the end of my tongue. Look." He lolled his tongue out, and Amber looked at the end with guileless curiosity.

"How did that happen?"

"I bit it."

"Must have hurt."

"I was unconscious. I was having a kind of fit. I get these sorts of fit. Epilepsy, it is called."

"You're *Davy*," Amber said, as if the full significance of his name had only just occurred to her. "Oh good gracious! And bad gracious too. Well what a surprise to meet you here, Davy."

"They had *me* tied up, yesterday," said Davy. Amber was pretty, and he wanted to ingratiate himself. "I guess they kidnapped you, like they kidnapped me."

"Kidnapping isn't how I'd describe it," said Amber, glowering at the women. "I'm one of theirs, you see."

"You're from Wycombe?"

"Born and bred. Although it's always seemed to me that that expression is the wrong way about. After all, a person is bred before they're born. Aren't they? I mean your breeding is what *leads up* to you being born. Isn't it?"

"So you left Wycombe? Didn't you like it?"

"Are you kidding? It's the best place on earth."

"Then why did you leave?"

Amber drew a great breath into her lungs, thereby pushing out (Davy found himself incapable of not staring) her chest, and let it all go in one long sighing whoosh. "Oh dearie me, Davy, my lad. Where to start?"

"Don't feel obliged to tell me anything if you don't want to," said Davy, who was a little rankled by the manner of cool superiority she appeared to be taking with him—as if she were a suave and assured adult and he just a little kid.

"I should tell you," she said. "I should tell the whole world. You know who Father John is, yeah?"

"He's in charge of an area to the north. Oxford isn't it? Or maybe further north? I'm a little hazy on the geography."

"He doesn't know what's coming, the poor man. I mean, people say he's a tyrant and everything, but just because he's a foreigner we shouldn't hate him. Just because he's a man we shouldn't hate him. When you become a man I shan't hate *you*."

Davy's heart did a strange little twerk at that, foolish though it was. *Not hate*, his solar plexus said, is the start of something positive; something that might grow into—maybe, *love*? "When you say when I *become* a man ..." he started. But Amber was on a roll.

"And anyway, even if he is a tyrant, then his people are just regular people. You know? Just people trying to get along. I figured they deserved to be warned. To be warned away, you know? Have it explained to them that they need to back off. Why, do you think it'll be *John* who gets killed if his troops try and storm the Chilterns? No, he'll be safe and sound far away. It'll be ordinary women who get murdered. And men, too! And that's the bottom line, isn't it? People talk about war as if it's different to murder, but it's not different, morally. I mean come *on*. If you kill someone it's murder and if you kill lots of people in war it's mass murder. Wouldn't you agree?"

"I guess."

"I tried to make *them* see that," she nodded at the women by the fire. "All of them. I mean, if Father John is a tyrant, what is Henry? I ask you."

"I can't answer you."

"A tyrant," she hissed. "Henry is as much a tyrant as John, except that we all swaddle ourselves in our moral superiority. Oh we're *better* than John. Oh we deserve to live and his people deserve to die. But how is that moral?"

"It," Davy said, in a tentative voice, as if unsure whether this was the right answer, "isn't?"

"Of course it isn't. I figured if John's people knew how stupid any attack would be then they'd leave us alone. It didn't quite work out that way. They weren't interested in what I had to say. They were interested in having a hostage. But, good golly and gracious, I don't need to tell *you* how little traction a hostage would give them, when it came to confronting Wycombe."

Abigail came over to them. "All right you two, we're going to make a move. Steph says John has parties out all over the landscape, looking for—well, looking for you, traitor-girl."

"Don't be horrid, Abigail," said Amber, poutily. "I've had a *shocking* rough time." She appeared much less like a grown-up, saying this.

"Brought it on yourself," said Abigail. "If we get you back and nobody gets killed it'll be a miracle, frankly. Then we can see what Henry wants to do with you."

"I had the best of intentions," sulked Amber, staring pointedly at the floor.

"You've no idea what you've started, girl," Abigail said, severely. "One almighty fuck-up. It may yet cost lives. It has *already* cost—" But looking down at her, Abigail seemed to change her mind on this last utterance. "Anyway, we can talk about all that when we get home. Jesus, girl, I only wish you'd take on board how serious this shit is."

"There's no call for that kind of language," said Amber, without lifting her gaze.

"Hark," said Abigail, putting a hand to her ear, "what is that I hear, ululating from afar? *Is* it the call for sweary language? I do believe it fucking *is*! None other than the fucking shit-shouting call for sweary language! Ah, how beautiful it sounds. The call has fucking well gone out." She dropped her hand. "We are going to try and creep away, nice and quiet, but if the shit," she looked pointedly at Amber, "hits the fan then we may have to gallop and scatter. Davy you ride with me."

"OK," said Davy.

"Steph needs her hands free, so Amber you'll be riding with one of mine. She's called Jojo and, Davy here can tell you, the amount of fucking-around she will tolerate is exactly zero. Give her any grief and she'll knock you down and drag you along behind tied to the steed's tail. You understand?"

"And we're supposed to be the good guys," muttered Amber.

"*Do* you understand?"

"Yes."

"All righty-tighty. Now, Davy: if all goes to plan we'll be in Wycombe before nightfall. Trust me, that's the eventuality you want. We have electricity, hot showers, warm beds and good food. The alternative is that you fall into the hands of Father John, and he not only has none of those things, he will take personal delight in making you suffer. That's just how he is. Come on."

Davy got to his feet and Abigail pulled Amber upright. It was only at this point that Davy realised Steph was the woman he had met at Rafbenson. He felt foolish for being so belated in his understanding.

"Hiya, Davy," Steph said, waving at him with her thickly bandaged hand. "Good to see you again. How's your Guz friend Daniel, by the way? Dead, I hope?"

"There's a reasonable chance he is," said Abigail, doing up her coat. "He went into the freezing water near Didcot and none of us saw him come out. I did mean to shoot him."

"I would have thanked you," said Steph.

"Yeah. Sorry. The moment somehow got away from me. He killed my horse."

"Well isn't that exactly the kind of shit move you'd expect from Guz?"

"Guz aren't our most pressing concern right now," said Abigail. "All right everyone. We all know what we're doing?"

Jojo raked the fire down, and they all went outside to where the horses were standing in a huddle. It was still very cold. Overhead the sky had filled with a layer of thin cloud, grey-white and crinkled like the roof of a dog's mouth. Breath puffed: cold steam.

They all mounted up and started away.

For a quarter of an hour things went without incident. The hills were in front of them now, slowly inflating on the horizon as they approached. But then—Davy was never sure what exactly provoked the panic, whether they were spotted, or somebody stumbled onto something—there was yelling, and spurring of horses. Abigail's mount leapt like a steeplechaser and went straight into a lolloping gallop. It was all Davy could do to cling on. They cleared a bush, and ran straight over a patch of open ground. Jojo's horse was close behind.

There was a snapsnap sound, and then another double-snap, much closer. Davy felt something being pushed into his hands, clasped as they were into Abigail's tummy. It was a leather strip—the reins. "Hold them," Abigail called, as she rotated herself in the saddle, stretched out her right arm to its full extension, reached over Davy's shoulder and reached her arm backwards. She was holding a firearm.

Davy craned his head round, looking over his shoulder. Jojo was guiding her horse to the right, out of the way. Two horsemen on white horses were in pursuit, a couple of hundred yards behind them. The sky split open and a chunk of thunderous noise dropped in one great mass onto Davy's head—he was so startled and scared that he shouted out, and flinched, and his ears sang a high pure note. Abigail had discharged her weapon. He watched the smoke from the shot hang in the air as they galloped away. Both pursuing riders were still after them. Davy wanted to say, *Could you warn me next time before you shoot*, but his ears were muggy and he couldn't be sure if he was talking or not. And then the gun went off again, and the sound clamped hard onto his skull again and he just shut his eyes.

The noise in his ears was now a *woo-woo* up-tone, down-tone sort of wave. He opened his eyes to see only one rider chasing them and saw that Jojo was aiming a crossbow. Abigail still had her gun. He felt, rather than heard, the click of Abigail squeezing her trigger a third time—a misfire, duff bullet, something wrong.

She turned to face front again, took up the reins and urged the horse on.

They rode over turf dotted with shallow frozen puddles, which threw up icy shards like shrapnel when the horses' hooves hammered into them. A hedge loomed up, shaking up and down like an earthquake, and then they were silent, mid-air, the horse's legs stretched out front and back—flying.

The impact when they landed on the far side was enough to compress his spine, and almost shake him from the saddle.

The next thing he knew they were in amongst trees, and the horses were walking, breathing heavily. Jojo was near. They were going uphill.

"Did we lose them?" Davy asked.

Abigail's answer: "Sh!"

They continued their upward walk, and at some point another horse came plodding quietly alongside: two women in the saddle, May up front and another behind whose name Davy had not yet learned. The tree trunks looked as black as leather, and there were a great many dark green ferns on the ground and around their bases, the pattern of their fractal leaves as intricate as any embroidery. The white sky flickered amongst the black branches overhead. The hooves of the horses made soft swishing noises as they trailed through the heaps of old leaves. Higher up there were more firs, like flaky teepees. The further they went, the more Davy became aware of a relaxing in the general mood of the small group.

"Well," said Abigail, to nobody in particular. "*That* was exciting."

"You can parcel all the excitement in the world into one bundle," grumbled Jojo, "and stuff it up your snake-eye."

"I will register a formal complaint," said Amber. "When we get back to Wycombe. Formal!"

Finally they came out on the top of this shoulder of a hill, and, looking back, were rewarded with an impressive vista of flat and intermittently flooded land stretching away north-west. Here there was a house, and the three horses and six human beings stopped there. Davy assumed it was an agreed-upon rendezvous, and that they would wait for the others to join them.

The house was in pretty decent repair, although there was obviously no glass left in any of the windows, and the roof was variously holed. The rooms inside were weedy, with ivy growing on the inside as well as the outside walls, and there was a smell of fox shit and general natural pungency inside. Jojo and May and the third woman—Mahvesh was her name, Davy discovered, by eavesdropping on their conversation—took positions by the northward facing windows with guns. Abigail brushed old leaves from an old leather armchair and sat down. "I think I pulled my shoulder," she said. "Twisted round and firing—it's not a good stance."

"Did you hit anything?" asked Jojo, from the window.

"I'm not sure."

"Yeah."

"I think I did."

"Yeah."

"This rope," said Amber, in a shrill voice, "is rubbing my neck. And I can't feel my hands—*actually* that's medically really dangerous, and tantamount to abuse you know. It's like torture? Yeah? If Wycombe stands for anything it stands for being better than such things. Do you really want to plonk me down in front of Henry with my hands all necrosed from being starved of oxygenated blood?"

"G. Susan Christ," muttered Jojo.

"My dear," said Abigail. "I genuinely think Henry will be less concerned about the state of your hands, and more concerned about the damage you've done to us all."

"I was doing the *right* thing," said Amber. "Always do the right thing. I thought that's what Wycombe stood for in the first place."

"The first thing Wycombe stands for," said Abigail, "is keeping us all safe." But she untied Ambers wrists, and Amber herself unspooled the rope from her neck.

CHAPTER TWELVE

THEY WAITED IN the house for an hour or more. Davy lost track of time. Mahvesh lit a fire in the corner of the room and boiled up water for some tea, which everybody drank. There was a little to eat, also shared: some cheese that was halfway to becoming yellow plastic, a third of a strip of beef jerky each and what was left of the damp waybread. It wasn't much. But then May went off to relieve herself, and came back with the news that one of the rooms at the rear was almost entirely overgrown with mushrooms; so the women picked a great many, peeled them and fried them in their own mushroom juice over Mahvesh's fire.

Then there was a flurry of not-quite-panic as May announced that somebody was approaching the house. Everyone rushed to the windows and picked up their weapons, but it was Steph on a horse. She came in and hungrily devoured what was left of the mushrooms, and drank very deep of the water.

"What about the others?"

"They may have gone otherwise," said Steph. "I didn't see anybody shot, so if they're not here it may be because they couldn't find a way through."

"Which raises the question," put in Jojo, "how long do we wait? Two hours' ride and we'd be inside the cordon. I'd feel a lot safer then."

"Oh the cordon's about to get a *whole* lot wider, you mark my words," said Amber, unprompted, with a voice halfway between a preacher and a whiny teen. "But at what cost, eh? That's what I ask you."

They all ignored her.

"Give them a half hour, yet," said Abigail. "And then we should probably push on for home."

"Good to be back on the high land," said Mahvesh.

"We're not safe yet," said Abigail.

Steph was given a mug of tea, and she found a space where she could sit, with her back to the wall. For a long time she simply sat, cradling the mug. Then she said, nodding in the direction of Davy, "I hope he's worth it." Then she drank.

"Near as I can piece all the elements together," said Abigail, gesturing at Amber, "she's the one who kicked over the first domino."

"You won't ethics-shame *me*," said Amber, in a high-pitched voice.

"She's awfully chippy," said Steph, "for someone who basically got her own sister killed."

There was an instantaneous, catastrophic silence in the room. Steph looked about herself, and then locked eyes with Abigail. "Christ, Abi, doesn't she *know*?"

"We were going to wait until we were safe back in Wycombe before we told her," said Abigail.

It was very cold, cold enough even inside to make their breath visible, but Davy could have sworn that the temperature dropped palpably. Nobody said anything for a while.

"What's that about my sister?" asked Amber. Her voice had lost all its confidence, all its high-pitched swagger.

"Kid, I'm sorry," said Steph, hiding her face in her

unbandaged hand. "My mouth runs away with me sometimes. I'm sorry."

"What," Amber repeated, "about my sister?"

"She went after you," said Abigail. "We tried to stop her. Hardman found her, and he—"

There was a long pause. Davy could hear the scrapy sound of rooks giving voice to their rookish chatter outside. A slurp as Steph drank a little more of her tea.

Davy breathed in quietly and breathed out again.

The rooks fell quiet.

"Why did he kill her?" Amber asked, in a small voice.

"He'd been hired to retrieve—well, this lad here. Davy. It should have been a simple matter. But he was always a devious old fuck, Hardman, and he'd got a sixth sense that something was up. He got—look, I don't know how. Nobody knows how. But he got some inkling that the boy was a key to unlock something. He figured Beryl knew what. Which she did, by the way. And he'd heard some story of a Wycombite going upriver on a particular boat. So he—look, I don't want to go into details."

"Dear god," said Amber.

"He killed her," said Abigail. "I'm sorry."

"And I killed him," said Steph. "And I'm *not* sorry."

"Jesus," said Amber, her voice hoarse. "But what will Mum say?"

"I think she knows, love," said Mahvesh.

"It's a bad business," said Abigail. "All round, a bad business, and no question. But we'll get you home, and bring the boy in, just as Henry asked us to. So we'll salvage something from this situation."

"Was Hardman working for Father John?" Amber asked.

Abigail blinked. "What? I don't think so. I think he was working for himself. Like he always was."

"He must have had a buyer in view," said Amber. She really

no longer sounded like a child. "For whatever it was he figured this—boy—would unlock."

"Can I just say," Davy put in, "I haven't the first foggiest clue about any of this. I'm just a regular boy. I'm not any kind of key. I really don't think I could unlock... well, anything."

"Speak friend and enter," said Jojo, standing by the window. "And what's the elvish for *shut-the-fuck-up*?"

"I don't think he knew what was, as it were, behind the door. I mean," said Abigail, "Henry has her plans, sure, but she wouldn't have told *him*. I assume Hardman just thought: I bet it's valuable, and I bet I can jump in before Wycombe and half-inch it. After that—maybe he was going to go to Father John. But if I had to bet I'd say he was planning on selling it to Guz."

"Guz?" Amber's voice had sunk to barely a whisper.

"I wouldn't have pegged them. They're based a long way away, on the south-west coastline somewhere. But they sent a force up along the North Wessex Downs couple of years ago, and they're still there. And the thing about Guz is that they're much more a high-tech sort of organisation than Father John. John is many men, and brute force. Rumour has it that Guz have a whole fleet of warships and submarines and who-knows-what. Nuclear missiles and everything. So if I were Hardman, I'd be thinking about selling to them."

"If you were Hardman," said Steph, sternly, "I'd have to kill you all over again, so it's good you're not." The she added, talking to nobody in particular, "That bastard."

"I'm sorry," Davy told Amber. She looked at him with blank eyes, and said nothing, and then looked straight ahead.

A sombre silence took possession of the room for ten minutes or so. Finally Abigail sighed, and said, "We can't wait here forever. The others know the way back to Wycombe."

"Let's go," agreed Mahvesh.

Everybody got to their feet and started gathering up bits

and pieces. Davy thought back to his time with Daniel, and wondered if the old man was still alive. A vivid vision of Daniel's wrinkled old face flashed upon Davy's inner eye. He had the sudden profound realisation that if he allowed himself to be taken to Wycombe he would never see home again.

The women were chatting as they got themselves ready. "So nobody knows," Jojo was asking, "what the deal is with shitpants boy?"

"Henry wants him."

"Because he's the new messiah? The new mess-his-pants hire? Why?"

"Ask her yourself when you see her. I don't know."

"It just feels contrary," said Jojo. "Don't you reckon, May? Personally escorting this *male* in through our gates."

"A bit off," was May's opinion.

"I assume Henry's reasons are legit. Unless you're challenging the whole basis of the authority on which our community stands?"

"Fuck off," was Jojo's reply.

"And anyway: he won't be with us for long. Soon as he turns thirteen, Henry will boot him out."

"Or chop his coconut head *off*," mumbled Jojo, "if she's any sense."

"I'm already thirteen," said Davy.

"Come on Amber," said Mahvesh, coaxing the stunned girl into a standing position. "It's hard. We all know. We've all been where you are now, lass. Each in our various ways. We know the numbness, and then the hurt. Let's all get home and then you can grieve."

"I am," said Davy, again, "thirteen."

"What?" asked Jojo.

"I'm thirteen."

Abigail turned to face him. "You're twelve."

"Well, OK. Whatever you say. I'm not though."

"Oh I had this bloody conversation with him at Benson," complained Steph.

"I'm thirteen," said Davy. "That's just a fact."

"Wellthischangesthecomplexionofthingssomefuckingwhat," said Jojo.

"Hold your horses, Jo," said Abigail. "It's just a number."

"He's thirteen, he's a man," said Jojo. "Our *rules*, Abi. Our rules."

"Henry specifically asked for him. Henry needs him—the future of the whole community depends on him."

"You know what, Abigail? I genuinely and honestly can't see how that can be. Look at him!" She swung an arm in the general direction of Davy. "He's nothing."

"Thank you very much," Davy said.

"I *would* say he's only a boy," sparked Jojo, "but it turns out he's *not even* a fucking boy. He's a man. I'm not going against one of the fundamental rules of our community and personally escorting a man under our battlements. Capiche?"

May said, "She has a point, Abi. Him being thirteen does change things."

"He doesn't *look* thirteen," Abigail said.

"And yet he *is* thirteen," snapped Jojo. "Funny how that works, sometimes, ain't it?"

"It's just a number."

"It's our rule! It's what defines us! Once you start chipping away at that then where will we be?"

"So then we're at an impasse, aren't we, comrades?" said Abigail, in a voice that suggested she was losing her temper. "Because Henry gave me very specific instructions to bring this lad in. Are you saying you won't help me do that?"

May walked over to stand behind Jojo. The latter said, "Not only am I saying I won't help, Abi, I'm saying I will do everything in my power to prevent you violating one of our fundamental rules by smuggling a full-grown adult male into Wycombe."

"Is that how you all feel?" Abigail demanded.

"She does have a point," said May.

"Jesus Abi," said Steph. "The cat's out of the bag now, though, isn't it? Maybe we could have smuggled him in as a kid, if nobody knew his age. He is kind of runty and small—"

"I'm," said Davy, "right *here*, you know."

"—but now everyone knows, it's not a grey area any more, is it? Rules are rules."

"Mahvesh?"

Mahvesh shrugged. "Me? I tend to think we ought to allow men in, anyway. Some men. The good-looking and kind-hearted ones."

"Oh don't start with that," complained Jojo. "Not again."

"Not trying to pick a fight," said Mahvesh, holding up both hands. "It's a matter we all should discuss, is all I mean. It's a medium-term thing for the future of the community to talk about, maybe. But for now? Well," and she laughed a self-conscious little laugh and waved a hand in Davy's direction, "I can't speak to how kind-hearted he is, but nobody would classify this one as *good-looking*."

"Might I once again take a moment to remind you all," said Davy, "that I'm *right here*?"

"You're really not making my life easy," said Abigail, rubbing her eyes with her wrists. "OK, we need to get going now. We can go to Fingest, I guess, and send word up to Handy Cross that we've brought the boy. Henry can come to us, I suppose."

"Or I could just go home?" Davy suggested. "Just slip away, westward? That way I wouldn't be a bother."

"Whatever it is that Henry thinks you can do," said Jojo, "better be sky-scraping *amazing*. You better be able to move heavy objects with your mind, or generate electricity out of your fingers just by standing in a bucket, or something."

"If you don't all start being nicer to me," said Davy, "I'll use my one magic power on you all. Which is to make you all grow—" He was going to say penises, but in the middle of the statement he suddenly had a crisis of uncertainty as to whether the plural of *penis* was indeed *penises*, or whether it wasn't something fancy like *peni*, and that they'd all mock him for not knowing this. Then, having stopped, he reflected back on what he was saying, in this room of full-grown women, and blushed.

"Grow what?" prompted Jojo.

"Consciences," Davy concluded, lamely.

For some reason, this was the prompt for Amber to burst into tears.

CHAPTER THIRTEEN

THEY CONSOLED AMBER as best they could, and gathered all their stuff together. Then they went outside into the pale afternoon light and mounted their horses. Abigail took one last look north, across the lowland landscape. There didn't seem to be anything going on. A few streams of smoke were visible from homes at the foot of the hills. Wood produces a thinner and more spectral smoke than coal, and homesteads visible in the middle-distance were probably burning fires in their grates, even if nothing was visible from their chimneys.

A kite flew, its long wings angled as it turned, like a mighty uptick in the sky. Circling out its imaginary arena below it, the space within which everything was prey.

"Things seem to have calmed down," said Abigail.

"Our best guess," said Steph, "is that Father John is quartering a pretty large force in Long Crendon. Hundreds of men according to some. Thousands according to others."

"Long where?" asked Davy.

"It's a few miles north of Thame."

Abigail saluted the distance, the better to peer into it. "Can't see any sign of that. Anyway, we need to get going."

They rode slowly through the trees until they came to a road. It had been cleared: the rusting wrecks of cars and trucks pushed off to the side, parked, as it were, in amongst the trees. Accessing a road made progress rather more rapid, naturally, and the horses moved forward at a sprightly trot.

Abigail turned her head, "We're going inside what we call the cordon—not into Wycombe itself, but the outer zones. At least inside the cordon we'll be safe."

"Safe," repeated Davy, and as he did so May, riding ahead of them, screamed. It wasn't a warning scream. It was more by way of being an agonized scream. There were several swishing noises, and Davy, looking around him with the abruptly adrenalised start-up of panic, saw one crossbow bolt hit the horse behind him—hit its neck and sink in deep—and caught a glimpse of another in flight—a blur of grey—before it jarred into the chest of that horse's rider. Mahvesh. She exhaled hard, as if she'd been punched, which, in a more fatal sense than is usually implied by that word, of course she had been. She slumped to the side, and her horse, in pain and consequent agitation, sprang into motion, shouldering Abigail and Davy's horse aside and galloping ahead.

Davy could see what was happening. The enemy was on them. They had chosen this cleared-away corridor of crumbly tarmac because it was perfect for such an ambush, and Abigail had blithely led her people into it. Abigail was already aiming her pistol to return fire. May was still howling in pain, up ahead, for whatever reason, and Mahvesh's horse, and its sole, probably dead rider, was careering away into the distance.

It was obvious what was going on. Yet something in Davy wondered: what is going on? He opened his mouth and shouted:

"What's happening?'—

—at exactly the moment Abigail discharged her weapon. The crashing, severing noise of the gun going off completely covered the sound of his voice. It also seemed to scare the horse they were riding, which arched its spine and leapt up, all four hooves off the ground so far as Davy could tell. It landed with such a hefty jolt that Davy was bounced up in turn, and when he landed back on the saddle he caught one of his testicles under his thigh.

This was not a pleasant sensation.

Now it was Davy's turn to yell. He writhed to the left, to free up the crushed organ, and the horse, as if in response, rolled its whole body to the right. The combination of these two motions shucked Davy clean off the saddle. He fell, hard, to the ground.

He didn't hit tarmac, but instead fell just to the side of the road onto a sedimented layer of old leaves and fir-needles. The horse was tall, but this softer landing ground meant he was not as badly hurt as he might have been. But his balls! Or, more specifically, his right ball. For a time he simply lay with his hand between his clamped thighs, trying to get his breath back. There was some kind of commotion going on around him, but he didn't have the mental space to pay attention to it. His entire sensorium was consumed by the pain in his testicle.

It settled, eventually, or at least the pain and shock withdrew to a more tolerable level. Davy rolled over, and got up, by stages, sitting up, pulling his legs round and getting onto a knee, and finally stranding upright.

There seemed to be a great many people in motion. Davy turned to look up the road. A few yards ahead he saw the horse he had been riding only moments before, with its head on the ground, kneeling on its forelegs with its huge rear up in the air, as if the beast was abasing itself, or praying, or doing some kind of callisthenics. There was a pile of something on the ground in front of it. The horse wasn't moving at all. Davy stumbled a few steps towards the beast, and started to walk round it. There was a great deal of black goo on its front, soaked into its hide, dripping into a puddle onto the road.

Something *tsinged* past Davy's ear.

People were yelling.

His ball ached.

Something went snap, very loudly, quite close. Davy continued walking along the horse's motionless flank, and brought the heap, whatever it was, into clearer view. It wasn't a whatever it was. It was a recognisable thing. It was Abigail, lying foetal on her side, a bolt through her throat and much blood underneath her, a dropped cape of black-red slick painted onto the road and glistening like wet leather.

Something else, somewhere nearby, made a very loud snapping noise.

The whatever. It was not good. Whatever it was that was.

Davy bent forward, to get a closer look at Abigail. There was no mistaking her lifelessness. Her un-status. He got up again, and looked around him—in the trees on the other side of the road, using the rusted hulks for cover, were many people. Somewhere something, or things, went *snap, snap, snap*.

Davy thought to himself, *You're smart, Davy, you know you are. You really ought to be able to piece together what is happening here*. But though he understood what all the discrete elements were, somehow they wouldn't gel into a meaningful whole.

There were many figures in amongst the trees on the far side of the road. These figures were dressed variously, mostly in clothes of tan and leather.

Davy turned about.

About a yard from him, a chunk of the crumbly tarmac disengaged from the road and leapt diagonally into the air, separating as it moved into a dozen small pieces of shingle, all going in different directions. Grit from this disassembled tarmac rattled against Davy's left leg as he turned.

He saw a running man in a bulky brown jacket duck his head, dive at the tarmac as if it were water, and lie motionless. Running at *him*.

Running at Davy.

It was—

Turned right around. Cars. There were lots of rusty hulks on the far side of the road, and fewer hulks pushed into the trees on *this* side of the road. In between the trees were lots of people, but dressed differently from the others—in tidy-looking black outfits, all alike. Something went *snap, snap, snap*, like the air itself was clacking its jaws.

Davy saw a figure, standing not far from him, hauling his rifle round to aim it. A bullet, or a piece of shrapnel, touched this person's belly with a glancing blow, and the whole gut opened as if unzipped. A mess of viscera slopped out and unfurled towards the ground. It reminded Davy strongly of the way cows shit, the way a great quantity of manure will simply slop out of the beast's rear-end and splash to the floor.

The person wasn't standing any more.

"Davy!" yelled somebody, and it was a man's voice, not a woman's.

Shreds of mist were drifting over the road. But they were a strange sort of mist that smelt not of moisture and cool but of a musty, sulphurous hotness.

"Davy," yelled somebody, quite near. "Cover, Davy! Come over to me."

Davy saw another horse lying on the ground. This one was on its side, and its chest was not moving up and down the way a living, breathing horse's chest would. It was very solidly static. Davy walked slowly over towards it, because there was a rider with a leg trapped under the horse. *I can help lift the horse and free her*, he thought. But then he thought, *No, no, a horse would be much too heavy for me to lift*. So then he thought, *But perhaps I could drag her out*. It was May, and she was still alive. He got to the horse and May's face was in motion and in pain but she was still alive, and then there was a flash-bang and all the air was instantly hot and hard and it bundled him over. Abruptly he was—*tzit!*—down, face down. How had that happened? The texture of the old tarmac was like stale baked goods, or old rubber, and it smelt strange. It was scratching Davy's face, and his head was filled with a strange song, maybe birdsong, very high pitched, and

—eeeeeeeeeeeee—

and he got in a spinaround way to his feet again. The spinaround was the whole road. It was obvious what was going on. He knew very well what was going on. Dizzy dizzy. You'd have to be moron not to see it. May wasn't moving any more. She was still stuck under the horse, but there wasn't as much to her head as there had been a little while before. The world spun around the sun and spun around its polar axis and how it was spinning around Davy's head.

Davy said to himself, *You are in the middle of a big fight, a proper war, and people are dying.* But because there had been no build-up, no advanced-warning, no preliminary, because he'd suddenly found himself in the middle of it, and because his ball still ached, and because all these people were dead, and because he was only just thirteen years of age, he simply couldn't make any meaning out of all these component events. Flashes and flickers. A breeze from the left, and then a much stronger breeze, hard from the right, making his hair struggle and writhe. Somebody had hands on him. Somebody had grabbed him, and was turning him away from the dead body of May. The *eee* inside his ears was sliding up a tone, and then up a semitone, and then *iii* with a sort of background roaring moaning rush, the whole yelling, roaring, snap-snapping world loomed back into audibility, and the man who had his hand on Davy's shoulder was shouting right in his face

"Davy! Davy!"

—and it was Daniel, Davy recognised his creased old face, and smiled, and then Davy said, with a resonant internal sense of comprehension (but in a croaky sort of voice), "Ambush."

"What?"

"It's an *ambush*."

And Daniel said, "I know, lad, come *on*."

And out of the mush of weirdness and disorientation and the fact that his testicle still ached, something more distinct came swiftly into focus. Something much more adrenalised. Something more like

"Shit!"

panic and

"Come *on*, Davy..."

Daniel, doing an awkward crouch-down lopsided-limping run, was pulling on Davy to drag him along, and Davy's heart suddenly upped its rate, and the fact of being-in-danger clattered home to his thinking mind. He was suddenly very scared, and he *ran*. Daniel hauled him behind an old van, once white, now a pattern of pale blotches over wine-brown rusted metal, as if camouflaged for life in the snowy tundra. Davy was panting now, and everything had become much more vivid. He could see with jittery precision all the little details of the scene, and here was Daniel dressed in black with a big cast on his hurt foot, and a gun in his hand, and all around were people keen to kill him, to kill *him*, Davy, who was so courteous and pleasant to everybody, who had always been a good boy, and yet here they were, and Davy was afraid and when a triplet of detonations slammed into the far side of the van, shaking it and making it chime like a muffled bell, he let out a shriek of alarm.

"Daniel," he gasped.

"Good to see you again," said Daniel, peering round the side of the van. "We need to get you out of here, my boy. Are you ready to run? Stick with me. I'll be doing a bit of a Quasimodo lope, but I can move pretty fast if I have to."

"What's happening?"

"John is happening," Daniel said, grimacing. He seemed to

have hurt his shoulder. "Trying either to grab you or kill you—or grab you prior to killing you."

"Why?" Davy asked. "I don't understand why!"

"I don't know suppose *he* knows why either," said Daniel, checking his gun. "Except that he knows, now, that Wycombe wants you so very badly, and he's made the decision that it's in his interests to thwart them."

"Oh dear God."

"It's bold," said Daniel. "It surely is. It's surely going to piss off Wycombe that John's actually put men up on their hill, and a pissed-off Wycombe is not a thing you want aimed at you. I guess he's actually making his move. Interesting times, as the Chinaman said. Was that a Chinaman? I'm not sure."

Davy's heart was now going so fast it was palpably uncomfortable in his chest. He was fidgety. All his instincts were screaming inside him to run. "What do we do?"

"I'm going to fire this," said Daniel, looking at the stub-barrelled shotgun he was holding in his right hand "and then we're going to make a run for the trees—over there." With his left hand he gestured. "Keep running, and don't stop, even if I—*Jesus*!"

This last came out as a shout, because a wide chested figure in a yellow leather coat was coming straight at them—was almost upon them. The pistol in this figure's raised right hand was aimed directly at Daniel's face. He pulled the trigger as he ran, and Davy heard the click of the mechanism very distinctly.

The pistol did not discharge.

Daniel hoisted his shotgun and fired one barrel. It didn't go off. *Clic-tac*. He pulled second trigger and that barrel too failed to fire. Davy saw Daniel's expression curdle in anger, and heard him say, "Oh forf—" before the running man crashed into him, and the two of them sprawled—"irk!"—backwards onto the road—"*sake*!" bellowed Daniel. The two men rolled over and over, struggling in an ungainly way that made it impossible to see who was doing what to whom.

Davy's panic was in no way diminishing. *I have to get away.* To his right the soldiers of Father John's army were coming closer, and seemed very numerous. He looked across the road at the black-clad soldiers of Guz. Would they shoot him, if he ran straight at them? What could he shout to let them know that he wasn't attacking them? Would they even care? He rubbed his face with his hands, made a little whimpering noise, and took a step away from the van. "If I shout *I'm not attacking*," he said aloud, to nobody, "then what are the odds they'll hear *attack* and shoot me down? Oh god oh god."

He took another step away from the van. Paralysing indecision. He turned to face down the road, strewn now with the bodies of human beings and horses. He turned to face up the road. Was that the direction to Wycombe? But why would he want to go *there*?

Which direction was home?

Daniel and his assailant were still grappling with one another. They had rolled completely off the road and were wrestling in amongst the old leaves and rubbish.

Somebody tapped Davy hard on the left shoulder. It was a very firm smack indeed, and, to be truthful, it was far from comfortable. It made him cough and take a step forward, to avoid falling over. Who would be so rude? But the sensation was one of pressure, not of penetration or pain—not, that is, in the first instance.

It was, however, a sense of pressure that did not go away. On the contrary, it intensified, and began to expand, like something boiling hot, or very icily cold, being poured over the whole shoulder area. Underneath the expansion was a prickling that, when he focussed on it, felt very much like pain. Felt very much like a sharp, unpleasant pain.

Davy reached round with his right hand, elbow at his waist, the back of his hand sliding awkwardly up his spine. His fingers fumbled on something straight and stiff and thin, like a pen, that projected straight out from the shoulder blade.

It was, Davy realised, quite hard to breathe. He was finding it harder to pull a breath in than he usually did. The pain in his shoulder was increasing, growing from ache to stab to something worse.

Davy took another couple of steps forward. He dropped his hand to his side. *This*, he thought to himself, *is not good. Oh no. Not good.*

Figures to his left, flitting between the trees. Those were Father John's men, and they were legion. They were going to kill him.

Somebody was shouting, and it was several somebodies who were shouting. God, his shoulder hurt! It *raged* in pain. Someone had sheathed a blade in his shoulder and by Christ it hurt. A paralallip rhythm. A paralallip. Rhythm of *paralallip*. Davy thought perhaps it was his own heart, galloping towards shutdown in panic and pain, but the sound wasn't inside his body. It was an actual percussive pattern, being beaten onto the ground, and resonating in the soles of his own feet.

Paralallip. Paralallip.

He tried looking over his left shoulder to see with his own eyes the crossbow shaft that had struck his shoulder blade. But it was not in his field of view. The shaft was too short, or perhaps it was too deeply buried in his body. He couldn't see it, as he tried to look over his own shoulder. It hurt to move his neck. Breathing in grated pain out of his left side and sent scattering sparks of agony all through him. Breathing out was sore, but not so agonising, like a release of pressure. Shallow breaths.

Shallow breaths.

Paralallip. Paralallip.

Out of the corner of his eye Davy saw the horse, at full gallop, and with no possibility of slowing or stopping before it ran him down. There was nothing he could do. The pain had paralysed his feet. He tried to snatch another breath, but the pain was so ghastly that he sobbed and stopped and sighed the little air out of his lungs again.

He recognised the rider on the big horse. The rider on the big horse was Jojo, the woman who called him shitpants and fuckwit and who hated men and hated him in particular. And now she was going to run him down with her steed.

Davy grimaced. Oh, how his feet were fixed to that spot! He couldn't run, or even turn. Death was riding him down, like in a fairy story. Father John's troops were coming out from the trees now, running at him, at the horse Jojo was riding, yelling, or making the sorts of gargoyle faces that people do when they are shouting, but Davy couldn't hear, he was deafened by his own pain, or else he could hear only the crescendo of Jojo's horse's *paralallip paralallip*.

It was a white horse.

The horse reached him and didn't trample him with its hooves. Instead the pain in Davy's shoulder suddenly intensified into something far worse, something simply beyond the capacity of flesh to endure, and what small air was in his lungs was jammed right out of them, expelled as if by a rocket, and he was *down*, to be trampled underhoof after all, except that he wasn't down, he was somehow *up*, swinging into the sky—he actually saw the trees shrink down and Father John's men go below his line of sight, as if he were a bird flying—but then he couldn't really see anything, because the pain was so very overwhelming it flooded through his whole body and brain and a cascade of sharp-edged sparks flowed through his skull, and he was gone again, gone, gone again.

Jojo had ridden right past him. She had, to give her credit, seen that this chance was the last chance, and she had *taken* that chance, despite the fact that she had lost two of the four fingers of her left hand moments before, and blood was spittering out from the wound, like a comet's tail as she rode.

There was no time to stop, and certainly no time to dismount and haul the lad up onto the horse, and remount and ride away. Father John's men had pushed back those fuckers from—Guz, she supposed, in their black combat fatigues—and they almost had the boy. So she didn't stop, and didn't dismount, and instead she reached down with her good right hand, and grabbed the handle now usefully protruding from the lad's shoulderblade, and good fortune and her own reflexes and most of all her horse's sheer weight and momentum meant that she was able to heave him up, scoop him almost, and she tried to ignore the way he was screaming, and put her own head down as gunfire sounded all around her, and urged the horse on with her heels.

She got him, just about, over the pommel, on his belly, and then she was able to concentrate on just riding as hard as she could. By the time he hit the saddle he was unconscious. Luckily for him.

CHAPTER FOURTEEN

DAVY DRIFTED IN and out of awareness, and each time he opened his eyes he was somewhere new. But each time he opened his eyes his pain was the same, and the perfectly linked-together line of physical agony took such precedence over his merely geographical whereabouts to render that latter spectral and unreal. The fundamental was: always pain.

He was being lifted down from a horse, and various hands were holding him, but the movement dragged the bolt's shaft against raw bone, and he howled, a long lupine sound. Then, with no sense of transition, he was in the back of a van or minibus. He wasn't screaming now, but his mouth was very dry and the pain was exactly the same, exactly as unbearable. There had once been windows in the rear door of this van, and the glass had long since disappeared, and Davy could see tree trunks swinging past and going behind. The angle made it look as though it was an endless line of columns tumbling down, one after the other, in time to the ponderous beats of his own heart. But each heartbeat was pushing pain, not blood, around his body. And with no sense of transition he was in a low-lit room and there was a smell of soap and bleach, and he was on his side. The pain was as bad and then it was much worse, a grinding drilling that opened his whole back and allowed all his innards to slop out and fall in fire and acid onto the table, and his soul fell out too, and he was floating around in an airy medium of pain. He would have writhed and struggled, but he discovered he was tied down with a series of buckled straps, and—the pain had prevented him from noticing this before—there was a wooden plug in his mouth, to prevent him biting his tongue, and perhaps to stifle his howls, and then with no sense of transition he was in a much lighter room, with ivory-white sky visible through an actual glass window, and electric lightbulbs on the wall. He was in a bed. His shoulder hurt, as before, but the thread of pain on which his experiences were strung was... Davy fished for the right word. Thinner? More silk and less wire? It was still there, but it was less. Breathing was still hard, and doubly hard because (he realised) he was lying on his front, with his face to the side. That meant that drawing breath involved lifting his whole torso as well as gritting his teeth against the pain. But the grinding of metal against bone—against *his* bone—had gone.

He was disembodied, but he had brought the pain with him. He flew, or floated, or fell in a strange horizontal trajectory. He saw the whole landscape below him: the dark green elongated wedge of the Chilterns, and to the north the parti-coloured spread of fields and innumerable small lakes and flows, flashing bright as the sun passed overhead, and retaining some wraith of illumination in the night, when the sun swung around the wall's edge of the horizon.

Then it was dark. Davy was very thirsty. He tried to ask for water, not to yell or demand it, but just to beg in a small voice, pitiably enough, for a little water. His voice wasn't working, though. What came out was a creaky, cicada burr. The thirst was so acute that it took Davy a little while to notice the pain again. But the pain was certainly there. More diffuse, now: the whole shoulder area cannibalised by a severe ache. Davy experimentally flexed a muscle in his back, and the pain started roaring, so he quit that pretty sharpish.

Eventually he fell asleep again, despite the pain, and despite the thirst. And in the morning there were two women, who fed him some water through a tube for which he was so grateful he actually wept, sobbed like a baby. He felt them peeling something off his shoulder and probing the wound, which was very far from a pleasant experience. There was a wash of something cold. The thing about this fluid, whatever it was, wasn't that it was cold but that it *stung like fuck*, and he wriggled and complained and they told him to button it. Then they reapplied the bandage and patted him on the head. "I'm still thirsty," he said. "I'm thirsty again." So they gave him some more water, and left him alone.

He was in a room. There was a big window, and it was glass, and it had bars in front of it. He was in a bed. The walls were white.

He lay still, observing from within (as it were) the way the pain in his shoulder burned like embers in a grate, and slowly diminished over time to a kind of distant moan. He tried reaching round with his right hand to explore the area, but even moving the muscles on the uninjured half of his back stoked up the ferocity of the pain, so he stopped trying, and lay still again. And lying still enabled the pain to settle, as agitated water restores itself to flatness.

There was a distant wheezing, rasping noise. It was faint, but once Davy heard it he couldn't miss it: a remote squeezebox whingeing, or sobbing. It sounded like the whole house was a ship at sea, and its timbers were creaking. Or else it sounded like the cosmos had broken its heart and was sobbing over and over *waah, waah, waaah*. What was it?

Was it him?

No, it came from outside him. It was something else. Too irregular to be a machine.

He couldn't work it out.

Perhaps he dozed, and woke. Perhaps he did that several times over; it was hard to tell. He became aware that he was hungry. If he concentrated on his stomach the hunger got worse, and if he put his mind elsewhere—out through the glass window, for instance, at the hazy white clouds that were visible—then the hunger got less worse. Reduced in worseness. Diminished in worsosity.

Better. Slowly, slowly.

He supposed he was mending. Slowly, slowly. The two women came back, and gave him some more water, and when he said he was hungry they fed him little pellets of something, maybe bread, maybe chicken, flavourless except for a faint saltiness. These he swallowed as he lay flat, and they did little to take the edge off his hunger. He told them he needed to relieve himself, and they didn't understand. He said, "I need to relieve myself," more slowly. But it wasn't his forktongue pronunciation that was throwing them, it was the idiom. Relieve myself was the kind of thing his Dad would say. So he tried again, "make water. Drain the bladder. Have a piss."

"It's gonna hurt, my boy," one of the women warned him. "We'll have to roll you a little onto your side to get a pan in under you, and that won't be comfortable. You sure you can't hold it?"

"I could just piss into the bed," he said.

"Well that would be smelly and nasty and, I think we'd have to say, unhygienic. Wouldn't you agree?"

The pressure in his bladder was quite severe now. "I don't think I can hold it."

So one of the women trotted off to get a pan, and when she brought it back the two rolled him towards his right side. Not the whole way over onto his side, but just enough to be able to slip the pan in. And it was indeed, as they had promised, excruciating, agonising, excruiagonising, and he cried aloud in pain. "Oh god, oh god, oh god."

"Do your business, boy," said one of the women, "and we'll put you back down and things will settle again."

But there was a problem. He was now lying on his right arm, and couldn't move it; and there was no way he could do anything with his left arm. There was no chance of moving his right arm at all; it was locked, paralysed, helpless. His left arm could do it, if it were free. He tried to explain this to the two women, but the combination of his physical distress and the rising panic that he was going to lose control and wet himself, added to the slit in his tongue, meant that he was not able to communicate his anxiety to them. Eventually one of them intuited what the problem was, and fumbled at his pants to get his little willy out, and he gratefully rang the bell of the pan with a hard little stream of urine, and finally they lowered him back onto his front and left him to it.

As before, he lay for a time in sheer pain, and over the course of a distinct period the pain slowly settled until it became only an ache. It settled enough to permit him to sleep, and so he slept and when he woke up it was dark.

He grew so bored, lying there in the dark, that he began experimenting with moving portions of his body. Seeing how far he could move without waking the slumbering pain in his shoulder. He could flex his toes, and his feet and even bend his legs at the knees, lifting his shins off the mattress. But turning his head was a no-no, and though he could fiddle with his right-hand fingers and move his arm a little from the elbow, his whole left arm sprang agony upon him if he moved any part of his right shoulder.

He listened to the silence. The creaking noise had stopped.

Light again. He slept odd hours, like a baby. In the morning he was thirsty again, and they gave him some more water. The irregular creaking noise was back. "We have a painkiller here," said one of the women tending him. Neither of them had told him their names. "It's a pre-Sisters pill, and you have to swallow it. Do you think you can do that?"

"I'm hungry," Davy complained.

"The pill won't help with hunger. But I tell you what: if its active ingredient hasn't dissipated over the years, it will take your pain away, as if by magic. And then we can get you sat up, and properly fed. You can eat, use the toilet, have a wash. What do you say?"

The pill was as large as the nail of a little finger, and Davy nearly choked on it—he couldn't speak and beckoned for more water, a gesture which first only puzzled the two women. But then they gave him more water through the straw, and he managed to get the pill down into his stomach. They left him for a half hour or so. He tried to determine, as he lay there, whether the pain was diminishing because he was lying still, or because the pill was actually working. Maybe it *was* the latter.

When the women came back they coordinated in a series of manoeuvres of his body in which he was a junior partner. Rolling him fully onto his right side—his shoulder hurt, and quite acutely, but not nearly so badly as it had done—and then swinging his legs over the edge of the bed and sitting him up. His head swam with prickly dizziness and his sight retreated down a sort of corridor towards blackness, except that the glowing ache of his shoulder pulled him back to consciousness.

He was up. The women gave him more to drink and fed him a little soup and bread. Then they took a photograph of him. An actual photograph! It was only when the camera clicked and the box was taken away that Davy realised that there was somebody else in the room. A newcomer, a stranger, had been standing behind him as the image was taken.

"On the mend?" this person said.

Davy couldn't see who it was, and didn't feel like taking the risk-of-pain entailed by turning his head to find out. The voice sounded old. "Better than I was, I think," he said.

"Good," said the person. "I'll come and see you again. There's a lot we need to talk about."

"Like why I'm even here in the first place?" Davy said, with some hostility in his voice. If he'd only had a bit more strength he would have allowed himself to get properly angry. Kidnapping him? Taking him away from his home? The person, whoever she was, sitting behind him didn't say anything. "Or won't you tell me that?" he asked.

After a while he realised he was alone.

The distant *waah waah* background noise. It went away at night, and returned during the day. What *was* it?

The two women helped him to shuffle to a toilet, where he sat, and the pain in his shoulder started to grow again. Afterwards he washed his hands and face, and shuffled back to the bed, to lie down on his front again. By this point the pain was quite severe, a pulsing, scraping sort of agony that started at the point of his wound, but disseminated itself all over his back, pinched at his heart, and made breathing very difficult. Davy was crying: little desperate tears, shallow sobs. "Can I have another?" he asked.

"Another what?"

"What you just gave me?"

"The painkiller tablet?"

"Tablet. That. Tabt."

"My dear boy," said the woman. "Those are gold! Rarer than gold. I'm afraid we couldn't waste another on—excuse me saying this, but—a man."

"It hurts! It hurts!"

"I'm sure it does." Was there a note of sadistic satisfaction in her voice? What had Davy ever done to *her*?

The other woman was a little more kindly. "Just lie still, my love," she said, "and the pain will settle down again. We have willow strips you can suck on, or chew. Chewing works best. I'll fetch you one in a bit."

The pain kept building, and then it plateaued, and then slowly it reduced in intensity. Finally it settled down properly, became background noise again. Eventually he drifted off to sleep.

A noise from somewhere—somebody dropping something with a clang—woke Davy. His heart was pummelling his ribs, and he was sweating. Anxious. He had a very clear visual image of Abigail's body, dead and bloody on the ground—Abigail who was once alive and was now dead. Davy was, he realised, weeping. His agitation was making him move his body, and that in turn was disturbing his wound and making it more sore, but that only made his anxiety and desire to run away stronger. He had to get away, or what happened to Abigail would happen to him. It was intolerable. The sobs were crushing his own throat. Tears gumming his eyes. He groped with his good hand, and the pain of his wound flared. His hand found the bars of the bedstead and he grasped and tried to pull himself off the bed—to get up, run away, find a place to hide from the fighting. Tensing his muscles appeared to rip something in the wound—flesh tearing open, bone snapped or shifting, something agonising, agonising. He screamed.

One of the women came through eventually. "What's your noise?"

"The fighting," he sobbed. "The fighting."

"We're miles away from the fighting here," she said, briskly. "You can't hear anything where we are. Stop making a fuss."

"Why do you hate me?"

"Me hate you? I'm not the one who shot you in the back! Nursing you back to health and this is the thanks I get? I'm going to petition Henry for a different duty, I honestly am."

She went out, and Davy lay on the bed sobbing. Eventually the panic drained out of him, and his heart-rate settled again, and the pain in his back settled into a less ghastly configuration.

He worried that he had done something to his wound, but after a while, exhausted with his own terror and worry, he fell asleep again.

He dreamed of his family: his two sisters, his Da, his Ma. He knew it was them, but because they were standing behind him he couldn't see them. In the dream his back was fine, and there was no pain. He was standing up, inside a wide, clean, bright room, and he could simply have turned around and greeted his family. He could have gone over to them and hugged them, and then all of them could have walked out and strolled down the valley and up the hill on the far side—in the compressed topography of the dream he was a short walk from home. But he did not turn around. "*Why don't you?*" somebody asked, and Davy saw that it was May, the woman he had first ridden behind on that big horse, when the Wycombe crew had first grabbed him and brought him here. He looked over at May, and saw she was naked, and an intense sensation of embarrassment at her nudity mingled with an equally intense sense of arousal. May smiled at him. "*Why don't you just turn around?*"

"*I don't know why I don't,*" said in-dream-Davy, but the main thought in his dream-head was, *Can she see how turned-on I am? Can she see my hard-on? Because that would be just too humiliating and embarrassing.* Dream-May smiled again, and came over to him, and reached out with a hand to touch the side of his face. "*You don't need to feel awkward on my account,*" she said. "*I'm dead, remember?*" And Davy remembered that this was indeed the case, and that fact made him feel a plunge of sorrow.

Davy awoke in the dark room.

CHAPTER FIFTEEN

FOUR MORE DAYS and Davy's wound had healed sufficiently to enable him to sit up, leaning his good shoulder into a mass of piled-up pillows, and so drink soup, and eat munches of cold roast parsnips, suck the little inch-long strips of willow bark that did (as he had been promised) take the edge off the pain, and look about him. On the fifth day they got him out of bed altogether and settled him into a large padded chair. From here he could survey where he was.

He was in a room inside a much larger building: a well-maintained relic of the pre-Sisters world. There was a radiator on the wall that got hot twice a day. There were two electrical light bulbs in the ceiling, and they came on in the evening, and poured out light in a ridiculous, prodigal profusion of brightness.

Through the barred windows the view was of a long sloping meadow, the grass kept short by a herd of some two dozen sheep. It had been their bleating that he had heard, from his bed. The mornings saw the whole stretch frosted over, but within an hour or two of the sun rising the frost melted. The coldest of winter was behind them, perhaps.

On day five he began to feel hot and uncomfortable. His two reluctant nurses scolded him for this, as if he had done it on purpose. The antique glass thermometer reported that he had a fever. The women stripped off his shirt, and made him bend forward and peeled away his wound's dressing. Even Davy could smell it. "That's bad," said the angrier of the two women. "That could be the end of you."

"We have antibiotics," said the other.

"We're surely not wasting those on a him!" said the first.

"We may not need to," said the second. "I've seen people recover from worse infections than this."

So they cleaned the wound, and it stung and sparked pain and Davy, leaning so far forward his chest was on his thighs, wept with the discomfort and the relentlessness of it all. "It comes," said the kinder of the two women, "from re-using the same dressing. We should put a new dressing on each time."

"I swear if Mary mother of God came to us with a hole in her breast, we wouldn't treat her with such lavishness!" exclaimed the first.

"Henry was very clear."

"How long since he took that photograph? A week?"

"Not so long," said the second woman, lifting Davy a little from his posture so as to be able to wrap a bandage around the front of his chest, and again round the back, fixing it with a pin.

"How long before we accept it's not going to work? Before we agree we have to let him go. I mean—look at him!"

"You're not looking at him," said the second, "with the right eyes."

"I guess we'll see."

This entire exchange sank into Davy's febrile mind, hot with feverish fidgetiness. He sat back in his big chair, leaning his good side into the cushions, and stared through the window, down the meadow and past its sheep to where the distance was fringed with winter trees. So many boughs, dividing into so very many branches, all subdividing and subdividing into finer and finer black lines against the white sky. Like the blood vessels in a retina, as if he was the eye looking at the eye that was looking at him. He replayed the conversation the two women had had over and over. It kept going through and through his humid brain. Not looking at him with the right eyes. Whose eyes? Not looking at him with the right eyes. Whose eyes? He had a fever, and he didn't feel well. His eyeballs felt molten in their skull-sockets. He was shivering with the heat. Sweat came out of him like grease. He was thirsty. His nurses had left him a bottle of water, and he grasped it with his one good hand, but it shook like it was a live grenade about to explode, and he grew very afraid. He was crying. It wasn't the bottle that was shaking. It was his hand that was shaking. His whole body trembled. His shoulder resonated with the tremors and made a song of pain out of the motion. Vibration was the source of all sound, he knew, and therefore of all music. The string that vibrated was his own taut nerve. Savage savage savage savage. He took a drink. Not looking at him with the right eyes. Whose eyes? His mouth was dry, and he tried to take another drink but realised that he had drunk the whole bottle.

Not looking at him with the right eyes. Whose eyes?

He managed to get to his feet, and though his shoulder hurt he was able to shuffle slowly, one foot over the other like a bear, to the little toilet room next to his one. He sat on the toilet because he wasn't strong enough to stand, and pissed the way women do, and then he filled his water bottle at the tap and drank some more, and then, because sitting on the toilet wasn't comfortable, in that it forced him to bend forward a little, which stretched the skin of his back painfully—because of that he somehow got back to his feet and shuffled back to his chair, and sat in it. His head was searing. He wept hot tears.

He dozed, and when he woke he was a little better. He was still hot, and the room still had an unreal quality to it, as if the whole experience was a dream. But his heart was calmer, and he wasn't sweating so much. He drank the rest of his bottle, and stared through the window for a while.

He felt—strange. Trembly and overheated and a little sick.

The door opened, and one of his two nurses came in. It was the crueller of the two, and she had a strangely triumphant expression on her face that made Davy wary. "You have a visitor," she said.

"I feel strange," Davy told her. "Hot and floaty, sort of. I don't feel all here."

"None of your nonsense, now. Didn't you hear me? You have a visitor."

In through the door came Davy's Ma. She walked right up to him, and bent over and gave him a hug, as he sat in the chair. He started crying. He couldn't help it. "Ma," he said. "You're here."

"How are you, my boy?" said Ma."

"I'm sorry Ma—I'm sorry I didn't get back. I missed Christmas, I know. Oh Ma you must be so angry with me."

"I'm not angry," Ma insisted. "Just relieved to see that you're all right. It's not your fault, my love."

That wasn't the kind of thing Ma tended to say. But Davy clung to the hallucination, if that's what it was. "Oh Ma, I've had such a time!"

"I know my love."

Her presence was turning him again into a little, little boy, a tiny kid, a baby. He wanted her to gather him in her arms and hug him. "I tried to get back, but they grabbed me."

"He feels very hot," Ma said.

"He has had a temperature," said the nurse. "But it's going down."

"An infection?"

"A small one. We've cleaned the wound, and it's good now."

"Have you given him antibiotics?"

"He's mending well."

"Don't shit me, Miranda," said his Ma, in something closer to her usual tone. "I know you have them. Give him the medicine, god damn you."

Miranda scowled, but didn't reply.

"Ma," Davy said. "I tried to get home. I'm sorry. Did I miss Christmas?"

"Yes, my love," said Ma, giving him another swift hug.

"I knew I did. I knew I missed Christmas." He began crying again, because none of this was real, and his Ma was an impossible distance away, and he would probably never see her again, and an hallucination was no substitute.

"But it doesn't matter," Ma said. "And I'm not angry. I'm not angry," she clarified, looking at Miranda, "with you. Get well—Davy, Davy, just you concentrate on getting well, and these people will help you."

"I got shot in the back! I got a crossbow bolt in the back, Ma!"

"I know. It must have hurt."

"It hurt like the world was ending," he said. And, thirteen years of age boiled away by the fever and the emotion to a mere five or six, he started weeping yet again. Ma comforted him as best she could, although that kind of thing had always been Da's business, really, not hers. Eventually she stood up and rubbed the small of her back.

"I've got to go now, Davy," she said. "But I'll see you soon. When you're well. All right?"

"Are you going Ma?" said Davy. "Don't go."

"I have to my sweet. But I'll see you soon."

And she left the room.

Davy sat in his chair, his head hot and his skin itchy with sweat, and he tried to make sense of what had happened. Miranda had gone out with Ma, but she came back with a cup of water and a new kind of pill: a parti-coloured lozenge of red and white, much smaller than the other one he had had to swallow. It went down easily, and Davy was helped back to the bed, and he lay on his front and dozed.

When he woke the fever was worse, and the bed was wet. Miranda and the other nurse got him up, and fed him, and gave him another red-white pill, and he lay down and slept again.

When he woke this time he felt a little better. Not so hot, not so shaky. He got himself to the toilet and pissed standing up, for the first time in who-knows-how-long. Then he got himself to the comfy chair and just sat, staring out of the window for a long time. The other nurse came in, not-Miranda, and took his temperature, and gave him another of the miracle red-white lozenges.

"Am I in Wycombe?" he asked her.

"We don't let men in there," she replied. "It's nothing personal."

"So am I on the Hill?"

"What do you mean, Hill? We're on *a* hill, I suppose."

"I mean, am I home? Or near Wycombe."

"Oh," said not-Miranda. "The second one, my boy. You're near Wycombe. You're at a place called Hughenden. Henry didn't say anything about not telling you, so I guess I can tell you. It's a few miles from Wycombe."

"I had a fever," he said.

"But you're getting better," she replied, and turned to leave.

"I had a sort of vision," he said to her retreating back. "I thought I saw my mother. I thought I saw my Ma, and she came right into the room and she told me she would see me again." But the woman had gone.

CHAPTER SIXTEEN

IN TWO DAYS Davy's fever had entirely evaporated, and though his shoulder still ached, and sometimes twinged so badly he cried out, it was clearly starting to mend. His main problem now was that he was very bored. He got up from his bed and shuffled slowly to the door, but it was locked. He tried the window, but trying to lift it made flames of pain lick out of his wound, so he gave up on that endeavour. Sat down again.

He watched the sheep meandering over the grass, heads down. He listened to their bleats.

A click, and the door opened. In came Miranda, and she was pushing a wheelchair in front of her. "All change for you, Davy my lad," she said.

"You sound jolly Miranda," Davy returned. "For a change."

"My stint here is almost done, lad," she replied, without losing any of her good humour. "And I can't tell you how pleased I am with that. Here."

It was another of the red-white pills. Davy took it placidly, and then looked at the wheelchair. "For me?"

It was only then that he noticed there was a second person in the room. She must have slipped in behind Miranda. Not the other nurse, but a small-statured and very old woman. Indeed, she was the oldest person Davy's young eyes had ever seen. Her face was so brown and wrinkled it seemed to be sculpted out of nothing *but* wrinkles, with the flesh in between creases reduced to fibres, and the whole shaped into cheeks, a chin, a thin mouth, and a wide brow. Her eyes were bright, though: blue and clear with that strange magic that keeps eyes young whilst the rest of the body shrivels. Her hair, white as old hay, was tied back in a bun, and she was wearing a plain blue dress, cut close to her slender frame. She was standing a few yards from Miranda, and though her head barely came up to the nurse's chest there was no doubt who deferred to whom.

"Hello Davy," this stranger said. "I came to see you once earlier, but you were quite feverish and I don't think you registered my presence. Plus, I was here for your photograph, of course."

"Who are you?" Davy asked.

"I'm Henry, my dear. I run this place."

"This hospital?"

"No my dear. This land."

"I've heard of you," said Davy. "I thought you were a man."

"Now why would you think such a thing?" asked Henry, in a level voice.

A dog was barking, a long way away. It stopped barking.

"I don't know," said Davy.

"I'm afraid you've got yourself caught up in some major events, my boy. And I know you were shot—in the shoulder. That can't have been comfortable."

"Un," Davy confirmed, "comfortable."

"I saw you when they brought you in. The quarrel was sticking out quite neatly, from the exact centre of your shoulderblade."

"The what?"

"It's the technical term for the bolt fired by a crossbow."

"Why not just call it a bolt?"

"I try to steer clear of *why?* questions, my dear," said Henry. "They rarely lead human beings any place good. Though it was almost a shame they had to take the quarrel out, I thought. They could, perhaps, have inserted a second one in your other shoulderblade, and then fixed wings to the stumps. Big eagle-wings, with feathers made of tooled steel. Think how magnificent you would have looked!"

Davy wasn't sure if the old woman was joking when she said this. "That doesn't sound..." he started, and then trailed off.

"But with your metal wings, my dear, you could fly! You could *soar*."

"You're pulling my leg?"

"I am pulling your leg." The old woman trotted to the side of Davy's bed and pulled herself up, to sit on the edge of the mattress, like a child. "I hope they've been looking after you? Miranda and Camilla?"

"After," said Davy, "is what they have been looking."

"We didn't expect you to be brought in quite so close to death. Knock-knock-knocking on heaven's door. In point of fact you were doing more than that. You were ringing heaven's door bell, hammering on the door, kicking its cat-flap with big booted feet, and yelling to be let in." When Davy stared at her in incomprehension she said, "My lad, we expected you simply to arrive, by horse. We have a little apartment ready for you, in a different place. In the event, we had to bring you here first."

"*Why* did you have to bring me here?"

"Because you were so badly injured, of course."

"Not to this hospital," said Davy. "To this land."

"Ah," said the old woman, nodding and smiling. "I see what you mean. Well, Davy, I'll tell you. Do you have any sense of what it entails, running a place like this?"

"The land, not the hospital? I honestly don't."

"A lot of it is mundane bobbins. Sorting out the facilities.

Making sure there's food, and shelter, disposing of sewage, looking after the sick, OK-ing work rotas and duty-lists. Work is prayer for us; people do as much or as little of it as they feel they need to get in touch with themselves and with what is beyond themselves—the community, the larger principle. The goddess, some people call that. Not all of us. Wycombe is not doctrinaire. But most people who come here are keen to pitch in, to make everything work. And I end up working very hard. I do delegate, of course. Although it's harder to do that at a time like now."

"What time like now?"

"Why, we're at war, my dear. A proper war. It may be the first this country has seen for a long time: actual armies and generals and pitched battles, advance and retreat, all that."

"War with Father John?"

"Yes. And with Guz waiting to see who comes out on top. They're sly, Guz. They've brought up quite impressive concentrations of troops and materiel, all camped out west of the Thames—your neck of the woods."

"Soldiers in my home?"

"Not literally inside your house, I think. They're mostly down by Goring. They've even put up a pontoon, so that when they think the time is right they can march straight across."

"Invasion."

"Well, if you'd ever spent time with one of the Guz higher-ups, you'd know that they don't like to talk in those terms. They'd say something about the loss of life, and the grave social disorder, and all the negative consequences of war. They'd talk about the necessity of restoring order. I would agree with them about that, actually. I'm just not all that keen on Guz's version of it. They make a desert and call it peace. Do you know who said that?"

"Did you say desert, or dessert?"

The old woman peered at him for a little while through her

gloriously wrinkled old face. Then she moved on. "Initially I hired a proxy to grab you: a man. That was delegating. I shouldn't have hired him. Delegation is always a thicket. He'd done good work for us before, but this time he got wind of something, and he did a little poking around on his own account, and then decided to grab you for his own purposes. We hired him because many people on our council like to think we can keep our hands clean, or at least distance ourselves from the dirty-work. We can't, though. We shouldn't have hired him. We should have gone over ourselves and snatched you."

"Or maybe not come at all? Maybe just leave me be?"

She didn't reply to this. "So," she went on, shortly. "Running this land means attending to a lot of petty day-to-day business. But it also means thinking strategically. It means thinking ahead, and knowing when to act—to act militarily, I mean, to defend ourselves. I don't have nearly so many troops at my disposal as does Father John, I'm afraid. But we do have some advantages, happily. We're fighting over defensive territory that we have well prepared, for one. And we have much better kit."

"Kit?"

"Not just weapons. Tech generally. Tech is our superpower. We're known for it, of course. We salvage old pre-Sisters machines and components and bits and pieces, and we study them. We run generators. We distil ethanol on a large scale. We have electricity. We have impressive libraries. There are limitations to what we can do, of course, and a lot of the stuff we salvage is junk, or so degraded and decayed we can't do anything with it. But we have managed a lot, and that gives us the edge."

"I suppose that's one of the reasons John wants to take you over," said Davy.

"You're not as dim as you appear my boy."

"Thank you?" Davy suggested.

"I've never met him, you know. But I feel I can read his mind.

He thinks like a man. He thinks, *I will capture the Chilterns, seize all the clever tech in Wycombe, persuade our technicians to run it and maintain it, and then use it.*"

"Use it?"

"To conquer the rest of the country of course. Conquest and power: that's how a man thinks. I don't think the country would enjoy such an eventuality. I grew up under Father John's authority and it was not a very *kind* environment."

"You grew up there?"

"Eons ago, of course. Wycombe has been my home for many decades. It was me, and my friend Amy. Together we built this place up. I don't mean to sound boastful, but it turned out I had a genius for running things. Organising, but also inspiring. Knowing when to encourage and when to punish. Thinking strategically, like I said. And Amy had a different genius: a genius for machines and tech. She was really never happier than when tinkering with all that old jetsam."

"Amy," said Davy.

"Indeed," said the old woman, and gave Davy a significant look.

"And you two founded Wycombe? I thought it had been around for fifty years or something."

"We didn't found Wycombe. There was already a community of women here when we arrived. They were strong in moral authority and weak in political power—paying a tithe to local warlords, in goods and sexual services. They were trying to make something beautiful in an ugly world and it wasn't easy. They were all about the justice, about the fairness. About community and helping others. It was a fine little world." The old woman was sounding almost wistful. "But," she said, altering her tone, "doomed. Absolutely doomed. There was no leadership. They sent collective prayers to the goddess, but they were within a year of being entirely wiped out. Probably less than that, probably six months. Soon enough some warlord was going to come driving through and carry them all away as chattel. Surprising, in fact, that it hadn't already happened. But then we came, Amy and I. And I was able to persuade them that justice could be a martial as well as a social virtue. I was able to train them, and give them the skill to fight. It was partly a matter of teaching them the basics, and partly a matter of getting them to see that exercising those skills could be a matter of the craftsman's pride. I did that. And Amy kitted us out. Amy and her crew. Plus we had geographical advantages, on account of the topography of Wycombe itself. So we defeated some of the raiders, and built up our defences, and then we had to start expanding."

"You did?"

"I'm afraid so. Standing still isn't an option, you see. But expanding modestly, really. It's either that or be swallowed up by some other expanding territory. My strategy is to expand a sphere of influence rather than to march into neighbouring lands and install occupying garrisons. But it amounts to the same thing."

"My mother's name is Amy," said Davy.

The old woman nodded at this, but went on with her narrative. "So as I was saying, my primary job, in terms of running this place, is having a workable medium-term strategy to ensure our defence, and therefore our survival. That means assessing the varying risks of the enemies that are ranged against us, on all sides, and having a plan to deal with them. There's a nasty little tribe that's seized most of Kent. They will probably become a problem in a few years, although for now there's London's wasteland between us. To the south is a patchwork of communes and small-time gangsters with little manors. To the west—well it used to be the various peoples of the Downs. But a few years back there was a big bust-up, and lots and lots of people got killed: farms burned, people gunned down in the countryside, guerrilla war and snipers. All in all a bad business, and a vacuum into which Guz marched a well-trained little army up from Portsmouth. So now we can say: to the west is Guz. And I have to give them credit, Guz is an unusual problem for me. For the moment they're just holding off, as I said. My best guess is that they're waiting to see if we beat John, or if John beats us. In the former eventuality they might then judge Wycombe weakened to the point where it makes it a reasonable roll of the dice to come across the Thames and take us over. If John wins, then maybe they'll come anyway, and try and eject his army from the highlands. Either way it makes sense for them to hold back for now."

"There were soldiers of Guz," Davy put in, "at the ambush where Abigail and the others died. Where I got shot in the shoulder."

"Indeed there were. An expeditionary force, you might say. Interested not in invasion but in snatching you."

"Me."

"They had identified you as an asset, although they didn't know *why* you were an asset. But they knew we wanted you, and that was enough. It's the same with John: he was happy to grab you, or kill you, and probably happier to do the latter, because he knew it would thwart me. He doesn't know why it would thwart me, but in the final analysis that doesn't matter to him. That's male thinking too: if it pisses off my enemy it must be good."

"I'm male."

"So you are! And now you're here."

"And that's good for you."

"That's *very* good for me. Good for Wycombe. I don't mind telling you I was *extremely* relieved when they told me you were likely to live."

"As was I," said Davy.

"Come along," said the old woman, hopping off the bed. "Situate your gluteus maximus in this little mobile chair. You need to come along with me."

"People keep saying that to me," said Davy, levering himself up off his bed. His shoulder twanged with pain, but he got to his feet. "Come along with me, they say. Where are we going this time?"

"I need to show you to somebody. He was very disbelieving when I said you were still alive. Told me, in point of fact, that he saw you killed."

Davy had a flash of insight. "Daniel?" He lowered himself into the wheelchair and let out a sigh.

"Hobbling along on a hurty ankle, poor fellow."

Miranda, who had been waiting by the doorway, stepped over to push him, and so he followed the old woman out of the room.

Immediately outside was a long, wide corridor, the walls of which were hung with a series of paintings much too large for them, and presumably salvaged from elsewhere. They were all very old, the surface of the paint overlaid with a network of irregular hexagon and spiderweb cracks. Beautiful women in blue silk gowns, with light shining from, presumably, an electrical light fixed in the backs of their necks just out of sight. Old men holding up clasped hands, either because they were praying at the sky or else because they'd just caught a fly in the space between their cupped palms. A barn filled with animals, including two cows that were, in Davy's professional opinion, very unlifelike, all crowding round a wooden box in which a bizarrely-proportioned fat baby sprawled.

They turned a corner and rolled down towards an exit. "It was all to do with Rafbenson," said Davy. "I know that much."

"What's that, my dear?"

"Rafbenson. Benson, some people call it. What's there? Daniel thought there were whole flights of magic machines that could swoosh humans through the air from sea to sea in the blink of an eye."

"That," said the old woman, "sounds rather more like a

fantasy than any kind of verisimilitude." She had stopped at a big door and was poking a code into an ancient keypad—silver metal buttons standing proud of a tarnished metal rectangle. Davy watched her, fascinated. They didn't have anything like this where he came from. The lock clucked open and she pushed the door open.

Miranda pushed Davy outside. The air was fresh, sweet in the nose and the mouth. The sheep were making their creaky calls.

"What *is* at Benson, Mrs Henry?" he asked.

"Nothing," said the old woman.

"So this has all been a wild goose chase?"

"Goose," said the old woman, flashing a rare smile at him. "Goose! Very good. That's closer to the truth, my dear." She was walking alongside the wheelchair now, and Miranda was making sure to push it at a slow enough pace.

"Goose," said Davy. "Goose-geese. What?"

"There's nothing at Benson. Nothing of value. Not any more. What—did you think I was going to leave all the valuable kit just sitting around those hangers, did you? We retrieved it all years ago. The issue wasn't the *kit*. The issue was always how to deploy the kit. And for that we needed—"

"Amy," said Davy.

"She has her areas of genius, and I have mine. She's a remarkable woman, she truly is, your mother. I have loved her as I have no other human being in my life. And I have had a long and varied life."

"So weird to think of her like that," said Davy. "I mean, of her having a life before—well, before us." They were rolling along a wide path, fringed with weeds, towards a blocky three story building made of red-orange bricks. Smoke was idling out of a chimney. The air was chilly, but not unbearably cold.

"I'm assuming she didn't talk much about her life before she started her family?" the old woman asked.

"Not with me. But then she never much talked about anything

with me. I was the son, and she reserved her most intense interactions for my sisters. Although, I don't suppose they know any more about Ma's earlier life than I do. Than I did."

"I would assume she didn't want to tempt them. If she spoke too enthusiastically about Wycombe, her daughters might leave her and make their way here. Plenty of daughters do."

"I guess she didn't want to lose them," Davy agreed. "Or not yet, at any rate. But, see, that's one part of it all that just doesn't make sense. I mean, me. I mean: *why* me?"

"I believe I already made clear my opinion of *why*-questions," said the old woman.

"Seriously, though. You wanted leverage against my mother, and I get that—I get why. No, I don't, actually. But I get that you might want such leverage. So kidnap one of my sisters. She loves them more than me."

"She doesn't, though."

"I think," said Davy, turning his face away because his eyes were feeling hot and pricklish, "I understand the emotional dynamic of my own family better than a stranger."

The fresh air stroked his cheek. Baa said the sheep. Hush said the air.

"I knew your mother long before you were born, my dear. She *values* your sisters more than she does you, perhaps. But she doesn't love them more. I've been a mother and I can tell you: that's not how love works."

His eyeballs weren't getting any less hot or wet or prickly. Davy stared into the distance. The meadows, with their sheep, looked smaller outside. The forest at the edge of the estate looked larger, the bare trees blacker and sharper-twigged.

"If we had grabbed one of your sisters," Henry said in a dispassionate tone, "Amy would have reconciled herself to the fact that her daughter was at Wycombe. It would, almost, not even be a hardship to her. She would miss the girl of course, but she would also know that she was in a good place. Her son—

now, see, *that* is a different matter."

"Because I'm not allowed in?"

"Well that was my mistake," said the old woman, with a wry look of self inculpation. "I miscalculated. I thought you were still a young boy. But in the end it didn't matter. We can keep you out here."

"Here isn't Wycombe?"

"There's a zone around Wycombe proper. We call it low Wycombe, though it's actually, topographically, higher. And we allow men to settle here, if they want to, and are prepared to work. Most of the men are just visitors—mercenaries, some of them; traders other. They come because women visit them for sex, when the women feel like it."

"Aye-aye?" Davy said.

"Women who give birth to kids raise them in Wycombe," said Henry. "If they're daughters they can stay. If they're sons they have to move out at thirteen. Either way, Amy would not be happy with you being here."

"Because?"

"Because she knows we would kill you, if necessary. And she knows that we could never do that with one of her daughters."

It didn't really strike home to Davy, the full weight of this statement. He understood it, but somehow it seemed abstract rather than real. He reflected, though, that it was surely a real thing. That he ought to feel alarmed.

"Ah," he said.

"It's nothing personal dear," said the old woman. As if that made it better.

They had reached another building now, rolling up a ramp to the main door. "Is my Ma, here?" Davy asked.

"No dear," said Henry. "I'm afraid not."

Inside the main building was a tall, chill hallway, paved with wooden tiles. The walls were crowded with many large, gold-framed paintings.

A woman sitting behind a desk nodded respectfully as Henry walked through.

At the rear of the entrance hall they opened another door and went through to another corridor, this one darker—still lit with electrical light bulbs, but walled and ceilinged in dark wood panels.

"Why did my Ma leave?" he asked the old woman. "Why did she leave you all, to have us?"

Henry was walking ahead of him now, since there wasn't space in the corridor to walk alongside his chair. When she didn't reply Davy assumed that she hadn't heard. But just as he was about to repeat his question she said:

"For a great many people, the strength of Wycombe is its principles. Your mother is one of those people. Most of us are, in one way or another. There are plenty here who would be surprised to hear me say it, but I'm one myself."

They'd reached a door at the far end of the corridor, but instead of opening it, Henry turned and faced Davy, in his chair.

"There is, I would imagine, a proof of it somewhere, like the proof about how you need at least four colours to colour a map, or that incompleteness theorem, whose name escapes me, and about whose details my memory is a little hazy."

"A proof of what?"

"Of the impossibility of political rule in accordance with absolute adherence to moral principle. Politics is always pragmatism, I'm afraid. The two words are almost synonyms. And although it is possible to *leaven* pragmatism with morals, at least a little—I'd say, indeed, it's impossible to rule if you set out to be *purely* pragmatic—nonetheless ..." She frowned, and stared over Davy's head for a while.

"Nonetheless...?" he prompted.

"I had to do what was necessary to keep Wycombe safe. Which meant: strong. Which meant: pugnacious. Do you know to what the word *realpolitik* refers?"

"I know what the word real means. But not the rest."

"Ah well. Long story short, Amy grew disillusioned. She grew disillusioned with many things: with me, with Wycombe... she would say with what Wycombe had become. She even became disillusioned with technology, and that was the most puzzling thing of all because that was a passion that preceded all the others. When I first met your mother do you know what she was doing?"

"No."

"She was fishing old tech out of the lake at Marlow. Good grief how she loved all that stuff! But she turned her back on it, went west, married some man and had children. A farm, of all things! Of course she had a crew under her, here at Wycombe I mean. And some of the brighter ones had even managed to learn something from her. So we carried on. But it's never been quite the same. Never quite the same."

She turned back and opened the door. "Davy," said a voice from the room beyond. "Is that you? Good to see you, my lad." It was Daniel, and he was in handcuffs.

CHAPTER SEVENTEEN

BEYOND THE DOOR was a wide, low-ceilinged room lit by dim electrical light bulbs—a row of them, all tucked away behind the rim of some ledge-like ceiling coving. There were many tables and many people sitting at them. A dozen, or so. On some of the tables were boxes—microwave ovens, perhaps, like the one Mother Patel had owned for about a fortnight, and which heated things up by the magic of electricity—but Davy wasn't sure.

When Henry came padding into this room all the people at all the desks stood up: no exceptions. Daniel, his hands tied before him, was already standing. Henry waved them all down, and they took their seats again.

"You all right, lad?" Daniel asked Davy. "I thought I saw you killed at the battle of Rout's Green. I'm genuinely glad to see that I was wrong about that. Can you walk, though?"

"Oh yes," said Davy. "Mine spine is fine. I mean, *my* spine. It's fine. I'm just still... what's the word?"

"Recuperating?"

"Exactly. Convalescing. What happened to you? Did they capture you?"

"Not exactly. Though, then again," he glowered at the other people in the room, "not everybody would consider treating an envoy like this to be *acceptable* behaviour."

"Not everybody," said Henry, "would consider Guz to be entirely trustworthy. Are we ready?" This last was addressed to one of the women manning one of the microwaves. Two switches were flicked, and the hum of a generator increased in pitch somewhere near at hand. Lights came on, and the front door of the box flickered with light.

It wasn't a microwave at all.

"It's a screen," said Daniel. "Do you see?"

Davy looked more closely. The screen was spittered with whiteout blotches, and there was a shimmering white line down one side; but the rest of the rectangle showed an animated picture of broccoli and a strip of fabric. The image was in motion, as if a camera were moving slowly across the surface of this still life. It took a moment for Davy to understand what he was seeing: a falcon's-eye view of forest, with a river in the middle distance. And when he realised that, the image revealed all sorts of new details. There were houses on the far side of the river, little boxy structures in amongst the trees; and boats moored on the riverbank like rice-grains. And there was a bridge. Was that the pontoon the old woman had mentioned earlier?

"It's Goring," said Davy. "You fitted a movie-picture camera to a bird."

"You're a smart one," said Henry. "And yes, this machine is a kind of bird, and it has a kind of movie camera in its snout. We brought home two dozen of these drones from Benson— decades ago, long long years. The engines run on a kind of sealed battery, and Amy figured out how to renovate and recharge it. But the hardest part was in speaking its own machine language to it. Programming, the books call it, and it's not like any human language. The pre-Sisters humans designed dozens and dozens of them—of the languages, I mean. A whole spread of different machine languages! Who knows why? To baffle their enemies, perhaps. They left us lots of books about them, the programming languages, but none of those books explain the reason for the sheer proliferation of them. Anyway, Amy solved it. She has a genius for such things."

The image of Goring was growing larger in the middle of the screen.

"Are there people inside the flying machine?" Davy asked.

"Wee free folk? No," said Henry. "No. This plane is four feet long."

"So it's a toy?"

"A special kind of toy."

"You're delivering a message to Goring," said Daniel.

"I am," said Henry.

"You could just have told me your message," Daniel offered, "and I would have undertaken to pass it on, you know."

"Well it's the kind of message liable to get diluted if translated into *words*," said Henry. "Much," she added, arching one eyebrow, "as I admire and respect the power of words."

The little moving pictures on the tattered old screen were hypnotic to watch. The toy flying-machine was coming closer to Goring, swooping down perhaps, like a bird coming in to land. Everyone in the room was silent, staring at the images. The houses were larger, and it was possible to make out details on the sides of the moored boats. Birds flew out of trees and away as the image got bigger. There was the pontoon. The flying toy was close enough now that it was possible to make out a gate and a guardhouse on the Goring side of the bridge. The pontoon was now filling the screen, and Davy just about got a glimpse of figures running on the far side. Guards, he presumed.

The screen went spotty-white.

There was silence. "Is it broken?" Davy asked.

"That depends," said Henry, "on what you mean by *it*." As she spoke the screen flickered, and a new image came onto it. A wall, with a tiny little door in it, like a dollhouse door.

"Going," said somebody else. "Going Goring, gone." Another woman laughed, a sound like rubber being twisted.

Henry and Daniel were having a conversation. It was evident that, whether he had come as some kind of envoy from Guz, or whether he had been captured sneaking around in Wycombe territory, Daniel was going to be released. He was taking *this* message—the strange little bird's-eye view of flight over the trees to the new bridge at Goring—back to his people. "Your demonstration," Daniel was saying, "has, of course, made it harder rather than easier for me to get your message back to my side."

"I'm sure you'll find a boat that will take you over," said Henry. "Or maybe you could swim? One might assume the cast on your leg would make that impracticable, but I'm told you can be a surprisingly persistent swimmer when you want to be."

"And there's another side for me to get over *to*, is there?"

"Side," said Henry. "Well. Largely. More or less."

"Your sweet little old woman act," Daniel said, "is something approaching a master-stroke, you know."

Henry didn't react to this. "The inconvenience to which you are now put when it comes to returning to Guz is very much the message I wish to send," she said. "I don't say I *want* a hard border on my western flank, mind you. I say such a border now exists, and I would encourage Guz to respect that fact."

"Whilst you make minced-meat of John's army?"

"I am disinclined to take instruction on that matter," said the old woman, brightly, "from a group who possesses not one but a great *many* of these nuclear weapons, sitting in your big boats and submarines." She pronounced this last word with a heavy emphasis on its second syllable.

"Subma*rines*," said Daniel.

Henry smiled. "I've only ever seen it written down. But, yes, yes. You and I know what we're talking about. Most of my drones carry conventional ordnance. I'm obviously not going to tell you precisely how many I have. Some of my drones—and again, obviously, I'm not going to give you a detailed itinerary, but is more than one—have these ... what shall we say? *Bigger* bombs. Bigger bangs."

"The mighty atom," said Daniel, and raised up his handcuffed wrists. Or perhaps he said, "the mighty Adam," and was making some Biblical point. Davy couldn't be sure.

"Father John," said Henry, running an index finger over first one and then another eyebrow, "is arrogant and greedy, but he is not insane. Once he grasps the destruction he is calling down onto his own heartlands, he'll pull back."

"Or you'll bigger-bang him," said Daniel.

"The important thing is that he understands that I do not bluff."

"Was it *you*," Daniel said, in a voice of dawning realisation, "who sent that young girl up the river, on that crazy quest to Father John? Jesus, Henry. Was it?"

"It's been a pleasure meeting you, Daniel," said Henry, gesturing to one of her people. "Don't take it the wrong way if I say I hope we never meet again. Jojo tells me you killed one of our horses?"

"Horses cost less than bridges."

"Well, yes, I was going to say: you'll be pleased to hear we won't be pressing you for the restitution of that debt. I'm sure you've heard how persistent Wycombe can be when it comes to recovering our own."

"Madam," said Daniel, bowing, "it is not despite but because I grasp how much of what you are trying to do depends upon maintaining a certain act, a certain attitude, that I offer you my genuine admiration and respect."

All this time Davy's eye was caught by the screen: the dollhouse wall, the teeny-tiny doorway. As Daniel was making this last speech Davy saw the door open, and a teeny-tiny figure come out of it and start walking towards the camera, swelling rapidly and prodigiously as she, or he, did so. Henry, noticing what Davy was doing, pointed a finger and the operator turned the screen off.

CHAPTER EIGHTEEN

DAVY'S NEW LIFE began. They took him by car (an actual moving vehicle, whose engine hummed and sputtered) along a repaired road, and he sat in the back peering through the window. Lots of soldiers coming and going, most of them women, a couple of armoured vehicles, and a great many horses. Then a turn down a bumpy track, past the weed-crammed shells of roofless old houses and to their final destination. It was a two-storey block building, behind a fence. Inside this compound Davy was helped from the car. He leaned on his guard's arm as he was shown around. A large room with a bed it in, and an annex with a sink, a toilet and a bath which had presumably once been white but which was now the colour of the heel of your foot. In the main room there was a bookcase against one wall, and a window looking across a stretch of wasteground to trees. The window had bars on it.

It was a prison.

Davy sat on his bed and fought to get his breath back. "Lots of books," he observed.

His guard was called Gabriela: a tall well-built woman with

white-yellow hair and a little scar shaped like an uptick in her left cheek, by her mouth. "Something to pass the time."

"I can't read, though," he said.

"Well, the time *will* pass," she said, "whether you read or not."

She laid out the routine: breakfast and supper in the room, lunch in a communal dining space followed by two hours in the central quad for exercise, or fresh air, "Or not if you don't feel like it'.

He quickly got used to things. He had no timepiece, but soon got the sense—judging only by how empty his belly was when breakfast or supper were delivered—that the timetable run by the guards was very loose. Sometimes they woke him early with bread and milk, or bread and hot tea, but sometimes he woke and spent a long time staring at the ceiling, or padding around the room, or staring through the barred windows at the view, before food arrived. Food did at least always eventually arrive, and there was hot water for about half an hour in the morning. So things could have been a lot worse.

Lunch meant unlocking his door and escorting him through to a sparsely-kitted room where four guards and three prisoners sat at the same table and ate. This, and the two hours that followed it in the building's twelve-metre by twelve-metre internal courtyard, were the highlight of Davy's day. The two other prisoners were both female: an elderly woman who said very little, and a young woman who was only a few years older than he was.

The young woman was Amber: the girl he had, briefly, travelled with. When Abigail and May were still alive. She looked different.

"You escaped the ambush," he told her. "I'm so pleased!"

She stared at him, not recognising him at all.

"I'm Davy. Don't you remember? When Abigail and the others were bringing you back to Wycombe, I was there too."

Nothing. She was, it seemed, in shock. Or perhaps she had never registered his presence there at all. Davy remembered that her sister had been killed, and that she was in some obscure way to blame for that, so he decided to give her space. Not to pester her.

After a week Henry came to see him. It was the last conversation he would have with the old woman. "Settling in?"

"How long will I be here?"

"You understand that we need to keep you around, for a little while," said Henry, smiling a thin smile.

"I don't, really," said Davy. "I'm much fitter now. I have hardly any problem with my shoulder. I mean, I have *some* problem with my shoulder. But it's much better."

"You're a clever lad," said Henry. "Too clever to believe that we're holding you for reasons to do with your health."

"I just..." said Davy, looking gloomily at the floor. He stopped.

"You just?"

"I suppose I just wonder if I'm ever getting out of here."

"Oh I'm sure you will," said Henry, in a tone that implied that her sureness actually ran in quite another direction.

"Will my mother visit me? Is she staying here?"

"She's gone back home. She has, after all, her pride. As I believe I said before—" The smile dropped from Henry's face, and then came back up. "Nobody has known her longer than I have. Not even you, and you've known her all your life."

"So you're just holding me in reserve?"

"It might look to some," said Henry, as she went to the door, "like petty statelets squabbling. It might look that way to some. But that's not what's going on." She paused, by the door, and Gabriela waited on the far side, with her keys out. "Most power politics is jockeying for position. But where we are *now* will shape the way this entire country grows over the next hundred years. Longer! Father John doesn't grasp that fact. I don't think even Guz understand it. But I do. Goodbye my dear."

And she left.

THE SECOND WEEK was the worst. A deep gloom settled, like a snowdrift, on all the roofs and gutters and crannies of Davy's soul. He would never get out of this place. Eventually his Ma would die, of course, and then he would be of no further use to Wycombe, so perhaps they would let him go then. But they might equally well just cut his throat and leave him in a ditch. There was no point in anything.

At lunch, everyone seemed to be in a similar state of misery. The guards chatted amongst themselves; the other two prisoners simply stared at their food. The weather took another turn to the icy, and the little courtyard was very cold, its stone flags so frozen that Davy actually slipped and fell when he tried to walk around the perimeter. A bruised arse didn't help lighten his mood.

One day the old woman was gone—released, they said. So now Davy and Amber were the only two prisoners. Just the two of them.

Days were interminable. Because he wasted much of the day in naps, nighttime sleep was unreliable. He often found himself in the dark, staring into nothingness. His room had an electrical light bulb, inside a little wire cage, but there was no switch on his side of the door, and it was only illuminated for a short period in the evening.

By the second week he had grown bored with being depressed. He went through all the books in his book case. A couple were so old and spotted with brown decay that he wouldn't have been able to get anything out of them even if he'd been able to read. With a couple more the pages simply crumpled to flakes when he opened the covers. Most of the rest were in reasonable condition: a few had a kind of waxy layer over the pages, and others were printed on sturdy old paper. The majority had nothing by way of illustration at all. One had old line-drawings on a dozen pages. Two of the books were illustrated with old black and white photographs, one of pre-Sisters humans doing peculiar-looking things with big machines—making some kind of food, it seemed, but on a huge scale—and one of lots of kinds of seabirds and coastal landscapes. He spent several days going over these pictures in detail.

One lunchtime he took a book with him to the table. As everybody was eating he asked Amber if she could read.

She looked surprised. But instead of ignoring him she looked him up and down. "Yes," she said. "Of course. Can't you?"

"No," he said.

They ate in silence for a while, as Davy summoned the courage to add, "Will you teach me?"

Amber stared at him and turned away. She said nothing more to him for the rest of the meal. He assumed he had offended her in some way. But after the meal, when two of the guards and the three prisoners stood arms-folded and stamping their feet in the little courtyard she turned to him and said, "I'd be a rubbish teacher, though."

"You know how to do it and I don't," Davy pointed out.

She looked at the guards, leaned in closer and hissed, "This is a *prison*, you know."

Davy was a little startled that she thought he didn't understand where he was. Without really thinking, he replied, "A place where I get to spend time with someone as beautiful as you can hardly be described as a prison."

She drew her head back. Then, after a long pause, she opened her eyes really wide.

"I'm sorry," said Davy. "I shouldn't have said that."

"There can't be anything between…" she said and stopped. "I

don't want to break your heart, kid, but I don't feel... Look: I'm *seventeen*—seventeen—and... Look, how old are you?"

"Thirteen," he said. "Look, I'm sorry. I don't know why I said that. It just popped into my head. It was a stupid thing to say."

"I'm just not interested in that kind of..." she said.

"It's OK—I won't. Look, I won't say anything like that again."

"It's not that it's not *flattering* it's just..."

"I understand. Really."

"It really really could never work out between you and..." said Amber.

"You can stop saying that kind of thing now," said Davy.

She stared at him with her bug eyes for a while, and then slowly lowered her eyelids back to their regular position. "How old are you?"

"I'm thirteen. Like I said."

"You're thirteen, and you can't read?"

"Can't read *and* in prison." He tried for perky. "It's hardly a surprise you don't want to go out with me!"

Perky didn't come off.

She looked at him closely, as if trying to determine if he was joking or not. Eventually she said, "I'm in prison too."

"True."

"I know why you're here. You're Amy's son. You're our insurance policy."

"You make me sound like a piece of paper."

"There are many paper men," said Amber, haughtily. "They outnumber the real men a hundred to one." It had the sound of an apothegm.

"We did meet before," Davy offered. "Do you remember? Abigail was bringing me up into the Chilterns?"

Amber shook her head. Then she said, "Abigail is dead," and she began to sob.

Davy stared at the table in an embarrassed sort of way, until Amy got her sobbing under control.

"It's understandable," he said. "You being sad, I mean. Locked up in here."

"It's OK," she said, without meeting his eye. "I'm not sad because I'm locked up in here. I'm sad for a different reason."

Her sister, Davy warned himself, in an inner-monologue so distinct it was as if one part of his brain was shouting at another part, *she's sad because of her dead sister. Don't, whatever you do, mention her dead sister.* "So why *are* you in here?"

"I was trying," she said, her voice back under control, wiping her eyes with the heels of her palms, "to warn some people that they could have been killed in their thousands and their land consumed by a dust storm of poisonous evil."

"You were trying to kill thousands of people and obliterate their land in a dust storm of poisonous evil?"

"Not me. I was trying to *warn* them that other people were... but, then, actually, yes. You're right. Not other people. I was. Because Wycombe was and I'm a part of that. Do you know how things are run here?"

"Henry, you mean."

"She wishes! No, there's a council. All adult woman serve a turn on it, and last year it so happened my lot came along, so I served, and we were discussing this poison weapon that kills men and women and children and animals indiscriminately, and leaves the soil polluted for generations, and we were actually talking about using it against Father John. Anyway, I said it was not moral, and that if Wycombe didn't stand for doing the right thing then there wasn't even any *point* in Wycombe, yeah? Anyway. Anyway, I tried to... tried to get word to John. So Henry has bunged me in here as a punishment. She may exile me, I don't know. I don't care if she does, actually. There is no shame in going to prison for a good cause. Do you know who said that?"

"I do not."

"Neither do I. I learned it in ethics class at school. I don't remember her name, except that everyone called her Granny, so she must have been old. And it's true, don't you think?"

Davy nodded, and tried to look wise. He was acutely conscious of the age gap between them: he a skinny, under-height kid with a nick in the end of his tongue, she this beautiful and assured young woman. There was no chance, of course. He knew there was no chance. Not in a million years. Even though he was technically a man now, she looked at him and saw just the kid. He had to play it cool, that was the main thing. So he decided to tell her that Daniel, from Guz, had explained to him what ethics was, and maybe he'd tell her about Daniel. That might impress her.

So he looked into her eyes and, somehow, instead of saying that, said, "I met him once, you know. He kidnapped me actually. Carried me off. I mean that man who killed your sister."

She stared at him. Then she started crying. Then she got up from the table, still crying, and, followed by one of the guards, left the room.

Davy sat in front of his lunch blushing. What had he done? Embarrassment filled him, as acute as grief. His stomach chewed at itself. It occurred to him to get up, rush after her and apologise but he couldn't move. He was as stuck to the bench as firmly as if he had been glued there. He was aware of a rushing, sparkling hum inside his skull. The other two guards were staring at him. They were staring. They were staring at him, and he was blushing so hard he could feel the heat of his own cheeks. He had to at least try to explain. He opened his mouth to speak, as electrical sleet swirled in the crosswinds of his sightline, and said:

"I'm—"

The dark angel was there, looking exactly as he had done on that icebound hill overlooking the Thames. The light faded and thickened. Shadows gurgled audibly. The dark angel rose, slender and terrifying, and when his metallic wings spread wide they clicked like beetle-jaws snapping together, and rustled like old paper and reached as far as a great tree. The ground was sand and the sky was white and there were no walls. The face of the dark angel opened—a vertical central seam that separated with thin rungs of spittle that broke and inside was black and the dark angel said—

—

—

—

The next thing he knew he was in a strange bed. He sat up and the action made pain swell at the back of his head. "There you are," said Gabriela. "I was just about to radio the hospital and have you transferred. And you're OK now?"

The sheer ordinariness of the quality of reality, its solidity and groundedness, made Davy breathe more deeply. It had something to do with the abruptness of the transition. Maybe it did.

"My head hurts," he said.

"You had some kind of fit."

"Epilepsy," said Davy. "It comes on me sometimes."

"Epilepsy!" Gabriela's voice was full of amazement.

"I've always had it."

"They might have told us! Well you thrashed yourself off the bench like a fucking dervish, clonked your head on the floor. We had to put a bandage on the bleeding."

Davy reached up and felt with his fingers: it was true. "I'm OK," he said. "I think."

"Can't keep you in here," said Gabriela. "This is the sick room and it's not secure. Can you walk? You need to get back to your bedroom and get locked in. Or should I get a wheelchair?"

Davy tried his feet on the floor, and found that he was able to stand. "I'll walk," he said.

CHAPTER NINETEEN

THE FOLLOWING DAY Amber was back at the lunch table. She seemed less upset. Davy swore a solemn oath, silently in his head, to be more tactful, and then debated with himself whether apologising for his tactlessness the day before would violate that same oath. In the event she spoke to him:

"You had some kind of fit yesterday, they say."

Davy smiled what he hoped was a rueful smile, but which probably came over as sheer goofiness. "Yeah. Epilepsy."

"Woh," she said, in a disengaged voice. "Sounds serious."

Not wanting to miss the opportunity to appear heroic and dignified in front of her, he pulled a solemn face and said: "pretty serious. I've had it all my life."

"You poor thing," she said.

Pity wasn't the reaction Davy had been trying for. It occurred to him that he'd only managed to make himself look more pathetic in her eyes—not only a kid and a runt but some kind of brain-cripple. "It's pretty painful," he lied. "When the fits come. But I've learned how to endure that."

She didn't seem very interested in his powers of endurance.

Instead she said, "I've decided, I will teach you your letters."

"Oh. OK. Thank you!"

"It'll be good practice for when I get out of here, and if I get a teaching duty. It's pretty likely I will get a teaching duty, you know, because I'm pretty good with kids." She patted his hand.

"Oh," he said again, feeling the press of disappointment.

"That's how things work in Wycombe, most people have stints doing most jobs. There's a rota."

Later, back in his cell, he lay on his bed and went over and over the exchange. It had been, in a strange way, more provoking and embarrassing than the episode the previous day. A *kid*? Was that really how she saw him? Was it because he couldn't read? If so, he would learn to read doublequick time—he would become the greatest reader in the history of reading. He would read so well she would *have* to take notice of him. She might have reservations about the viability of a relationship between them right now, but the time would come, one day soon, when she would look across and see him turning the pages of a prodigiously big and complex book. And then she would think to herself, Wow but that guy can really read!

The following day he brought a book to the lunchroom, and in the courtyard afterwards she started with *Birds of the British Coastline*. He was soon recognising B and C, but then was rather thrown by the fact that letters—Amber said—came in large and small forms. "Why?" he asked, but she didn't know, and indeed the question propelled her into a characteristically rambling disquisition on how illogical and stupid spelling was, and how she planned one day to write out a standard book of logical spellings that everybody could use and so save all that effort and make the world altogether a better place. But the lesson broke down when Amber picked out some examples of small-form Bs and Cs, and Davy asked why it was that the small-form c looked like a smaller version of a large-form C, but the small-form b did not look like the large-form B. She didn't know, and began speculating on whether it would be possible to start from the ground up, with a whole new alphabet.

The following day Davy got all the letters of the book's title, and their order, fixed in his brain. *Birds. Coastline. British.* Then he was able to go through the main body of the text picking out examples of those letters. He was even able to read the word *for*, by piecing together the three components.

By the end of the week he had his vowels, and most of his consonants. It wasn't clear to him if all of these latter were actually needed. X, say, was just *cs*, J a sort of *dge*, and lots of words seemed to have *gs* and *hs* in them that didn't really contribute anything to the overall effect. But he wanted to impress Amber, and so he worked hard.

He dared to hope that teaching him this elementary stuff was distracting her from her sorrow. She made no mention of remembering him from before. Perhaps she'd blocked the memory, or perhaps she really hadn't noticed that he was even there. But, he thought, *I am speaking to her! We are having conversations! That's the start of something, surely?*

One week turned into two. By the end of the month he could sit and read aloud to her, in a halting voice, often going wrong over pronunciation. The exercise appeared to be having a calming effect upon her too.

The weather grew milder, although for several weeks winter persisted more or less stubbornly. Sometimes he would chat with the guards and ask them what was happening outside. He didn't learn much this way, except that Father John had retreated into his own territory with 'a bloody nose', whatever that meant in practical terms. "So the war's over?" Davy asked Gabriela one day. A small hope buzzed in the empty cavity of his breast that peace might lead to his release.

"No," said Gabriela. "Not by a long way."

So that was that. And the real facts of his existence had nothing to do with the routine, or the possibility of release, or the larger events. They didn't even have to do with the slow progress he was making in terms of reading and comprehension. The real facts of his existence in that place had to with the enormousness of the crush he had developed on Amber.

He lay in bed at night thinking about her. In his room, alone through the morning and afternoon-evening longeurs, he thought about her. He was desperately, hopelessly, heedlessly in love with her. At the same time he was—because he wasn't a complete fool—perfectly aware that love was something else, something grander and more grown-up, and that what he was experiencing was an infatuation. But how powerful the infatuation he was in! How all-encompassing. How it flavoured every feature of his day!

He had enough control over himself now not to blurt anything out. He couldn't prevent a certain amount of cow-eyed staring at her in quiet moments. She must have been aware of his feelings, but she said nothing and engaged in no flirting, kept him courteously but unmistakeably at arm's length. Still, she was pleasant, and helpful, and interested in his progress, and he was as completely under her spell as her faithful pet dog.

One consequence of this was that her moods now governed his. When she was tetchy, or sad, or withdrawn, his self-esteem would collapse and his heart sink. When she was upbeat or cheerful or chatty his whole mood would lift, and the world would seem full of possibility again.

Still, Amber was scrupulous about not encouraging his crush. One month turned into two, and blossoms began to appear on the trees. Davy's reading abilities continued to improve.

One lunchtime Gabriela let Davy out of his cell, and followed him as he padded through to the lunch-room.

Amber wasn't there.

"I forgot to tell you," Gabriela said, "she's been released. It's just you, me and Louise now, kiddo."

The other guard, Louise, smiled blankly at him. The boulder

that had fallen from the height of the moon all the way down to this precise spot in the middle of the Chilterns had flattened Davy so completely and so rapidly that he didn't even feel it for whole, long minutes.

CHAPTER TWENTY

THE SIMPLEST WAY to describe the weeks that followed would be to say: Davy gave up. He stopped reading, although he had acquired enough fluency to make out whole stretches of any of the books on his shelves. He ate less. He spent all morning, afternoon and evening lying on his bed, doing nothing, thinking nothing.

"Cheer up, lad," said Gabriela, bringing his breakfast one morning. "She hasn't been executed, at any rate."

That his hopeless passion for Amber had been so very obvious to his guards dampened his already sodden spirits even further. It's not that it surprised him. If he thought about it, it must have been obvious to anybody who so much as glanced at him. But for his profound and deathless love to be the matter of amused gossip was almost worse than the bruise of his broken heart.

He wanted to ask for more information, but something that was either pride or else the sheer inertia of his misery prevented him from doing so. After Gabriela had gone he told himself that he was going to hold out. He would claim that his refusal to play into their narrative was strength. He would ask nothing about her, and say nothing, and become granite, and endure. At lunch, though, he broke down straight away.

"Where did they send her? Did they exile her?"

Louise laughed, and Gabriela's indulgent smile was rather too wide. "Don't worry about her—she's fine. You won't be seeing her again, though."

"You mean she's gone into Wycombe proper?"

"Even if you *did* see her again," Susan told him, "it wouldn't make any difference. She's never going to go with a geezer like you."

"Susan!" rebuked Gabriela.

"Well it's the truth."

Another week passed. He let it pass. He unclasped his fist and let the time dribble through his fingers. Was it a whole week? How long had he been in this prison? Months and months.

How long was he going to remain in this prison? Years and years.

Nothing to be done, and everything to be endured. He could, he told himself, fret himself into exhaustion and despair, or he could accept the situation. Go, as Mother Patel liked to say, with the flow. And remembering Mother Patel, and wondering how the old lady was doing now, took his thoughts back to Shillingford Hill, and home, and his depression melted with the winter outside. The weather alternated sunshine and April showers.

He didn't cry for very long, in the end. There didn't seem a need to prolong the performance of grief. And as he washed his face in the sink, he did feel better. *Senses working overtime* had been his Da's phrase. But the *work* part didn't need to be quite so strenuous, and the *overtime* could soar like a falcon rather than drive him to exhaustion and collapse. The only thing he needed to hang on to was his sense.

Sense. Sensible.

Him. Use your senses, Davy. Make them work for you.

The rat-in-a-hole scratch of a key being turned in the lock of his door. And here was Gabriela to take him through to lunch. "Will they keep both of you on duty here," he asked her, as they wandered down the corridor. "It seems like a lot of bother, just for one kid."

"It won't be us," said Gabriela, opening the door for him to go through. "But it will be somebody. Somebodies. And what I'm hearing is that you may not be alone for very long. Father John has thrown a great crush of people at our defences. A huge army. We're knocking him back, of course, and I wouldn't be surprised if a few high-profile people from the north didn't come inside to join you."

"Fellow hostages," said Davy. "Company, at least."

"Not that I think Father John will care. The welfare of hostages doesn't concern him."

Davy took a look at the way the lunchroom was laid out. It was as it generally was: a bench at the table, and one chair, with a couple of free chairs scattered around the room. Sometimes these were stacked in the corner, but today two of them had been put out. He saw that he wouldn't be able to check, later in the meal, without looking suspicious, so he clocked the room as he came in.

He took his seat on the bench by the table and ate. He wasn't hungry, but he figured he should probably eat as much as possible.

Sensible.

"Is there any more?" he asked.

"Hungry today? I think there's some more. After all, it is just you."

Gabriela came back with a second plate. "Good to see your appetite's picked up," she said. "That you're not so down in the dumps."

"We all get a little heart-bashed," agreed Susan. "Especially when we're young. It's nothing to be ashamed of."

Davy's put his fork beside his half-finished plate. He stared at the table. His expression very plainly said, *This is an actually painful matter to me*. It said, *Please don't make fun of me*. Susan chuckled, and Gabriela said, "Oh, lad, don't take on so. You were doing so well!"

It was time. He had to do more than accept. He had to embrace. He had to commit to it completely. His only worry was that he might commit *so* wholeheartedly that he actually ended up injuring himself. But there was no other way.

He made a low growling noise. He wasn't sure why, but it seemed appropriate. Then he made as if he was getting up from the bench. Susan opened her mouth to say something, but before she could Davy shut his eyes and threw himself backwards.

It was, in a way, a leap of faith; although the proximate focus of his faith was: *I hope I don't actually break anything*. Like his skull. Like a fatal crack, killing him dead. Nonetheless he had to kick back as hard as he could, or it wouldn't work. He tried to let himself go limp, but he couldn't help tensing a little. And when the back of his head and his good shoulder connected with the chair it was a painful shock, and the willpower he had to employ in not crying out was considerable.

Bang, clatter, and he hit the floor. This second impact was even worse, because he bounced off the chair onto his bad shoulder, and though the speed with which he hit the floor was not so great, it sent shock waves of pain through his whole left flank nonetheless. He writhed on the floor and made a sort of low groaning to try and vent his agony. Some of his half-chewed potato mash spilled over his lips and may have looked like foam. He counted to seven, and then lay still.

This was, in a way, the hardest part of the whole process. The pain was difficult, of course—his shoulder burned and the back of his head was very sore—but worse was the need not to adjust his position to get more comfortable, not to scratch the itches that flittered over his skin, not to open his eyes to snatch so much as a glimpse.

He just lay there.

He could hear the two guards coming over to him, and felt their hands touch him. One felt for a pulse in his neck—that tickled, but he fought down the reaction—and the other lifted his head and held it at a strange angle. Whoever was holding his head lowered it to the floor.

"He's had another fit," said Gabriela.

"That was quite an acrobatic one," said Susan, with what sounded like admiration. "Let's get him back to his cell."

"I don't know."

"Don't know what?"

"What, leave him there? I don't *know*."

"He'll come round. Come on, we need to clear up the lunch stuff."

"I tell you I don't know."

"Bung him in his room. He'll be fine."

"We need to take him to the hospital," said Gabriela. "I received very specific orders from Henry herself: his well-being is paramount. He's no good as a hostage if he dies."

"He's not going to die, though," said Susan, confidently. And then, less confidently, "Is he?"

"*I* don't know, I'm not a doctor. Are you?"

"Christ on a bicycle *must* we, though? The hospital?"

"Let's not take any chances. Think how fucked we'll be if he dies in our custody. Look, *I'll* take him to the hospital," said Gabriela. "OK? You help me carry him to the van."

There was silence and inaction for a few minutes, and then Davy felt hands gripping his ankles, and other hands under his armpits. He willed himself to go as limp as a bonefish, and suffered himself to be hauled along, round a corner, straight along for a distance, round a sort of dog-leg and then—the air cooler on his skin—he must have been outside.

He was lowered, none too gently, onto the corrugated floor of a van, and was able to eavesdrop on some more rather anxious conversation. "Is he still breathing?" "I think—I think so." "Christ you've got me worried now, Gabe. Get him to hospital—if he dies, better that he does it there." "He's not going to die. I don't think he's going to die. But you're right, yes, of course, you're right." The back door of the van slammed like a cannonball hitting a giant gong and it was so loud and close and unexpected that Davy twitched in sheer terror. He hoped he hadn't been seen.

Soon after he became aware of the van rolling into motion and picking up speed. It was bumpy for a while, and then the vehicle took a corner at such speed that Davy slid hard against the side. Then a period of further acceleration. An anxious slow-down, another corner taken too fast, and then the grinding bluster of the engine accelerating again.

Davy tried to concentrate on breathing steadily and readying himself. The van finally came to a full stop, quenching its speed on a gravel drive with a sound like a wave crashing on shingle. The door was yanked open, and Davy felt cool air again on his skin. There was a pause. Then he was hauled, none too gently, onto a bed, or a kind of hammock—a stretcher, perhaps, or gurney. And then he was rolled up a ramp and in through an echoey space, where many voices were competing. Out of the throng he heard Gabriela saying, "We have to make sure he's OK, there are specific instructions from"—and a great bang-clang and jolt as the gurney ran over some ridge in the floor.

They were in a quieter space now. "Last time he had one of these fits," said a voice, "he came round in, like, twenty minutes. But he's been out for longer than that."

Was that Gabriela? She sounded different.

"Epilepsy, is it?"

"Epilepsy. What if he doesn't come round? Can epilepsy leave you, like, in a coma? Like, forever?"

"I'll check the book," said the second voice.

The gurney swung to the right and stopped. "We should put him in a room?"

"Busy," said the second voice. "Real busy. I don't know if you've heard but—there's a war."

"Talk to Henry," urged Gabriela. "She'll confirm this is a priority situation. Priority situation for the war effort."

"Like I can just crank the radio and talk to Henry!"

"Come with me," said the second voice. "We can sort something out, I suppose. I don't know."

Then: a lengthy silence.

This was the most ticklish part of all. He peeped through a millimetre open-eyelid gap and saw he was in a corridor. He hadn't been restrained. He seemed to be alone.

He lay still for a while longer and listened carefully for any signs that Gabriela was still with him: any breathing, or sniffing, or shuffling sounds of motion. Nothing.

He opened his eyes and moved his head. He was on a gurney in a corridor with pale-yellow painted walls, and he was alone. He sat up.

Nobody left or right.

He slipped off the gurney and padded to the nearer end of the corridor. There was a door with a glass pane in it—intact glass, with a graph-paper pattern of wires running through it. The other side was more corridor. It seemed empty.

He tried the handle, and it gave.

He went through. Halfway along was a branching corridor on the right that ran down a slight slope. He went down it to the door at the end, and this one was locked. And there was the keypad, like the one Henry herself had keyed when he had first been wheeled out of this very facility. Had Davy been paying attention, sat in that wheelchair, when she pressed those buttons?

Of course he had.

Say what you like about Davy: he was neither stupid nor unobservant.

Davy pushed the top left button, the middle one, the bottom left and the middle one again. And the door snicked open.

CHAPTER TWENTY-ONE

HE WORRIED ABOUT the dangers of the part that now lay ahead of him: escaping the hospital grounds. But this turned out to be a simple matter. He hurried across the wide lawn, through the scattered flock of oblivious sheep, and down to a hedge. This was an untended barrier that had sprawled, kept in check if at all by sheep nibbling tender shoots. Thick and dense. He made his way twenty yards along it before he found a hedgebush stem broad and bent enough to give him a leg up. The branches scratched at him, but he hauled himself up, and through the thinner leaves near the top, tumbled out on the far side to lie on his back.

He was in woodland on a bed of bluebells, bluebells, bluebells. It was the middle of a warm spring day, and he was in woodland, and the trees were stark trunks whose upper portions were vivid with spring green, and the ground was a summer sky of bluebells. He lay for a long time simply staring at the richness and beauty of this thick haze of distilled blue-purple. It was as if he had tumbled through purgatory and into heaven itself.

It was quiet. Somewhere deeper in the woodland he could

hear some birds tutting him. The spread of blue in front of him was hypnotic. In places sunlight came down to lay jewel-gleam patches over the whole. In the shade of the trees the blossoms darkened to a brackish purple and smouldering cyan. The bluebells grew in humps and valleys, following the forest floor beneath maybe, or else just marking places where some plants were taller than others. The myriad blue dots and atoms swelled into a fuzz of extraordinary intensity around one particularly thick and strong-looking upstanding trunk.

Davy couldn't delay. It was early afternoon, and the sun was high, so he couldn't tell his direction. But the thing to do was get away from the hospital and lie-low—to get his bearings later and find a way west.

So he got to his feet, and started off through the miraculous colour, a blue the colour of God's own eyes. He felt as though he were wading through the shallow sea of dream-stuff. He felt he was floating.

In five minutes the woodland changed its character; the trees became more closely spaced and more varied in kind, and there was a great deal more dun-coloured and dark-green undergrowth. Bluebells still shone like magic lights here and there, but they became fewer and fewer and finally he could see no more of them. Now the quality of light in the wood had changed: darker, with a quality of menace—or if not menace exactly, then certainly an unshakeable indifference to Davy's fate. It was harder walking too, picking his way through banks of compacted leaves, weed tendrils that gripped his legs and scrub that came as high, in some places, as his waist.

Eventually he left the old woodland behind and passed into a more open space. This had once been a farm, or perhaps the large-scale garden of a handsome house—the house was visible, reduced now to a ruin, like a rotten tooth poking up above the undergrowth. What had been lawn was now a varied scrubland of low bushes and saplings and broadsides of nettles. The sun was lower in the sky now, and by the time Davy reached the old house he had a good sense of which direction was west.

A brown bird flew low past him, and rose to settle on a platform of the broken house-wall. Almost as soon as it had landed it started singing: a scribbling gush of sound that distilled itself into distinct rising bubbles of song before spreading into its gabbling music again.

A skylark.

Davy's heart shrunk for a moment and then expanded hugely, as if it was a lung breathing out and then inhaling Joy. He kept blinking. Blinking. He didn't understand why he couldn't stop blinking. The bird flew off, and he turned to watch, but it seemed to blur and jolt about the sky, elongated into bizarre shapes and only then did he realise that he was crying.

Why was he crying? He felt happy. He was free! It was crazy.

Eventually his tears dripped away and he was his old self.

There was an old road associated with the house, and though its surface was broken up like crumble and grown through with a great many spear-length pale green weeds it made for easier walking than fighting through undergrowth. The road wound round and down, and then rose up the far side of the valley through another copse of woodland. Here a car had been abandoned, its doors pulled off, discarded on the ground beside a chassis wine-coloured with rust. A little ahead was another long-abandoned vehicle, of a completely different shape—the first car a collection of rectangles and squares, this later one all curves and an arch-shaped main body. Why had the people of that bygone age made their cars in such a variety of shapes? It made no sense. It was one of the many things about them that made no sense.

He kept his ears open, and although he heard various birds, and the occasional snort of an animal away among the trees, he heard nothing. Nothing human. A squad of rooks flew overhead, preceded by their wheezy, croaky rooksong.

After a while the road improved, and soon it was clear of weeds. Round the corner Davy same to an unruined house—a whole farm, in fact. He came off the road, went into the trees and crept alongside the main building. He thought about giving it a wide berth but something in the set up intrigued him. So he stayed to have a proper look. The roof was intact, there were two barns in good condition and there were even chickens in a wired-in enclosure out the front, and sheep in the fields at the back. But there didn't seem to be anybody about. There was an old tractor parked down a driveway that looked to be in working condition, but no cars or horses.

The sun had sunk close to the south-west horizon, and the sky behind Davy was the colour of charcoal. But there were no lights in the farmhouse, and no signs of life. Where was everybody? Off at the war, maybe? Or had the war come here, and claimed the inhabitants? But what kind of marching army would leave good chickens scrabbling about in the dirt when they could carry them off to eat later?

It wasn't that Davy felt hungry, but he was conscious that he might be many days on the road and that it would be a good idea to pick up supplies if the chance presented itself. Dare he risk breaking into the house? There might be a lovely full larder inside. But what if the inhabitants returned? What if they were inside now, just being very quiet?

Eventually timidity overcame daring, and he left the farm alone, making his way through the wood. The sun went down and the forest became murkier, although the westward sky still glowed with a deep blue that reminded Davy of the bluebells, and lifted his heart, and the moon sitting high in the sky looked like silver fruit plucked from a tree of light.

There was a rustling sound off in the undergrowth that might have been a deer, or a wild pig, or maybe even a big badger: Davy couldn't see what was causing it. It didn't sound like a human.

Soon, in the very last of the light, he reached a row of old houses, all roofless, a few with beams still pointing their black fingers at the stars. It was markedly colder now, and the night was filling the land like floodwater. He had no blanket or sleeping bag, and it wasn't much warmer inside the wreck than out. But he found a wall at the base of which he could lie, and hugged himself, and tried to sleep.

He did sleep a little, too, although he woke often with the cold, and once he shivered so fiercely that he rolled hard *into* the wall and jarred his bad side. There was no sleeping after that, so he sat up and tried to concentrate on anything other than the shining pain from his shoulderblade. The dawn percolated slowly through the woodland, and into the shell of the house, and eventually it was light enough to see.

It had been too dark to see any of the details of the room the previous night, but the dawn revealed the domestic fashions of a vanished age. Patterned paper was on all the walls, and where it hadn't peeled off it showed different sizes and colours of fish. The ceiling was a tangle of cobwebs and the carpet a thicket of ferns. But near where Davy had lain down was an ancient sofa, and from this sprouted a little forest of impressively tall-stemmed mushrooms. Davy went up to them with the half-formed idea of picking and eating them. He saw, in amongst the roots of the mushrooms, the shape of a long dead body, collapsed in upon itself. He couldn't make out any specifics beyond the shape.

He came out of the house and looked around. It was a brisk morning, with white-grey clouds overhead and the smell of coming rain. He set off on an empty stomach.

He made slow progress at first through dense scrub and woodland, and then he came down a hill through trees and almost fell into the margins of a deep lake. The trees grew right up to, and indeed over, the lip of the lake, and it was narrow but wide. He had to turn right—that is, north—and pick his way along it. A slight breeze tickled the surface of the water into those transient shudders Davy remembered from the flanks of cows when he had been a herder-boy. On the far side of the water a great many ducks congregated. Rusting metal pylons poked their upper portions out from below the water. His stomach gnawed at itself. He chewed a little grass, but it didn't really help.

As he went on the trees thinned, and gave way to sedge and a squelchy kind of turf, and here for the first time Davy ran into people. He crouched down, and hoped he hadn't been seen: three or four individuals. He couldn't tell if they were women or men. They were standing around talking. The burble of their voices was just about audible, although what they were saying was impossible to discern. Davy lifted himself a little and took another look: four of them, not three. One was smoking. All four wore similar clothes and all four carried rifles. That didn't necessarily mean they were soldiers, of course, but military was Davy's best guess.

Creeping slowly and keeping his head down as far as possible, Davy retraced his steps. Back in the cover of the trees he felt less exposed.

The clouds were thinner now, and the water shone with a bright crinkled blue, wavelets like a painter's brushstrokes. Davy decided he was being ridiculous. Did he hope to get all the way home to the Hill without getting his feet wet? It wasn't winter any more: the water might be bracing, but it wouldn't kill him. So he took off his shoes and socks, bundled them in a parcel made of his trousers, and slipped into the lake holding his clothes out of the water in his left hand. With his right he half-doggy-paddled across the stretch of water. Progress was slow but steady, and soon enough he was making the ducks complain in their ratchety voices. Below him, through the waters, he could see the tops of submerged buses and lorries— all lorries, all buses, no cars. That was odd.

On the far side he climbed out and lay on a heap of turf as large as a bed, letting the thin but palpable spring sunshine touch his skin. He dozed. He woke with a start when a woodpecker, standing on the grass not far from him, began a series of falsetto barking noises. He got dressed, and left the bird grubbing for ants in amongst the grass.

Davy made reasonable progress through the rest of the afternoon. That night he slept in the wreck of an old bus. It was two storeys high, like a house, and although the lower floor was wholly overgrown and choked with weeds the upper floor was clear. About half the windows had gone and there were quite a few old leaves littering the floor, but though the upholstered seats were a little damp and smelt odd they were also comfortable.

Davy was woken the next morning by the sound of people outside. He lay very still, and heard voices recede into the distance. He crept to one of the glassless windows and peered out. Down the track he saw a dozen soldiers. Looking the other way he could see more coming this way.

His heart rate scrambled to a sprint. Stay low, don't be seen, hopefully they would pass by. Surely they would just go past? Wouldn't they? Why would they be interested in the top deck of an old ruined bus? He would be fine. Davy crouched down in the space between two seats, with just enough clearance to be able to peer out. There were, he could see with increasing panic in his breast, dozens and dozens of soldiers coming down, and they weren't walking. They were jogging. With their weapons out.

They were all men.

There was a distant sound of detonation: a crumbling low-note resonance that came over like a bell tolling at a funeral. And then, much closer, a much louder and sharper explosion. All the men turned to look back the way they had come, and in an instant they scattered into the trees or took up positions behind the wrecks of cars. Davy's heart was already racing and could not go any faster. It went faster. Away in the distance a new set of soldiers was moving, darting in and out of vision, and soon enough the snippy sound of gunfire was audible.

Another explosion, closer still, and the whole bus rocked. Davy put his hands over his head. Men were yelling, and the discharge of weapons smacked the air over and over. A lower sort of sustained rumble might have been an armoured car, or a tank.

Davy was breathing rapidly and shallowly. His stomach was molten. There was a real risk he was going to lose control of his bowels. The complex of noises from outside the bus intensified abruptly: bangs, rattles, yells, and one voice—male or female, impossible to tell—hooting a long scream of pain.

The bus shuddered. Had it been hit? Not that. A crescendoing *boom-boom-boom* was somebody hurrying up the curlaround inner staircase. Davy was far too terrified to do anything except stay where he was, breathing so shallowly it almost wasn't breathing at all, his heart going like a gnat's wings. It was a man: one of Father John's soldiers. He was on the top deck now. He thumped his booted feet down along the central aisle, didn't notice Davy, and hurriedly took up a position at the back of the bus.

Davy was motionless. He was carved from wood, set in stone. The soldier at the back of the bus picked a target down on the road and fired his rifle and the sound was so sudden and loud Davy couldn't stop himself twitching. He might even have let out a little whimper. The rifle spoke again, a furious bellow, and another.

Gunfire from outside struck the bus and rang it like a gigantic gong. At this, Davy completely lost composure—he couldn't control himself to hold it in any longer. He put his hands over his head and crouched lower down, yelling. He knew he shouldn't yell, but he had to make some kind of sound to vent the terror inside him. It was stupid, though. It was the most stupid thing he had ever done in his life. Now the soldier would know he was there and would come back and kill him. But he couldn't help himself.

After a minute, or perhaps eighty hours, Davy uncurled and looked about. The soldier was lying on his back, and not moving. Then the bus started shuddering again, and again there came the *boom-boom* of booted feet on the inner staircase, and Davy's fear tipped over into a mess of sparks that consumed the back of his head and took his consciousness away.

HE WOKE IN silence, and late afternoon light.

It seemed he had been out for the rest of the day.

He was still on the bus, but he was no longer in between the seats. Instead he was lying on his back in the aisle. His ribs hurt.

When he sat up, slowly, wincing at the soreness in his chest, the other soldier was still lying there a little further down the aisle. He was wearing a monocle of crusted red-black blood and matter. He was grinning. He was utterly motionless.

There was no human sound, although in the world outside birdsong was filling every crevice of air and life. The song of life and of being alive. Davy looked down at his own body and saw, in the middle of his chest, the print of a muddy boot.

Somebody had dragged him out from between the seats, treading hard upon him as they did so. Since Davy's unresponsiveness had not been of the sort that could be shammed, the individual— whoever it had been—had concluded that he was dead, like the other man. Davy's sham fit had enabled him to escape Wycombe once, and now a real fit had enabled him to evade Father John as well. Luck working overtime. He remembered Mother Patel telling him that he was blessed, "I tell you, three times these fits will save your life, young Davy. Three times!"

Two down. What else remained?

He was genuinely curious.

He was also very thirsty. He made his way gingerly down the stairwell, left the bus and hurried away from the old road with its litter of dead male bodies.

CHAPTER TWENTY-TWO

DAVY WENT THROUGH the forest into what had once been an open field and was now turning into a wood. He found a shed as the sun went down, rusted metal walls, doorless, floored with a layer of old leaves, and curled up inside.

He slept awkwardly, thirsty and hungry and uncomfortable. In the morning, woken by the dawn chorus, he stumbled out. No humans were around.

There was enough long grass here for him to be able to wipe dew into his mouth and take the edge off his thirst. He chewed some stems, even though it made his stomach ache worse. Then he made his way west through a circle of ruined houses, up a road lined with other architectural wrecks and round a corner. There were various objects containing standing water, but he wasn't so stupid as to drink from them.

The sky was an ashen white, and once the birdsong settled it was weirdly quiet.

One bird was making a different song from the others: a continuous humming rattle-buzz noise. Davy looked up and caught a glimpse of an impossible gliding bird—long and thin, black-bodied and apparently headless, with stubby little wings too far back on its torso. The wings did not move.

The flier passed from south to north and was soon out of sight. It took quite a bit longer for its drone-like call to fade away.

The old road up ahead was choked with rusting cars and seemed to go into the wasteland of an old deserted town. There would be nothing to eat or drink there, so Davy cut left, into the trees again, and made his way, best as he could tell, east-south-east. His night's sleep had not left him rested, and he experienced a flicker of light on his retina, as if another fit were coming. But instead of building into the whole storm of sparks and vision, it was just that one flicker, and its strangely persistent after-image, on the back of his eye.

Maybe it was lightning?

He was halfway into the woodland when he heard a great rumble, away to the north: thunder. It sounded like a vast door being slammed shut, far and far and further away. So maybe it *had* been lightning? He checked the sky, but the white haze was thinning and blue was beginning to show through. It didn't seem like storm weather. The one great roll of thunder echoed and resonated, and then died away. Davy waited for a second, but it never came.

He walked. As the day went on the sky cleared, and turned a smoky blue, intermittently visible through the canopy of spring green overhead. A big, bent tree had fallen over, perhaps a year earlier. Now it looked like a tree on its knees. Beyond it the forest started thinning out. Davy heard something and stopped, anxious, but it wasn't people. It was four deer, running. They passed twenty yards in front of him, less galloping than flowing from right to left, their backs a slow sine wave up and down as their legs hurried. In moments they were gone.

He came to the edge of the wood and looked down a long slope to the big river. The Thames, at last. A scatter of ruined houses, and a few broken roofs poking out of the water's edge, but no people around. The sky was pale blue and the sun was actually warm on his skin.

His first instinct was to run straight down, plunge into the water and swim to the other side, but something in him made him hold back. Caution, caution. Who knew where the dark angel might be? Waiting for him to show himself, always.

So instead Davy found a vantage point and sat for half an hour. Birds came and went, and at one point a fox appeared, red against the green like a flame in the field. But no people.

He let his eye wander over the flank of the hill on the far side of the river. His hill. The whiskers of his mind twitched: nervous, anticipatory. A great breadth of green and blue-green and brown, slotted here and there with darker patches and blobs. No motion. Textures of intricacy in amongst the bigger spatches of colour: millions of individual leaves. Davy watched, and watched. Near the far bank branches strained down towards the river's surface as if tugging at their own invisible leashes to reach and drink. There was a tremble in the canopy and one crow, black wraith, big as a dog, his wings moving so slowly it didn't seem possible he could raise himself upward on them, broke from the cover and flew. Davy watched him go.

Enough. Or too much.

He couldn't hold back forever. Davy trotted down the slope and folded his shoes and socks into his trousers, as before. He waded into the water and swam one-armed. River water went into his mouth as he went, which was all right, because he was thirsty. The current pushed his trajectory into a long diagonal, but he reached the far side without incident.

He climbed a tree, and waited to dry off in the warm air. Nobody came up or down the river. When he was dry enough he dressed and moved north.

Within an hour he had come to a part of the riverbank he recognised. From there it was an easy path inland and up

Shillingford Hill. Familiar sights greeted him like old friends. And here was the path that led to his own farm—his home. He could even hear the cows lowing.

Round the corner and there was the house. Nobody seemed to be about, A memory of the whole yet strangely silent farm, back in the Chilterns, came to him. Where was everyone? Here were chickens in the yard, and there were three cows in their enclosure. They trotted over to greet him, and he stroked their noses.

He took a breath and opened the door to the kitchen and went inside.

He found Gal, sitting on a chair near the kitchen table, and nursing a young baby. She looked up, stared at him astonished and said, "You're Davy. You're Davy come home again. They all think you're dead!"

"Hello Gal," he said. "Where is everybody?"

"Your Ma is away. Somebody blew Goring up, you heard, I guess you heard, yeah? A bomb was dropped from the moon, people say. Your sisters are away with her. Your Da is up at Hellington, trying to buy another cow. My god Davy, I can't believe you're alive! You look so grown-up now! Where have you *been*?" Her nipple, thick as a finger, slipped from the baby's mouth, and the bairn made a sound of deep satisfaction.

Of all the strange reversals and violent changes of fortune that had characterised Davy's life over the last few months, this abrupt arrival home was the strangest and, in its way, the most violent. Everything was the same. Nothing at all was the same. Who would have thought that the unstrange spaces of home could ever estrange themselves?

Davy looked about. Home, home, home. "Oh the places I've been," he said, and sat himself down on the far side of the kitchen table.

ABOUT THE AUTHOR

Adam Roberts was born in London two thirds of the way through the last century. He currently lives a little way west of London and teaches English and Creative Writing at Royal Holloway, University of London. He is the author of sixteen SF novels, including *New Model Army* (Gollancz, 2010), *Jack Glass* (2012)—winner of the BSFA and Campbell awards—and *Bête* (2014). His most recent novel is *The Thing Itself* (2015). He is also the author of various works of literary criticism and review, including the recently expanded and updated *History of Science Fiction* (Palgrave, 2016)

DISCOVER NEW WORLDS

2018 marks the launch of Solaris's boldest new project. We've invited your favourite writers to explore new worlds *together*, weaving new legends and laying the groundwork for years to come.

THE AFTERMATH: A hundred years after asteroid strikes wiped out civilisation, the new communities rising from the ashes struggle to survive.

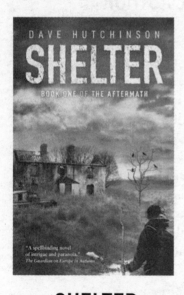 

SHELTER
Dave Hutchinson
June 2018

HAVEN
Adam Roberts
August 2018

AFTER THE WAR: The Armies of Light gathered, and after a long, bitter war, the Dark Lord was slain. But glory is easy; true peace is hard, and bitter.

REDEMPTION'S BLADE

Adrian Tchaikovsky

July 2018

SALVATION'S FIRE

Justina Robson

September 2018

FIND US ONLINE!

www.rebellionpublishing.com

/rebellionpub　　/rebellionpublishing　　/rebellionpub

SIGN UP TO OUR NEWSLETTER!

rebellionpublishing.com/sign-up

YOUR REVIEWS MATTER!

Enjoy this book? Got something to say?

Leave a review on Amazon, GoodReads or with your
favourite bookseller and let the world know!